Penguin Books

The Colours of War

Matt Cohen was born in Kingston, Ontario in 1942 and educated at the University of Toronto. He taught religious studies at McMaster University before becoming a full time writer.

His first novel was published in 1969. Since then, he has received critical acclaim for many books, notably "The Salem Novels" — *The Disinherited, The Colours of War, The Sweet Second Summer of Kitty Malone*, and *Flowers of Darkness. Café le Dog*, his most recent collection of stories, was published in the Penguin Short Fiction series, and *The Spanish Doctor*, a novel, is also available in a Penguin edition. Cohen has contributed articles and stories to a wide variety of magazines including *The Malahat Review, The Sewanee Review* and *Saturday Night*.

Matt Cohen now lives in Toronto, Ontario.

MATT COHEN

The
Colours
of War

Penguin Books

Penguin Books Canada Limited, 2801 John Street, Markham,
Ontario, Canada L3R 1B4
Penguin Books Ltd., Harmondsworth, Middlesex, England
Penguin Books, 40 West 23rd Street, New York,
New York 10010 U.S.A.
Penguin Books Australia Ltd., Ringwood, Victoria, Australia
Penguin Books (N.Z.) Ltd., Private Bag, Takapuna,
Auckland 9, New Zealand

Published in Penguin Books, 1986

Copyright © Matt Cohen, 1977

First published by McClelland and Stewart Limited, 1977

Manufactured in Canada by Gagne Printing Limited

Canadian Cataloguing in Publication Data

Cohen, Matt, 1942-
  The colours of war

ISBN 0-14-009302-8

I. Title.

PS8555.038C63 1986   C813'.54   C86-093618-X
PR9199.3.C63C63 1986

Verse on page 224 from *Last Year's Girl* by Leo Feist, © 1933.
Verse on page 226 from *Till the Boys Come Home*, © 1932, Chapelle
and Co., New York

The author would like to thank the Canada Council and the University
of Alberta for their support.

For K.

The
Colours
of War

ONE

I have to tell you this story.

My name is Theodore Beam. I am in an old stone church, trying to set down these words. They have their own invisible laws. I have to begin in the right way. I almost chant. I almost close my eyes and pray.

My story begins in different places – in the times of my life that were special and stuck up like sharp mountains through the comfortable dream of lies, the dream of everyday. Now my stomach aches and my throat is tight and choking. Trying to hold this back. Trying to push this out.

The story begins now with the telling.

It began on the morning of my twenty-seventh birthday when the police knocked down my door and woke me up.

And again, ten years before that, when I left home.

But for now, it is slow. For days I've stammered over this first page, listening for the sound of my own voice.

I stop. I start. I almost chant. I almost close my eyes and pray.

In the silence I can feel the power in me. I surround it with remnants of my soul, cupping it with care, as if it were a candle.

I sit and I listen for the sound of my own voice. Not the voice I hear when I talk. Nor the voice that sounds in my mind as I say the things I should have or didn't dare to. Not even the voice that I will have when I am old.

Maybe it is only the sound of the beating of my heart. But now I can hear it, though for most of my life it was silent. This is my voice: the sound of past and future singing through my bones.

Finally I can believe I exist. I can believe in you too. There will be moments when we touch.

Lise used to say that the only thing that tells the truth is a fuse while it is burning. Tonight it is too late for violence. It is the second night of a long spring storm. Before it came, the hills had already begun to melt, showing great expanses of brown-stained winter grass. There was snow in the bush and rabbits were easy to catch. Foxes too; but I'm afraid to eat them because they are rabid.

In the old days I would have thought the storm was only a coincidence, a random collection of clouds and pressure areas that had settled over the continent. Now I know better. For decades we waited our turn; while bombs and cannon exploded all over the world, this continent rode out the century like a fat eunuch king on a velvet pillow. These past few months our time has begun to come. Even the weather is helping.

I'm writing this in the attic of an old stone building, an old church that stands near the village of Salem. It's a long time since anyone has prayed here. I close my eyes: in my dreams the village has been destroyed, the frame houses are missing walls and roofs, as if there had been a hail of rocks. I open my eyes: on the wall I see a St. Christopher's medal. It catches the yellow light like a fish. It reminds me of things I need to remember.

Even in the storm I'm afraid the soldiers will come for me. At night I hide here in the attic. I'm kneeling on the floor, writing this by the light of some candles which I've placed in a half-circle around the paper. Once Lise and I made love in this room. Or at least made almost-love. In the corner the mattress is still as it was, the blankets and sheets unchanged. But the only safe place is here, in the absolute centre of the room, kneeling in the midst of these candles. The warped boards dig into the bones of my knees. I use the pain to keep myself awake. Half my mind is on the page. The other half is cast about the church, listening for sounds in the storm.

The snow and wind hiss against this old stone church. It will outlast them. Soon it will be summer and the grass will turn bright green. During the day I hunt for food. Sometimes I listen to the radio. There's hardly any news of the war: only government propaganda, music and old soap operas.

It is only starting. The state has grown into a giant, irrational beast. It roams the countryside hungrily, searching for enemies. Trucks, tanks, airplanes. They are between us. They are what we have to believe in. Every time I hear engines I feel them as if their highways were my veins, as if it were my blood and my brain that fuelled them.

But I don't have to tell you this. We already know each other. We've caught flashes of each other in a thousand movies, out of the edges of newscasts, between the lines of books and magazines. We've seen each other rushing in opposite directions at airports, standing in line for permits and licences, waiting for the elevator. We're stuck together and we know it, like a zillion ants on a giant honey-covered planet. We know each other so well we can no longer sleep together without love, or kill each other without guns and bombs.

If I can believe you exist, I can tell you the truth.

With Lise I shared this mattress in this old attic. Our bodies jumped together like magnets. Where she began, I began. Most of the time I cannot even summon her face into my mind. When I'm trying to recall her eyes, I see flashes of her arms and belly. She only appears whole when I least expect her. When I'm waking up from a nightmare. When I'm skinning a rabbit or a ground hog. I've almost had to give her up. My only consolation is that when they catch me, when they line me up against the wall to shoot me, I'll finally have it all over again, every sensation of my life flooding through me at a crazy jumped-up speed.

My knees are sore. I close my eyes and say my name. Theodore Beam. It could have been anything. Theodore Beam. We live one life after another, forgetting everything in between. Last time I was a tree. Or a monk, living in Italy, perhaps even Rome, spending every hot and dazzling winter day on my knees, like this, scrubbing the steps of some old church that had survived too many earthquakes. Theodore Beam. The next time round it will all be different. I'll be a memory chip in some computer. When they press the button, I'll recite old poems until my current is cut off.

Theodore Beam. If you want to hear your own voice, you say your name, over and over, until it all disappears, until all the sharp points and the vowels, and the places where you press your lips together, and the pauses where your tongue rests on the roof of your mouth, all melt together into one long primal grunt. My voice, for example, my own true voice, lives in my belly. Not my stomach – which is jammed up into my ribs, a weird but predictable leather bag that squirts itself with acid when I eat food it doesn't like – but my belly. I know it lives there because I've heard it. And I've felt it opening me up from the inside when it wants to. Or closing everything down tight. Not everyone's voice lives in their belly. Lise's lived in the middle of her skull, suspended precisely between her ears. It was a shrill, high-pitched voice that wanted to shatter everything it touched.

Theodore Beam. My father's name was Jacob Beam and my mother's was Elizabeth Malone Beam. Now the storm is howling louder than ever. We are all locked together. The electricity in our brains is causing this freak storm. When it's over, the village of Salem will exist again. I'll be able to look out the window and see the house where my mother's cousin still lives: Katherine Malone, the woman who delivered me into this world. For one afternoon Lise shared this church with me. We began and ended on this mattress. Now it's just a pile of sheets and blankets. A rifle lies helplessly on top. I've gotten used to guns on beds.

When this freak storm ends, the snow will be piled up in six-foot drifts. At the worst moments I can smell spring in the air. The wind smashes into the stone and mortar but it is warm. Now even the weather is conspiring to tell the truth. Theodore Beam my mother named me. I was born long and thin, barely alive. Who knows where Jacob Beam was then; it was years before I noticed him – a stocky, bearded presence who slowly edged into my life – and by then he had already become ridiculous.

I was born in October. When the ground freezes deeper every morning and summer begins to stutter – that is my season. Jacob Beam was away, looking for his war, and there was no doctor, so my mother was attended only by a cousin by marriage – Katherine Malone. I've always been able to picture them waiting for me in the big master bedroom with the four-poster bed. The window would have been covered by the white gauze curtain that was considered the ultimate touch in home décor. And the sun, low in the October sky, illuminated the room, turned it bright yellow, its glare so strong that Katherine Malone had to sit with her back to it on the edge of my mother's bed, playing cards and counting between contractions. My mother, a thin, pale woman who was ready for everything else in life, was not ready for this. When the pains began to close in on each other, and she began to hate Jacob Beam and the empty house he had left her, she decided there was nothing to do but move herself and her stomach to the spare bedroom. So they took everything into the room at the end of the hall, my mother stopping with every few steps, and set it up in the narrow iron bed already waiting for me.

Theodore she called me, after some long-lost favourite uncle who died hunting snakes in South America. The next day they aired out the room and turned the mattress over.

Strangely, on the very afternoon I was born, Jacob Beam wrote home to my mother.

This war is different from the others. We are all mercenaries or true believers. For weeks we've been trapped in the midst of these mountains; I've been creeping from valley to valley with a map I don't understand. The days are short, but at least the nights keep us invisible.

Somehow I learned the origins of the strange red-stained continent on the underside of my mattress. And so when I lost a sock or a toy, I could lie beneath my bed and contemplate my humble beginnings.

I shut my eyes. I'm lying on my back now. My ears are close to the wall and the storm whistles through these old stones, sending in cold sprays of air. At least I can use the stove; no one could see the smoke, so I'm warm, almost sleepy. The old smells of our loving heat up and rise from the bed, surround me like a warm and faithful blanket.

In the end I begin to get tired. I've learned how to starve and I've learned how to live without Lise. But I have no talent for suicide. Can a book begin with such a confession of mediocrity? I want to live in the world, any world, even a world like this.

Nietzsche said that thinking about suicide is the surest way to get from midnight to morning. Now the world is swept by war. Countries are torn apart and die. History has finally succeeded in changing something: suicide is obsolete.

But Nietzsche doesn't have to be forgotten. At least he made one true prediction: in life you have to go through everything twice – the first is tragedy, the second, farce. That is all I remember from him. I'm sitting cross-legged on the bed now, writing this down as if it mattered. In front of me, pressing into my knees, is the rifle, muzzle pointed towards the trap door. This is how it is. And this is how it was —

TWO

How it was. When I repeat words to myself, they gradually turn into a smooth shining surface, a barrier between me and whatever I want to say; so finally I'm forced to stretch them out, break them apart, try to change them from short easy units into long messy sentences that can let the world through, like old rivers that have finally consented to let the rocks push through to the air. "You can't trust words," my father used to say. But he dealt in them anyway, laying them down in long inky lines, day after day, long parallel lies flung across the pages of his newspaper.

What I like about words is the secret connections they make. Of course they can't be trusted. They reach under the surface and draw things together; forbidden images pop out like raw clams, like people making love when they're still strangers. You can't trust words, but it doesn't matter because between them and all the ways they collide there is always something happening: because of them, in spite of them, in the secret ways they meet.

The way my knees meet the floor here, digging painfully into the wood of this old attic. Even with my eyes closed I can't imagine people singing downstairs, praying for rain and sun and easy births – the prayers that farmers have. But I feel at home here in this old outpost of Salem. I'm kneeling down in the middle of the continent – an old church near a diminished town in the centre of Ontario.

I've spent most of the winter here, hiding, sometimes mark-

15

ing time and sometimes right in its midst. But a few months ago I was living in Vancouver, in the first-floor apartment of a house edged halfway into Chinatown. The summer had been cold and wet, the winter already in the air. It was a barren time in my life, one of those strange seasons between friends and activities that sometimes settles over me.

It was fall. Fall always seems narrow and brittle, a sharp colourful time when things begin and end, and I feel the edges of myself pushing out. I was born in the fall; and when I imagine my mother sitting with Katherine Malone in the bedroom, waiting for me, the sky is always that red-tinged blue of autumn afternoons, a warm-cold colour that excites me, hovers between living and dying.

On the night before my birthday, my twenty-seventh, I went drinking in an old waterfront tavern. There were people I knew and my loneliness melted a bit as we sat and drank beer and rested our hands on the wet tables. I had been living in Vancouver ten years and it was familiar to me: the wet air that caught in my chest, the sour salty taste of beer, the men and women with their jeans and wool sweaters stained and shrunken by the sea. It was familiar to me but it wasn't mine. When the evening and the beer were done, I walked home alone, kicking the first scattered leaves off the sidewalk and reminding myself that my birthday had come round again, another year to be measured and forgotten. I almost felt as if a hole were opening up in my existence to receive the war that everyone said was coming.

My father, Jacob Beam, had gone to his war. In Spain and all over Europe he had travelled around like a crazy mercenary in search of something – I never knew what. But this war was supposed to be different. There were no sides and no armies, or so the papers said. Just illegal underground groups that had been collecting weapons and now seemed to be systematically wrecking whatever was left of the cities in the South. Every day it seemed there were new declarations of emergencies and martial law. Not exactly a new war: things being the same as always but carried one step further.

In Vancouver, like the rest of Canada, life was still vaguely serene. I'd heard of the food shortages and crop failures, but winter was still only a threat and my own life had not been touched. That night, walking home from the tavern, the city streets seemed almost comfortable. There was a yellow-grey mist, promising the beginning of the rains, and the smells of the city were mixed with the sea.

At this strange time in my life, it seemed as if past and future hardly existed. All my projects and plans had exhausted themselves; and with this birthday I could feel a new sensation – the years piling up in me, age beginning to surround me like a stone fence surrounds an old and trampled field.

Coming to my apartment I took a newspaper from the box at the corner. Once inside, the warmth revived the beer in my blood, and I sat on the floor in my living room without turning on the light. Upstairs I could hear the scratching of my landlady's slippers as she made her way along the hardwood floor tracing out the great circuit of her life: from kitchen teapot to the bathroom and back. I sat and dozed. Vancouver is three thousand miles from the town of my birth, Salem; but this night the two places spun around in the sky, human settlements breathing out their time. In the dark, I tried to summon my parents' faces. At times I think I can almost remember the hour of my birth; a vast rushing erupts from the back of my mind and I can see myself as an infant, pushing and clawing through the hot noisy tunnel, wriggling and struggling with the cord around my neck.

I fell asleep, sitting against the chair. And then woke up in the middle of the night, just long enough to straighten out my stiff back and walk to the bedroom, still dressed, where I lay down and sank into a long confused dream about Salem – bombs falling, the town laid waste as if the violence in its guts had finally erupted and torn apart the stone and cement in one easy gesture. The sounds of this war, my own breathing, the beating of my heart, all melted together in a long insistent drumming, a muffled tempo that resolved into fists pounding against my door. I was on my feet and into the hall by the time the lock gave way.

There were two of them, obviously police, dressed in suits and ties. They rushed towards me, like characters out of a jerky old movie. One carried a gun in his hand. The other slammed me against the wall, his hands searching frantically for concealed weapons. My forehead and face were pressed up tight against the plaster. His hands were like sharp rocks digging into me: ribs, thighs, belly, groin. Then they slapped into my kidneys – a brief flash of pain – and suddenly pulled me around, away from the wall. "Fucker," one of them whispered, then shoved me down the hall to the living room. They were both short and stocky. Their hair was cut close and their necks were wide and muscular. Even their faces were lumpy with muscle. Through the remnants of my dreams and sleep, they looked completely evil – unafraid of anything I might do to them or they might do to me. Old professionals, I thought, taken off prostitutes and petty gambling and put onto drugs. The one with the gun had cut himself while shaving: two small nicks above his Adam's apple. They jumped around while he demanded my identification and asked useless questions. His flesh was a strange cooked colour and lay on his face in endless tiny layers, like pastry that had been sogged and crushed. His partner ransacked the apartment. There were only three rooms: a bedroom barely large enough for the bed, a combination kitchen-living room and a bathroom.

Scattered all over the living room floor were newspapers and magazines, a book about people who consume each other after an airplane crash, tools for an old truck which I had finally given to the wreckers.

"Theodore Beam. Theodore Beam. Theodore Beam." Each card from my wallet had its name read out loud. I opened the curtains. My apartment, though small, had one perfect feature: a wall of large windows and glass doors that looked out onto the backyard and garden which my Chinese landlady kept. She was standing in her red-and-purple padded slippers, a matching kerchief wrapped around her head – her only vanity, for she was bald. The day was bright and cold, the kind of fall day Vancouver seldom has, and beyond the yard it was clear enough to see the mountains. It was still so early that the dew lay on the lawn like broken glass: a perfect time to be arrested. In the lower drawer of my dresser, hidden by a false bottom, was a plastic bag containing six ounces of cocaine. I was keeping it for a friend.

I offered my guard coffee.

"Sure," he said, "two coffees with cream and sugar." His teeth and even his tongue were stained with tobacco. Filling the kettle I noticed my hands were sweating. I washed them surreptitiously, as if this nervousness might be held against me. I felt stale and musty from sleeping in my clothes. The policeman with the gun stuck close, crowding me between the stove and refrigerator.

Inside my chest a demon of fear had come alive, showering sweat through the pores of my skin, sending panic from my belly up to my throat. I was trying to imagine my landlady appearing in court to give me a character reference. Perhaps she would say some words about my slowness. The persons who judge me fall into two categories: those who think I'm slow and those who think I'm lazy. In this, as in other things, I'm afraid I take after my father.

I set three mugs of coffee on the counter and put sugar and canned milk beside them. The sound of metal against wood startled my guard; suddenly he was pressed against me, his gun poking into my chest. The demon froze. I stood still. Even in my stocking feet I was much taller than this agent of the law. Over his head I could see my newspaper from last night; the headlines were thick and black.

In the tavern last night people had been talking about the police; they were making more and more of these strange raids, breaking into places where they conducted useless

searches. As if they were now so frightened they had to terror-
ize at random.

My landlady had come in the door and joined us. Aside
from the fact that she had no hair, she was also extraordinarily
short. Perhaps she was not over four feet. She seemed unim-
pressed by these forces of the law. Without speaking, she
began tidying up the apartment, as she always did when she
came to visit me. When she had piled up all the papers and
magazines onto the card table, she came into the kitchen
alcove and began putting things back in the cupboards.

Her presence made everything seem safe again. The two
policemen and I were standing in the living room, drinking
our coffee and looking out at the garden and the mountains.
Now they were becoming ordinary men.

"I need a cigarette," I said. The one who had been searching
reached into his pocket and drew out a leather case. He
snapped it open. As I took out a cigarette I saw that one of his
fingers was too short: the tip, where the nail should have been,
was missing, and the surrounding skin was brown and porous,
almost mouldy. Noticing I was watching, he held his hand up
in front of me as he lit my cigarette.

The gun had been put away. Like a patient in the dentist's
chair, I was gradually growing used to this new reality. Somewhere I had read that human intelligence is the ability to
adapt. If so, that morning must have been the peak of my
genius; I was already accepting the inevitable march to the
car, handcuffs around my wrists, months in jail.

Then my genius began to go downhill and I wanted them to
leave. As they had entered and pushed me against the wall, I
could vaguely remember them flashing their wallets.

"What am I charged with?" I asked. "You must have a
search warrant or something."

They looked suspiciously at me and at each other.

"May I see your search warrant, please?"

"What the fuck," said the one with the defective finger. He
smiled brilliantly. His teeth were white and sparkled as if they

20

had been polished. He rubbed his finger in his ear to improve his hearing, then turned to his friend.

"Hey," he said, "did you hear that?"

"I heard that," said the one with the gun. "Listen to the lawyer." He patted his pocket and looked at me. I wanted to be wearing shoes. Without further warning, his fist shot out like a thick piston. I twisted slightly, but as I went down the breath popped out of my lungs with a loud snapping sound.

"We'll see you," he said.

"Yeah," said the other, "we'll see you." He laughed. "Don't call us, we'll call you."

And then they were down the hall and out the door, slamming it behind them.

I lay curled up on the floor, my eyes closed, filled with the image of the policeman's cooked face. Bit by bit I managed to push my stomach out. I didn't feel surprised or angry; now that my life had been crossed this way it only seemed amazing that I had remained protected for so long. Finally I stood up and brushed off my pants. My eyes were full of sleep and I wondered if for once there would be enough water to last out a shower.

Then, turning around, I saw that my landlady was still in the living room. She was sitting in the one comfortable seat, the armchair, her slippered feet stuck straight out from her short legs. She eyed me almost sympathetically, as if she had come in to protect me from worse. Her eyes, pitch black, possessed a strange ancient look, as if she had seen the whole world pass by. In her hand she held the bag of white powder which had been in my bottom drawer.

"I'll keep this for you," she said. She smiled happily. She always seemed happy. She slid out of the chair, smiled so widely that her compassionate black eyes almost disappeared, then walked out with my bag of cocaine.

I was supposed to be a free-lance journalist but in fact I was unemployed. It was three months since I had paid the rent; in another few days it would be four. When the police had pushed me against the wall, I felt like a coward for not resisting. Now my stomach was sore and my throat dry from fear. I took a sip of cold coffee and began the search for something to eat.

The apartment had been ransacked – pillows ripped open, clothes flung to the floor, drawers emptied and overturned. I made a fresh cup of coffee and sat down in the armchair to begin my birthday all over again. Miraculously, the newspaper from last night was still intact. The headlines, though, didn't refer to the war at all but to a scandal — it seemed everyone these days was so nervous they were trying to embezzle enough money to put together a bomb-proof, chaos-proof shelter out in the middle of the forest. I always wondered what these hundreds of millionaires thought they were doing as they sat out in the woods day after day, eating vitamins, doing calisthenics and listening to the radio for news of the apocalypse. In this new scandal a prominent official of the public works department had stolen and sold twenty-four bright-yellow bulldozers.

As I made my way through the paper, I noticed a curious item buried in the back pages:

An official from the Ministry of Agriculture said today that there will be a minor shortage of food for the next few weeks. It may extend, at worst, until early in the spring.

The shortage is due to unusually high grain exports to famine-stricken countries in the southern hemisphere and a series of strikes in railways and ports.

The army is now engaged in moving supplies of powdered milk and grain to the poorer areas of the country.

Citizens are requested to remain calm and place voluntary restraints on their consumption of food.

Emergency legislation will be introduced to make the illegal sale or purchase of food a crime punishable by life imprisonment.

Though I am thin and never get sick, in those days I

thought of myself as delicate and fragile, in need of exactly three meals a day. I put down the paper and went out to the corner grocery. Maybe it was only my imagination, but the shelves looked half-empty; and it seemed that the woman who ran the store, sitting hot and panting as always on the stool behind the cash register, wrapped in sweaters and eating chocolate bars, was even more suspicious than usual, her tiny eyes searching me for hidden pockets and bulges in my clothes. A shortage until spring, the official had said. It was unlike the government to think ahead – maybe we were almost out already. If the delivery trucks stopped coming to the corner stores and supermarkets in the middle of winter, it wouldn't take long for people to get hungry.

When I got home I stood in the spray of the lukewarm shower and tried to remember old books I had read about the depression, stories my parents and others had told me about those times when it was impossible to afford food and clothes. Of course in those days everyone could at least heat their houses with wood, which was free and available; and if they lived near a lake or on the coast, they could go fishing even in the city. Now there was no wood and the harbours were polluted. Outside of the city the game had been hunted out and the ground torn up for airports, subdivisions, industrial parks. In the tavern last night I had met someone from California. He talked about the cities as vast and intricate jungles. No matter how bad things got, there would always be some people who had hoards of food — and some with plans to take it away.

As the lukewarm water ran to cold, I started to soap myself, washing my eyes, trying to convince myself that the water was actually hot and relaxing. My stomach twinged, and looking down I could see a bruise starting to form just below the V of my ribs – and in a perfect bluish halo. Theodore Beam. Now it would come out of my stomach, like a spotlight. As I was inspecting my navel with perfect contentment, and congratulating myself on this new sign, the telephone rang.

I went into the living room, hoping it would be money. It was my father, Jacob Beam.

"Happy Birthday," he said solemnly. It was ten years since I had left home – without returning to visit – and every year he called me, as if to acknowledge some old and unrepayable debt.

"It's nice of you to call."

"My pleasure," Jacob Beam said. His voice is deep, almost hypnotically convincing. It sounds completely sincere, as if his whole being rests on every word. "I hope you are well."

"Very good," I said. "And yourself?"

"As always." Then he added, as always, "Your mother is also well. She sends her regards to you."

My mother never took part in these conversations. Somehow in her mind I had become an extension of him, perhaps even his property. If I'm slow, he's worse. He is at his best, my mother once caustically remarked, with his eyes closed.

Our annual ritual was now complete and it was time to hang up. "You could come home sometime," he said. "Why don't you come home for a visit?"

"I don't know. Maybe I will."

THREE

I got dressed and stood in the middle of my living room, drinking coffee again, the voice of Jacob Beam still ringing in my nerves. Then I opened the door to the garden and let in the wet morning air. My landlady's garden grew thick and fast, full of strange vegetables that crowded up against each other in a blinding mixture of reds, purples, greens – all shades of green from those bruised by blue and gold to those that were lime-bright and almost hurt the eyes. She and her granddaughter tended it; but every morning of the summer I was the one to give it the inspection, stepping out onto the grass in my bare feet to test the day, to bend over and watch for flowers, new growths, even the bugs and worms that squirmed green and happy in this infinity of food. Years of care and compost had built the garden soil several inches above the grass; edges of it could be seen crumbling down onto the lawn – black and wet, rich between the fingers, easily crushed into thick black cream.

"You could come home," Jacob Beam had said. Why not? In my mind it had already begun – the police had opened all the drawers and now I only had to pile what I owned in the mid-

25

dle of the floor, decide what would fit into my suitcases and what would be taken to the second-hand shop on Hastings Street. I had lived here ten years but I didn't own much, not even a bed.

My landlady had come out again and was standing beside me. In the house she seemed short but out here she was just right, stubby and thick, jumping up out of the ground like one of her own plants, an autumn plant, tough and withered with cold but still strong going into winter. Both her hands were full. In one she held a warm loaf of bread. I took it from her and let the steam sift into my palm. In her other hand she held four bits of orange paper, a dull complicated orange that wavered in the bright sun, the colour of a fifty-dollar bill. I took the bills and put them in my pocket.

"That's fair," she said. She smiled. Her face was leathery but hardly lined, and even when she smiled, stretching her lips towards the corners, only small brackets would appear on either side of her mouth. Brackets: as if to say this smile was only an unavoidable exception. But the money felt good in my pocket.

"I'm going home."

"Good," said my landlady. "It's good to go home."

I looked one last time at her garden, contemplating each remaining leaf, each remaining day, until the frost finished it or the fall rains drowned it. Then I went back into my apartment. It was already a mess from the police; nothing much would be required to finish off what they had begun.

By noon I was in a rented car, driving slowly north on the highway that winds up the narrow ledges facing Horseshoe Bay, climbing up the sides of the mountains I could see from my landlady's garden. The day was half gone now; the sun high and burning its way through the perfect sky, shining in long silver ribbons on the streams that rush down from old glaciers into the sea, making the snow on the mountains so white that it pulsed against the sky's blue. I drove slowly and breathed each breath carefully, each breath marked by the pain in my stomach, heavy and sore, branded by the detective's fist. I had been watching his eyes while he hit me, and it seemed they had opened wider at the last moment – drinking it all in.

The fall air was cold and heavy with the mountains. In all my years here I had been waiting to feel at home, truly rooted. But nothing seemed to pull at me, to live right in me: nothing but the imprint of one man's violence and the voice of my father, more real to me than any of the dozens of views that kept presenting themselves with every turn of the road – flashing in an incredible series of perfect moments as if the god of postcards had gone berserk.

Sometimes I turned on the radio. Between the endless advertisements were announcements about the food shortages, further statements and proclamations. And, so that listeners wouldn't get too nervous, there were the usual songs of true love. It's discouraging to hear the mournful ballads of love won and lost when you've been celibate for months. In my glass-and-steel vehicle, belted in, I felt like a one-man erogenous zone sneaking through the mountains. I once read about something called Black Holes: places in the universe where stars have exploded inwards and swallowed themselves. Anything that goes there is swallowed too and disappears forever: the ultimate male fear. In my mobile zone I was looking for its opposite – Soft Holes: places in the universe where stars have disappeared into ecstasy and everyone that comes into them has a billion-year orgasm.

I stopped at a service station and had coffee in their restaurant, looking out their plate-glass window at another dazzling view of the mountains. It was all completely beautiful, completely pure and tough – the earth's crust wrinkled up into rock and jabbing up into the air so high and so strong that even the weather fell into place around it – but it didn't have anything to do with me. Stirring at the half-empty cup I saw myself sitting alone at an endless succession of tables: eating, drinking beer, typing, reading, as if my whole ten years on the

Coast had been like this. Of course it wasn't true – not on the surface of my life that covered everything like a thick busy skin, busywork that sometimes filled whole months, places to go, friends to visit and sometimes even share things with. But somewhere beneath – in that place frozen with fear the moment the police walked in, in that part of me that felt encased, alone, untouched by anything except dreams, old memories and vague promises of the future – it seemed I hadn't grown at all in ten years. At least that's how I felt sitting in the restaurant of the service station, staring past the new-cut cedar panelling to the mountains. I didn't know myself very well then: I hadn't learned to see myself in other people, or how to betray, or to kill, or even to love. I only felt vague stirrings beneath the surface, a half-knowledge that the policeman's careless gesture had tapped me into life again.

The person I had felt closest to that whole summer was my landlady's granddaughter – a tiny four-year-old with stick-thin limbs and an amazing mind that swum around like a misplaced genius fish. At strange hours of the night she would come down the back stairs and scratch at the window of my bedroom. I would let her in and offer her a cup of juice or tea. She would sit with me at the kitchen table on a special chair I had for her, a high chair with a red cushion. Her name was Mona Oh No, and she often would refer to herself in the third person.

"Mona Oh No is sad," she would say, as if referring to a doll. Or, less often, "Mona Oh No is happy tonight." She had oval black eyes – like the eyes of her grandmother, they had already registered all there was to see – and translucent skin that held the light like the surface of some mysterious golden liquid. Though she never complained, there was about her an air of unnatural frailty, and I assumed she had a fatal disease. She was extremely shy and would hardly talk until I had poured her second cup of tea. Then she would take the cards I always kept for her on the table, shuffle them carefully in her small fingers, and spread them out in front of her, looking for all the world like a miniaturized fortune teller. Making all the right faces – her eyes squinted in concentration, mouth all screwed up and pushed into her nose – she would inspect the outlay. "I see a big mess," she would say and push the cards off the table. Or hearing the eternal rasp of my landlady's slippers, she would announce that her grandmother was going to the bathroom. Then she would tell me about the pictures she had seen that night while trying to sleep.

War dreams, she only had war dreams, long scenes of tiny figures running across the screen of her mind and being exploded up into the sky, like firecrackers, like seeds, like herself; and afterwards nothing at all, bare ground, showing no sign of anything. Some nights she saw only the battlefield, no people at all, just pictures of dirt bursting into huge umbrellas, like the magic mushroom that once cracked the basement floor in our house – huge umbrellas of liquid dust that turned into rains of snakes and frogs and lizards, plagues that would crawl over the whole world. "Will they swim the ocean?" she wanted to know. "Will they swim the ocean and come here?"

Some summer nights she came so late that it was beginning to get light by the time we were finished our tea. So we would walk down the steep misty hills to the beach and watch the men in their hip waders netting fish by the shore, inspect their catch for new strange animals. On those mornings the beach would glow with colour as we approached it, the grey logs soaked black with mist and dew, the blues and greys of the morning sky turned red at the edges, staining the grass that wet our shoes. And through the mist that held everything together, old wooden houses to the hedges that surrounded them, earth to clouds, sea to shore, we could see the freighters in the harbour, lined up for loading and unloading, patiently sending long sprays of smoke up into the mountains, the mountains we could barely distinguish across the bay, so green in the summer morning it was possible to believe they had not yet been touched. And winding among the freighters, like small fish in a school of whales, the tugboats moved with confidence, sending out orders, sergeants marshalling the supply lines for the next battle.

When I had finished the coffee I left the service-station restaurant and stood beside my rented car. The day was mild, the air a warm weight against my face. There are feelings and places foreign to me: that is how the mountains are – foreign. In the mountains I feel overwhelmed by the violence that created them, by everything that's so new and fertile that it bursts out with the slightest encouragement, and by the spirits that seem to inhabit them. Not grand and awesome gods, but mischievous and unreliable spirits; that's what puzzles me about the mountains – they're too busy being themselves and don't care about people.

At least not people like me, who don't belong there. When Jacob Beam came home from his wars and unknown adventures he decided he belonged in Salem; and aside from the occasional train journey to Toronto he almost stopped travelling altogether, his most frequent trips being to the shops and the tavern. In the summer, when people from Salem liked to get away from the tourists and go on vacation, Jacob enjoyed sitting in his back yard, in striped nylon lawn chairs, absorbing the sun in his undershirt and baggy pants, reading old books and drinking from an endless supply of beer he'd keep in the shade of his chair. He could sit in the chair all day, until the sun had burned its way through his hair and turned his skin red; and then he would sit there in the evening, rooted, as stuck to his yard as my landlady was to hers, as if the grass growing into his bare feet had secret ways of feeding him.

I got into the car and began to drive back towards Vancouver, now hardly aware of the scenery, all the perfect views condensed into one postcard I had bought and sent from the service station. It had a picture of the station taken against the mountains. The sky was of course absolutely blue, except for two fluffy white clouds that adorned it like expensive cats. On the back of the card I had written my message, brief, not knowing how to say it:

Dear Mom and Dad:
Home soon for visit.
Love,
Theodore

And then I had added, just before pushing it into the scenic cedar postbox:

P.S. Don't worry

Thinking they'd be afraid I must be sick to be coming home, giving in after all these years. Don't worry. When I lived at home, and in the first years after I left, it was almost impossible to believe we had cared for each other at all, rattling around like strangers in the old stone house that could have been a jail, was a jail for me with my father's drunken tantrums and my mother's inexplicable happiness – delighting in him, liking him better the crazier and drunker he was, encouraging any excess and sitting placidly through his occasional bouts of sobriety, knowing they couldn't last. I always felt there that I was the only mistake they shared, an accident in timing. There had been no other children, only me, a son for Jacob Beam to be proud of, swivel his attention to a few times a week; a son for my mother to clean and bathe and dress, and then finally to send to school so that my times coming and going from the house marked the boundary of her freedom. We were a solemn, ridiculous family. It suited us perfectly that now, in retrospect, with my father telephoning on my birthdays and me telephoning home at Christmas, we were trying to invent a normal past for ouselves, a home we had all shared and that could now be visited.

There was a place where the road humped over a wide stream. I got out of the car and followed the stream across a small field and into a patch of spruce and rocky gravel. Here the stream widened, ran fast and shallow; the water roared in my brain, the sound of time passing, the sound stars make when they come close to each other and begin to circle around a common point, drawing closer, waiting to see which will fall into the other. The afternoon sun reflected off the white-grey rocks and grew hot as summer. I lay down and let it soak through my clothes, the bare skin of my neck. Warm air and the sound of water. This place wasn't mine, didn't know me, but I was allowed to be here, for now, now that I had promised to leave.

The sound of the water seemed to grow right into my bones, dissolving the years I had spent here, stripping away the present and cutting loose thousands of jumbled memories of Salem – times and places I hadn't thought of for ten years, but most of all, images of the town itself: a dozen streets carelessly laid out, not quite square at the corners, dotted with old stone houses and newer ones of brick and clapboard, marked in the centre by a few stores, my father's printing shop, the Salem Hotel. The biggest buildings were churches and schools: three churches and two schools for the few hundred people who lived there and the few hundred who lived in the surrounding farms. With the sun on my back each breath seemed to last forever; I hadn't breathed like this since I was a boy, face down in the grass with the smell of cattle and maple trees so familiar they were laced through my nerves, mixed in the scent of the grass, the soft earth. The memory is perfect: at the time it alternated between paradise and unbearable boredom.

I stood up and stretched, kicking stray stones; this gravel was less giving than the ground near Salem. A hawk was circling above the stream. A few beats of its wings, then a long tilted circle. Round and round it flew, gradually moving closer to me until I could see the glitter of its eyes. It was a large square-winged hawk, with mottled brown feathers and claws that could be heard cutting through the air. I found myself backing away. The hawk glided in a long effortless swoop down the centre of the stream, exposing it like a wound, then began to circle upwards. It climbed higher and I watched it, the magical way it had collected the whole day around its flight, opening it into ever-widening circles, making me feel the wind combing through its feathers: as if they were mine, as if for one moment there was nothing for me to do but fly towards the sun.

In the legend the father teaches his boy how to fly and makes him wings from feathers and wax. The boy flies too high, the heat melts the wax, he and his feathers fall tragically into the sea. At least I could know that with my father, Jacob Beam, printer and citizen-about-town, there was no danger that history would be repeated: he always stayed close to the ground and far from the ocean – and advised others to do the same. Jacob Beam – sticky, almost bald and bearded – would be quite a sight in wings. Even Salem would be startled to see him flying above the town, wearing his printer's apron and smoking his inevitable cigar. Like a hawk he too would have to fly in circles because he had nowhere to escape.

By the time I got back to Vancouver it was almost twilight; and as I drove from the upper levels down into the city, the light changed from yellow and red to red and dark blue, settling in heavy layers across the mountains, the days growing shorter now. I checked in the rented car and paid with one of my landlady's burnt-orange bills. Then walked back to the apartment feeling warm and nostalgic – not for Vancouver, though this would be my last day here, but for Salem.

The evening was still warm and my pocket was full of money: money from my landlady and money – not much – that the second-hand store had given me for my old books, clothes, sheets and blankets, odd tools and equipment. As I got to my apartment I began to feel tense, wondering if the police would be hiding nearby, waiting to get whatever they had first come for. I went inside, nervous in the long dark hall, stopping at the spot where they had pushed me up against the wall. And standing there felt a swarm of mysterious forces and pain – as if a ghost had already taken possession of the apartment. It felt empty, emptier than it had been since the day I moved in; nothing there except the landlady's furniture and, in the living room, my remaining clothes and papers and the two metal and cardboard suitcases the second-hand store man had sold me – five dollars each and not a bargain.

With everything gone the fine dust of vacancy had already started to settle in, layering itself like the pastry flesh of the policeman, telling me the obvious: that no one lived here now. On the counter separating the kitchen from the living room my landlady had left a plate of food: delicately filled buns and vegetables, all covered in clear plastic. I made myself some tea and ate; being in the apartment was making the panic come back. I chewed and swallowed; the food pushed the panic down. When I was finished, my stomach was full and sore at the same time, too confused to protest. Suddenly I felt tired and realized I had hardly slept the night before. I went to bed and wrapped myself up in my landlady's quilt. As always I could hear the scrape of her chair, the rasp of her slippers against the floor. Twice I got up to check that the door was locked, then finally drifted off, my stomach knotted tensely around its bruise, my knees pulled up like a baby's, hoping to be born again.

In the morning I felt better. I got up and shaved; and then, to practise impressing my parents and also because I was afraid of being arrested again, I disguised myself by dressing in the only respectable clothes that remained to me – an old brown tweed suit that looked at least vaguely acceptable. I'm tall and thin, with reddish hair and sharp features. In the suit I looked foxlike, a young lawyer who had stumbled on seedy times. At least it surprised my landlady, who came down to say good-bye – quite pleased with me now that she was more than recompensed for the rent I owed her.

We stood at the door and I bent over her. "Come back when you like," she said. For this, as for all other formal occasions, she was wearing her best wig – a whirling grey mass with braid piled on top in the Dutch style. In the years I had lived there we had learned how to ignore each other. But now that I was leaving, I felt only sentimental.

She reached out and touched me, her hand smooth and

cold, tiny but surprisingly heavy, as if her bones were made out of rock. She looked at me through her strangely accepting eyes, to confirm that indeed she had seen me come and now she was seeing me go. One more human being passing through her life. It seemed almost as if she was assessing my limits: reaching out to touch me. I bent down and kissed her forehead. Her skin cold stone against my lips.

"Be happy," she said.

FOUR

The sky had turned a soft puffed grey. I looked at my landlady once again, almost smiling beneath her wig, then dragged my suitcases down the steps to the taxi that was waiting. As it drove, I read the newspaper: the announcements of food shortages had been moved up to the front page. And everyone seemed to have had the same quick reaction – because the Vancouver train station was absolutely jammed. The line-up to the wickets stretched through the whole building and it took me several hours of standing and kicking my battered suitcases forward to reach the front. When I got there a sow-faced man with a blunt nose and jug ears told me that all the coach seats and berths were sold out for two weeks ahead. So I traded three orange bills for a ticket for their smallest compartment. The agent's sow face scowled at me, as if disappointed I had been able to make the fare.

Not only were the departing trains completely booked, but the station was further swollen with those who were arriving. And for every one of us who was fleeing to some more certain home in the East, it seemed there were several who hoped that the mild wet winters of the Coast would be easier to survive. I was reminded again of old stories of the depression and the vast armies of the unemployed criss-crossing the country: when nothing else is possible, motion promises to fill the stomach.

When I finally had my ticket and was making my way

towards the coffee shop, crippled by the two suitcases, I was suddenly caught up in a knot of people and stopped, turned around. There was a rush of panic – an electric panic that filled the whole station – everyone's complete uncertainty about what they were doing, about whether they should be coming or going. Through the shouting, the announcements, the whining of nerves, strains of Muzak could be heard. More love songs, all mashed together into one long, plaintive, syrupy nothing. The Muzak was playing, lights were flashing red and green at the baggage counters, porters and officials were running about the station like newly dead chickens – but the total effect didn't work, it wasn't convincing; the station seemed like a long chaotic dream that we were all being forced to share.

In the coffee shop most were frantically ordering as much as they could, and it seemed as if soon people would begin snatching at each other's food. Even the Salem Hotel, where every Saturday night the locals drank themselves into the depths of their eccentricities, seldom could have equalled this. But in Salem, with all the farms, there would be enough food. I sipped at my coffee, trying to convince myself I could starve for a week, and looked at my reflection in the mirror.

Though my father is short and stocky and my mother small and frail – at least that's how I remembered them – I'm tall and seem almost gigantic in comparison. I try to believe that my face must be a map of dissipation and laziness; but in fact, with my suit, my newly combed hair and shaved face, I looked completely well-adjusted, like a man about to undress for an underwear advertisement. From a distance. In the mirror, aside from my own disappointing image, I could see the door to the coffee shop. Sometimes police came through and each time, predictably, I jumped. Then one of them swung through the door and made directly for me.

Before I could react, he was sitting on the stool beside me. Now I saw that he was not a policeman: his uniform was difficult to place. It was of expensive blue serge extraordinarily clean, with gold braid on the sleeves and decorations over the pocket. The waitress came immediately and stood in front of him.

Everything about him was careful and precise; even his hair was perfectly cut – black and thick, it rested exactly on the edge of his white collar. When he spoke, it was in a strange musical tone, an accent I couldn't place. "I'll have one cup of coffee," he said. "And one salmon sandwich." He recited this like a formula.

Nodding as if she had expected this all along, the waitress wrote it down on her pad and went to the kitchen. When she came back with the food, she put it in front of him and after a brief hesitation withdrew an envelope from her apron. She put it casually on the counter. "This came for you." Typed on the front was a name only: CHRISTOPHER PERESTRELLO.

Perestrello smiled and tucked the envelope under his plate.

"Will the train be on time?" This from the waitress.

"The train is always on time." Perestrello's accent was beautifully flamboyant, like his uniform. And now I realized he must work for the railway – perhaps a conductor, or even a chef. With his olive skin and black eyes, he seemed Spanish. His face was big boned and wide; his nose, almost too strong, was softened by a thick black moustache.

We sat in silence, drinking coffee and smoking. The restaurant was becoming increasingly noisy. A constant throng of people pushed in and out the door, jostling around the cash register. I began to wonder if the train could possibly be this crowded and how they'd be able to feed us all. The thought of food made me hungry.

I looked down at the untouched sandwich in front of Perestrello. There was a certain power about him. His voice and features were so strong he seemed almost dangerous, even cruel: not the careless cruelty of the police but something more purposeful. His hands were scrubbed clean, the nails so perfectly cut and polished they might have been manicured.

In the mirror I could see that the doorway had cleared.

Then a big man, wearing a windbreaker and workingman's pants, filled it up. He looked around the shop and as his gaze settled on us I began to stiffen. The fear that had broken through with the police was alive in me again: this time it was already a familiar companion, something I would need now that all the rules had been changed. The man in the mirror came towards us. He had a wide, fleshy face, he was smiling. Then, only a few feet behind us, he leaned beside a booth of teenage girls who were playing around and laughing. My eyes were locked with his in the mirror. Perestrello was still looking down at the counter, apparently engrossed in his coffee and unaware of the man.

He stepped towards us again. As his hand moved by the pocket of his windbreaker, I thought I saw a flash of metal. Yesterday I had waited to be hit; today I was prepared. I turned on the stool. Then Perestrello, as if cued by me, swung round with incredible speed, leaping to his feet and flashing his hand out to the stranger with such force that he was pinned to the side of the booth. A knife clattered to the floor: in the new stillness of the coffee shop, the sound was anti-climactic.

Perestrello and the stranger seemed glued to each other, unsure what to do next. The faces of the girls had become a comical, uniform white. They were pressed against the wall and each other, holding their breath like a chorus. Finally one edged out and picked the knife up from the floor. Then the police came in, surrounded Perestrello and his assailant in a maze of blue, and led them away.

As they left, Perestrello turned and looked at me as if to thank me. In fact, I was thinking that it had all happened so fast I still didn't know if the man was pulling a knife on Perestrello or if it had just fallen out when Perestrello jumped him. On the counter was the envelope the waitress had left. I put it in my pocket.

When my father made his occasional trips to Toronto he liked to travel first class. He would climb on the train at the end, in the carriage reserved for passengers like himself, and then the train would pull slowly out of the station, leaving us a last glimpse of him sitting contentedly at his window, smoking a cigar. That's how I felt when I finally got into my compartment: like Jacob Beam, escaped from the crowd, isolated at last in this long metal machine that was already quivering, ready to be ridden.

My compartment had two chairs – one wide and soft, somehow turned into a bed; the other hard and narrow, lifted up to reveal a toilet. I put my suitcases on the floor and stretched out on the would-be bed. Almost the whole day had gone; it was now late afternoon and only a few stray beams of light filtered through my window. The train, preparing to leave, was sighing and groaning like an old woman unwilling to get up. Through the soot of my window I could see the platform still filled with hopeful passengers trying to get on the train. A warning whistle sounded, a long bird-like shriek that died in waves of echoes. The chaos on the platform increased. The train shook and jolted, then finally reached some kind of plateau as the hum of the motors picked up, vibrating smoothly through the floor.

I felt dry and exhausted. In the old days Jacob Beam had always come home from his journeys mildly drunk. Even when I was with him – twice he took me to see my grandfather – he would spend the whole time drinking slowly, balancing his dislike of drinking in strange places against the boredom of sitting in a big machine. "We need a drink," he'd say. "This train air isn't good for you." I hadn't noticed it then, but now I did: the air was thick with smoke and stale smells. There was nothing to do except explore the train in search of a bar.

The first car I came to was a dining lounge. If there was a food shortage, no symptoms showed here. Every seat was taken, and most of the passengers were eating elaborate meals, accompanied by bottles of wine propped up in ice buckets. To enhance the illusion of prosperity, each table had its vase of flowers in the centre, and the plates were flanked by rows of heavy silverware. I had to make my way slowly through the car, dodging the innumerable waiters who were carrying heavy, steaming tureens. The scene reminded me of a book about survival in the desert where, after a long succession of stories of men and women shrivelling to parched sticks, the author warns travellers to glut themselves with food and water before setting out in even the most modern of airplanes. "You might as well carry it in your stomach," he warns. "That way it can't be lost or stolen."

After the dining car came a series of cars like my own: long narrow corridors with numbered metal doors. Some of the doors were anonymous, as their numberplates had been removed. Through the windows of the corridors I could see dejected passengers struggling on the platform. The train whistle sounded again, this time a smooth piercing note, as loud as the first but almost mellow.

By the time I found the bar, I had decided it cost too much to eat on trains; I would drink until I arrived in Salem.

In our house where we had lived as eccentrics and strangers, Jacob Beam and my mother would feed me. There had always been enough to eat, food for months ahead: frozen, salted, pickled, canned. There was nothing our house could run out of from one season to the next. As the train whistle blew for the third time, I could hear through the shouting in the car the hiss of the brakes being released. Steam swirled up beside the windows, barely visible through the layers of soot and grease. The train shook itself and began to move, crawling at first, then in a slow glide. As it did, a crowd ran beside it, some pounding unhappily on the windows, others shouting last messages to friends and relatives.

By luck I had a window seat in the bar car. With my can of cold beer, my suit and my blessing from the most inscrutable of landladies, I felt almost dignified. The beer quickly went to my blood; and as I drank it I could see the lights going on all over the city, a long electric garden in the sky. And by the time we got to the suburbs, it was so dark the lights were all that could be seen.

It must have been my day for mirrors. As my eyes grew tired of the lights, they focussed on the window and I noticed the reflection of the woman sitting beside me. She sat with an amazing and unnatural stillness, her face half hidden by a veil of hair. She resembled a portrait I had once seen in some obscure gallery, a portrait of a woman sitting contemplatively by a window, wearing a shawl and waiting with almost inexpressible patience for the artist to finish. She was looking away from me so I shifted round in my seat to see her better. She was small – not as short as my landlady but thin, her hands folded together in her lap, long and finely boned, her cheeks suggesting shadows. The dimmed lights in the bar car gave her face and hair a golden translucence: she looked very young and expensive. In her leather boots and her long skirt and jacket, she resembled one of those precocious government bureaucrats that are sometimes seen in downtown Vancouver; or even a graduate of a fashionable private college. She didn't seem to belong on this train, in this car with me. And she wasn't even drinking.

"Excuse me," I said. She turned. Her eyes were large and wide apart. Green-grey eyes, the colour matching her clothes, so deep and intense in this light I was distracted. "Do you have the time?"

"No," she said. And looked away.

I felt so awkward I couldn't help laughing.

"You shouldn't laugh at strangers," she said. She had a very grave, almost childlike way of speaking. Then she smiled. Her mouth was wide, less innocent than her voice, and her lips seemed full, almost sensuous. Her face straight-on was not as placid as the portrait; it was calm, but as in a mask, thin-fleshed and intense. She wasn't beautiful – her mouth and wide-set eyes seemed intended for someone larger – but there was something she gave off, an impression of energy and con-

42

trol, that made her compelling. She smiled at me and there was a jolt of recognition, as if secret parts of us already knew what would happen.

A few minutes later she stood up to leave. As she rose, her hand brushed against my shoulder. When she was halfway out the car I stood up and left too.

Now the train was moving quickly. The clicking and hammering of the wheels were starting to work into me, driving in the length of the day. I made my way down the narrow swaying corridors, aware that I was slowly catching up to the woman. Then she stopped outside one of the compartment doors, resting her hand on the polished aluminum handle. She turned around, staring directly at me. Standing beside her I felt unfairly large, perhaps even menacing.

"Excuse me," I said again. In this stronger light her skin was amazingly pale and delicate. Later I learned it was always turning different colours, washing through with pinks and reds and greys, changing with every feeling. But at the beginning, during the first few days, I never knew what was happening with her. She seemed nervous, perhaps even angry. I felt as if I had been caught out, as if she were accusing me of trying to force something with her.

Compared to my own cheap compartment, hers was palatial. There was a wide bed covered with a thick quilted spread. At its foot were two ugly leather-and-iron armchairs. Beside one of them was an open briefcase bulging with papers and maps.

We sat down in the armchairs, the new leather squeaking as it received our weight. In this room the regulation green train blinds had been replaced by red velvet curtains. A huge and ancient flower-filled brass vase stood on the floor.

"What do you expect?" she asked. Without waiting for me to answer she jumped up nervously and opened the curtains. Then she crossed the floor and checked the lock. She stood by the door, undecided for a moment, then shut off the light. The compartment filled up with the moon.

"I don't know who you think you are," she said. "I went into the car for a drink, not to be picked up and followed. Don't worry, I'm not afraid of you." She leaned forward and smiled – in control of at least this moment. In the moonlight her hair was silvery white; her eyes shone. We had begun the journey by the sea. Now we were already in the midst of the mountains, travelling along the inside of a deep canyon. Through the window we could see the river twisting and running in the moonlight. I felt embarrassed, as if I were being scolded.

"I'm sorry," I said. "Look at the river."

"It looks like a big silver snake," she said. "It's trying to run away from something. Rivers always remind me of great romantic escapes." She reached under the bed and pulled out a bottle. "Do you want some brandy?"

It seared my tongue, then settled in the stomach, spreading slowly through my blood. For the first time since my birthday I felt calm. "I could leave now," I said.

"Don't."

We passed the bottle back and forth, not drinking much. If my dry season was ending, it could end slowly.

"It's no use expecting anything," she said. "People always ruin things by trying to make them into great romances." She lit a cigarette.

"Great romantic escapes," I said.

"That's right." She laughed. Then looked at me, her head to one side, suddenly professional and expensive, ready to make cocktail conversation. "Tell me," she said, "do you think I have a secret?"

"I don't know."

"You have to guess."

"A secret war," I said. "You have a secret war." I don't know why I said this; I have a weakness for old songs and the bottle was making us friendly. I knew I was supposed to seduce her, but somehow she didn't seem to be playing the part. It was enough to sit and watch the river. A silver snake, yes, running from the mountains to be sucked up by the sea.

I watched the river awhile, then noticed she was crying.

"What's wrong?"

She hid her face in her hair, then lay down on the bed.

Later I went to sit beside her. Reached out and pressed my hand on her belly. By then we were at the bottom of the canyon. Percolating through the metal bangings of wheels and rails we imagined we could hear the sounds of the rushing water. And because the river was closer, the moonlight was now more pronounced, streaming neon white through the window, freezing us as we lay on the bed. My hand on her looked suddenly like my father's hand, Jacob Beam's hand, stiff and wooden, thick with age, cunningly reincarnated on the end of my younger arm.

While I watched her in the evening I thought that in the dark her lips might taste like flowers; moist crushed violets, or at least smooth and silky like out-of-season rose petals. But her mouth was only curious. A warm bizarre continuum between the innocent and the practised. Where is the line between truth and gossip? I didn't think those things, but I remember them. Solemnly she lifted my hand to her counterfeit mouth. She licked the tips of my fingers: once, then again and again. She took my hand.

And it was still my father's hand. I spread my fingers apart. Veins popped up, thick blue rivers laced together with my father's blood. Sometimes he catches me this way, unawares, in the midst of irrelevant movements. Where my skin has suddenly begun to fold, where the bone has grown into my elbows and turned my arms and hands out, so they hang at an awkward angle from my shoulders. Now I can hardly believe I was ever young enough to be disguised as myself.

I can remember the first time my father took me inside a synagogue. They were singing, a strange humming chant that seemed infinitely sad and familiar, like all the funerals I had ever imagined moved into one place, the different voices swaying and diverging from each other, some of the old men turned into their own corners, each faced in his own mysterious direction, towards his own Jerusalem. They were all different sizes, but about them hung a definitely foreign smell, bits of old history clinging to them. Their beards were tough and wiry, thick with thousands of meals and more thousands of prayers: each chanting out his own version of God, each assured only he held God's ear, only he suffered as it was intended.

While the train followed the bottom of the river canyon, I told her I was a salesman. I didn't know how else to explain my suit. I tried to imagine what I might possibly be selling. "You know," I said. "Educational materials. Textbooks and visual aids. My specialty is tape recorders. There's no substitute for the spoken voice."

"Myself," she said, "I'm a librarian." Her name was Lise. Despite everything I believed her.

"Oh yes," I said sympathetically. "So you work in a library. It must be very quiet there."

She reminded me of a woman I had once known, a woman whose ambition it was to starve herself to death. In the beginning she was seventeen years old. Her hair was luxurious and blond, her body slim and lithe. For some reason she believed she was fat. She claimed that her mother had told her this. Her muscles ran like warm fish over her bones. Somehow she stopped eating. Her flesh fell away. The last time I saw her naked she had almost disappeared. She moved across the room, towards me, her bony feet scraping on the bare wood floor. Wanting me, her cheeks hollow, her fleshless forehead shining. Only her genitals had retained their shape.

"I almost came," she said afterwards. "Maybe I did come." We had violated the Geneva accords.

In the moonlight Lise's green eyes glinted, their edges lined with light: fish's eyes. In the moonlight we sat cross-legged on her bed, facing each other, her long leather boots running beside my clothed legs. We were taking a long time to get started. And yet I hesitated, unsure. In her clothes she was still safe; and I, in mine, uncommitted. It seemed forever since I had slept with someone new. And that only reminded me I was going home as a failure. I had brought just two suitcases: one full of books and the other jammed with odds and ends I couldn't give away. I no longer wished to be a genius. I could hardly remember my own life. And yet, despite this, despite my parents' sadness at my lack of success, a woman would restore their faith in me. I could already imagine their shocked and happy faces at the train station.

"Son," Jacob Beam would call me, and wrap his arm falsely about my shoulders while gloating over Lise. Even my mother would be impressed. Fortunately my old room is now furnished with a double bed, a brass antique that Jacob Beam once bought at an auction. Not for profit, of course, but for pity of the owners who needed the money.

In the mornings we would wake up and look out my window at the old twisted apple tree that doubtless still survives in our garden. Then, after a suitably late breakfast, my mother would take Lise touring in the town. They would drop in on Henry McCaffrey, who used to be the schoolteacher in Salem. He would read to them from his notes; his lengthy research into the origins of, well, nothing is too insignificant for the inquiring mind. In the meantime I would be left to myself. Of course they would ask nothing of me. "A child is God's guest," Jacob Beam used to say.

"What are you thinking?" Lise asked.

"My parents would be happy if you marry me," I said. Perhaps fate had arranged that at this last moment something might finally be possible.

Lise looked at me, puzzled.

"I'm sorry," I said. "I meant, I haven't been a perfect son."

Lise took my hands in hers, pressed them – her fingers were strong and sharp. But although she was holding my hands and our legs were touching, almost touching, the tension between us was draining away and I felt again as I had when driving on the mountain – a one-man zone in search of a miracle.

In the moonlight she bent down to retrieve her purse from the floor. She pulled out her wallet, and even before it was opened I knew she was going to tell me that this first night which hadn't yet happened would have to be our last because regrettably – here she would show the pictures of her two young daughters – she had other obligations. No doubt the daughters would have her mouth and eyes, smiling innocently for the camera.

Instead she showed me a picture of a man dressed in a uniform. With his moustache and clean features, he might have been a younger version of Christopher Perestrello.

"Your husband?"

"My secret war," she said. Looking almost smug at having drawn this out of me. "It began with him, when he was killed. They said it was a mistake." She pulled the picture from its plastic folder. The paper was slick and thin, magazine paper. She lit a match and leaned closer over the strange face. It might have been a photograph of a statue. I have always wondered who will preserve me in their mind, who will keep me as I am. I had to blow out the match before it burned her fingers.

"I didn't love him," Lise said. "Maybe sometimes I did. He was in the navy for two years. They didn't make him go anywhere. He just stayed at home and designed explosives. He was very clever with them, really. He liked blowing things up. He could make bombs out of anything: gasoline, odd ingredients lying around a kitchen, anything at all. He was so crazy about it that he used to carry fuses around with him in his pocket."

My mother hid me from strangers. Her belly was innocent. It was she who would meet me at the station, make sure I knew I was forgiven for everything, everything in advance, backwards and forwards.

"He had all these crazy games," Lise said. "He had this game that on the last day of his service he'd go down to the harbour

– he was stationed in San Francisco – and he'd blow up one of the nuclear submarines. He had charts and blueprints, maps of how the submarine was put together and what he'd have to do to make the reactor start. I didn't really understand. It was just a crazy fantasy he had, the same way other people dream of winning a lottery or meeting their perfect romantic love."

"Everyone has crazy ideas."

"You don't have to tell me that." Her eyes were filled with tears again and shone in the light of the moon. "He *was* crazy though. He wanted to stay in the navy forever but he failed some psychological test they gave him. He said he didn't care." She rummaged around in her purse until she found cigarettes. "One Saturday he was just wandering around the harbour, making plans, probably imagining how great it would look as it exploded out of the water, and – for no reason – a guard got nervous and shot him. It was a mistake they said. It happens all the time."

"I'm sorry."

"You don't have to be sorry." She wiped her eyes and then, with her wet fingertips, touched my dry cheeks. The train's wheels clicked and clattered over the cold iron tracks.

"I like trains."

"Theodore Beam," Lise said. "Theodore Beam. What a name for a Jew."

FIVE

It's always hard to look back and say: There, that's how it was. I liked the jumpy green colour of Lise's eyes, the quick ways her face could change, the expensive way she dressed – so exaggerated she seemed to be wearing a costume. And I liked the way she insinuated me into her compartment, made me drunk on her brandy, edged along the question as easily as I, as easily as our legs half touched as we sat – never pushing or retreating – ending it all by saying she never slept with anyone until she had known him for a week. At least a week. And by the time I folded down my ridiculous compartment bed, almost breaking my knees, I was too drunk and tired to care; it was so late the sky had already begun to turn and the sides of the mountains glowed pink and blue – candy mountains.

And when I woke up I thought of Lise, of meeting her, and wondered if I would find her on the train again. By late afternoon the colours of the sky had deepened to black and grey, and the mountains were half hidden by fall mist and clouds. The train passed through them slowly, sighing and swaying on the long graded curves like an old drunk, like my father when he would make his way up the stairs to his bedroom: drunk and good-natured, but only safe because of my mother's presence behind him, her hands dug firmly into his back.

It was almost twenty-four hours since I had eaten and I suddenly remembered the envelope I had taken in the restaurant. CHRISTOPHER PERESTRELLO it said on the outside – no address. When I opened it, there was no letter – only a map, a map of the whole continent stretching from the isthmus of Panama up to the Arctic Circle. Criss-crossed on the map were irregular grids of red and blue lines. Some of them, the east-west ones, were railway routes – our own included. The others might have been anything – airplane paths, transmission wires, more railways.

I had finished with the map and folded it up when Lise appeared in the doorway of my compartment. Her eyes were bright green in the light of this day and her hair hung down her back and shoulders; it was fine and blond-white, like masses of corn silk. On her wrist she wore two silver bracelets: thick dull silver, side by side. It seems important to tell about how she dressed, the money that went into her clothes, the impressions the costumes were supposed to give. We were both wearing jeans but whereas mine were old and baggy, still marked by grease from cars long scrapped, hers were new and embroidered. She always dressed expensively – she and Perestrello and the others. It was more than a disguise; it was some kind of half-intended statement.

She came in the door and sat down. Every time I looked at her, her face changed. In the bar car it had been calm and serene. Later she had seemed nervous, almost sharp. Now she was flushed, the skin about her eyes stained by lack of sleep, her wide mouth pulled tight in concentration.

"I hate it when people lie to me," she said suddenly. "Promise me you'll always tell the truth." Her voice was tense, as if she were on the verge of breaking down, or as if something terrible had happened.

"Of course," I said. Knowing better.

She reached out her hands and I held them in mine. Then, both embarrassed at once, we turned away. She gave off an air of fantastic intensity, as if her skin could burn right through denim and wool. Her spirit energized her body like an oversized motor in a tiny car, and there was nothing she was afraid of, nothing she wasn't strong enough for. But when she collapsed she fell into almost a coma, sometimes sleeping ten or twelve hours at a time, her body completely relaxed and unaware of anything, as if it had been abandoned by her mind.

Sitting on the chair which converted into a toilet, she was looking at me. I shifted position and there was a twinge in my stomach. The first thing I saw when I awoke that morning was my bruise, deep blue, the edges tinted yellow.

Lise was so tense it seemed her nerves might jump right out of her skin. Her long hands moved through the air like small birds. She took out a cigarette and lit it, the dull silver of her lighter matching her bracelets – it was as if she had been planned by a store. The smoke seemed to calm her, and she relaxed and grew more confident. The pink flush of skin receded and she leaned forward to talk as if nothing had happened. "You know," she said, "there was some interesting news on the radio this morning. Do you ever listen to the news?" Her eyes were so bright they glittered; fish's eyes, animal eyes. "Do you ever think about politics? They say there won't be enough food to last the winter. What do you think?"

The truth was that although I read the newspapers, I didn't know anything at all. Not in the way of understanding. When she said there wouldn't be enough food, I thought that not only were there more people than food but that there were more bombs and bullets than people. Even our own peaceable country was said to have stored enough nerve gas to wipe out the entire world population in dozens of different ways. Each of them hygienic. Weather permitting, of course.

"It's going to be a long winter," said Lise. Still waiting. Her mouth wide, her sharp teeth showing, waiting for whatever might come out.

"I don't know," I finally said. Feeling stupid. "I used to think there'd be a big war and that whoever survived all the bombs and radiation would build a new world – like Noah after the flood. Then, when the war didn't happen, I thought there'd be revolutions sweeping away all the bad governments, and the oppressed would rise up and throw over the system." The oppressed, the masses. The crowd on the platform that hadn't made the train. The people Jacob Beam avoided when he sat in the first-class section.

"There have been wars," Lise said. "And there have been revolutions. In some places the new government is just like the old; but in others it's different, a people's government." As she said this she watched me closely. And I watched her. These words seemed like her clothes: stylized and decorative. I couldn't take them seriously, couldn't take seriously the fact that this expensive sharp-edged woman was giving me these tired clichés. It was as if she had suddenly started showing me dirty pictures. After all, who cares who owns the government if your belly is empty and war destroys your house and kills your friends? I remembered what Jacob Beam had once said on the subject: "If everyone ignored each other the world would be a safer place." But he had said this twenty years ago; now there are twice as many of us; we are getting harder to ignore. I took one of Lise's cigarettes and tapped it on the window sill. It was almost dark.

"People's government," I said. "I hate politics. I don't want to be the government."

Lise laughed. "I hate politics," she mimicked. It had started to snow and the train was quickly surrounded by whirling white blankets. We sat and smoked our cigarettes. Through the train windows we could soon see nothing but snow pressing against the glass in the dark grey winter light.

"I didn't mean to jump at you," Lise said, "with the questions."

"That's all right. I just don't know about politics. I never think there's a big plot to keep us all as we are – not a big conscious plot. We might be better if we were different; but we're not."

"Were you ever married? Do you have children?"

"No," I said. "Were you?"

"I was never married," Lise said, "but I had a baby once, a boy. I didn't know what to do with him. I couldn't work and keep him, so I gave him up for adoption."

"Do you ever wish you still had him?"

"Sometimes."

"How old are you?"

"Twenty-four," Lise said.

Twenty-four. Three years younger than myself. But while I was still shuffling through my choices, living out my time so carelessly and so cut off from myself that I now had to retreat to Salem to start all over again, Lise's life had already divided in its centre. Somehow this all seemed vaguely romantic: the creation of life, living through death.

Lise looked at me, reached out her hands again for mine. Have I told you that her hands were always warm? It seemed today she was always reaching out for me, touching me. "I have to tell you," she said. "It didn't end after he was killed. Some of his friends kept coming to visit. I suppose they thought since we lived together, I must be involved in his plans. I found out he was part of a secret group planning various sabotages – though I never knew if they were serious. The idea was that on a certain date, decided years in advance, they would all set in motion some spectacular explosion or destruction, and this would be a catalyst to encourage other groups to start surfacing, to show them the government could be vulnerable." She looked almost apologetic as she spoke, playing nervously with the silver bracelets. Isn't this stupid? she seemed to be saying. In the end we all have the same secrets, the same fantasies, the same desire to burn down the house. "To tell the truth, I thought they were crazy. I moved north to Vancouver, wanting to forget them and him and live a normal life. Then I found out I was pregnant."

"Did you want the baby then?"

"No."

"Why didn't you have an abortion?"

"I don't know. I thought I was going to. I arranged it with a doctor, then I changed my mind. I was confused. Maybe being pregnant gave me something to do."

"What about now?"

"Don't worry," Lise said. "Now I know all about birth control." Her face was calm again, the way it had been when we first met. "Yesterday, in the coffee shop, you took an envelope from the counter. I want you to give it to me."

"What do you mean?"

She smiled, the same smile she had used when she showed me into her compartment. Then she reached into her purse and took out a small black revolver. "Give it to me."

And I began to feel as I sometimes do when dreaming, the feeling of moving through thick clouds of energy, the feeling that we're connected by long invisible strings, the feeling that everything is on purpose, planned. Lise and I: we were part of someone's dream. Because Perestrello had sent her, she had come to discover me in the bar car. To make me follow her. To draw me into her expensive clothes and the small universe her hands made and unmade as they folded and unfolded between us. Or perhaps we would have met anyway. The philosophers say we're brought into a network of circumstance. I would have met her anyway. We would have fallen in love. I would have ended up here, on my knees in this deserted church, writing down these words, feeling the power cupped in me: my mind and body focussed while outside the storm still blows its guts out against the stone walls, blows winter and spring together in one last explosion before the ground melts and the sun pulls out plants the way birds pull out worms. This moment would have passed.

I gave her the map. At first I hesitated. I'd like to say I resisted, but I was too curious to see what would happen. She opened it and flattened it out against her knees. She ran her fingers over its surface, as if to read it by touch, then pointed along a blue line, the route our train was following, stopping at places where arrows had been pencilled in. "Every place an arrow crosses the track, the train stops. It's arranged that we leave supplies there. Perestrello is in charge of the movements of the train. There are other trains too, but I don't know how many."

"And you're part of this?"

Lise smiled widely. Her secret war seemed to be getting out of hand. "I am," she said. "But you don't have to be, Theodore. You can get off the train any place it stops. They don't have time to look for people now – and there's no one they're afraid of." Her hands and voice were calm. "I'll tell you the truth," she said. "I want you to help me but I won't blame you if you leave."

The train wound through the mountain night, wheels hammering like iron drums in the cold high air. There was snow on the ground, but the sky had cleared, revealing a hard, almost full moon that shone so brightly it showed the shadow of the train; and the long plumes of smoke that the engines trailed hanging low and white in the sky. To the deer and mountain elk that saw it pass, the train must have looked like a sterile metal river, leaving nothing behind except the smoke and the noise of our passing.

We sat in my darkened compartment, Lise and I, smoking and watching the snow out the window. In the light of the moon, the snow in the valleys that the train followed was blue grey. As it got higher, it was lighter, until at the peaks it shone like ice. Of all the coastal ranges, this was the easternmost and newest. The peaks were so jagged and rough it seemed that even at this moment they were still being formed, pushed up out of the soft earth with massive force to break apart the sky.

A set of footsteps, light but almost militarily precise, stopped outside our door. There was a knock. I switched on a lamp and opened the door. Wearing a uniform that was a miniature replica of Perestrello's, smiling brilliantly and pushing back the glossy black hair from his brow, a boy just verging on adolescence stepped into the room.

"I'm Daniel Perestrello," he announced. Dann-y-ell, he pronounced it, as if he felt the very blood of his ancestors in his veins. He was overflowing with good spirits, confident that the future was his, simply waiting for him to possess it. And in fact the bones of his hands and feet had already started to grow announcing that soon the rest of him would follow.

"I'm supposed to bring you to dinner," he said.

He led us to a region of the train where I had never been. Some of the first cars were composed of bedrooms and compartments, and we could see nothing but their long narrow corridors lined with faceless doors on one side and the shiny handrail on the other. Spotted among these were two dining cars, like our own, with old-fashioned linen on the tables and passengers happily eating sumptuous meals. Then we entered a section of coach cars. Here it was suddenly crowded; in the first two coaches there were more passengers than all the costlier cars contained among them. I realized that this was where the hundreds or maybe even thousands of desperate people at the train station had finally ended up. At the start of the journey, the racks above the seats must have been neatly piled with luggage and boxes, but now, after only two days, they were a dishevelled mass of clothes and bags of food which people rooted through for what they could find. The aisles were jammed with children and garbage. Slogans had been scrawled on some of the walls and windows. In most places the seats were turned together in groups of four. Some of these areas were covered with coats and blankets, like a tent, for privacy. In others, families and groups of friends sat crammed together, at least three or four in every seat intended for two, playing cards, eating, joking, passing the time as best they could.

After going through more than a dozen coaches, we came to a closed-off car with a locked entrance. Daniel produced a large key, opened it, and led us down a narrow corridor until he came to the one door.

In this compartment the rug was so thick that the noise and

57

vibrations of the train were almost entirely absorbed. It was as if we had entered an underwater world; even the furnishings fostered the illusion of the sea. Bolted to the wall were mahogany bookcases, each shelf with a glass window to protect the books against rolling and pitching. On a table in one corner were various instruments of navigation, an old brass telescope, an astrolabe. Looking strangely at home in the midst of all this paraphernalia, on a table of their own, were radio transmitters and receivers, their multi-coloured lights shining out from behind the glass like exotic electrical fish. As we came into the room, Perestrello was sitting at the table, wearing a pair of headphones and staring intently at the lights. "Come in, Red Thomas," he was saying. "Come in, Red Thomas." There was a blast of static. He fiddled with the controls.

"All systems are in contact," a voice blared out. "Tonight's junction will be delayed by two hours. Repeat. Tonight's junction will be delayed by two hours. Please confirm."

"All right," Perestrello shouted into the microphone. "Two-hour delay is confirmed. Call back later."

"Call back later," said the voice. Despite the static, it sounded young. Then Perestrello removed his headphones and turned off the switches.

Whatever gap had been created by the silence and the space, was filled up by Perestrello. As in the restaurant, he was immaculately dressed, and his olive features and wide dark eyes radiated confidence and determination. Shaking hands he squeezed mine firmly – firmly enough to let me know it would take only a small mistake to crush my bones. "Excuse my modest quarters," he said. "It was kind of you to come." He clapped my shoulder heavily with his free hand.

"Our first meeting was so brief," said Perestrello. "It's fortunate we can now get to know each other. Especially as I am in your debt."

I couldn't help wondering what my father, with his beer belly and sloppy hair and beard, would have thought of this man – Christopher Perestrello, revolutionary in an expensive uniform from nowhere. He was impeccable and anonymous. His strong face seemed to belong to another century. His hair, thick and black, glistened in the light, and the dark ghostly blue of his uniform spread through the room like the living pulse of old family fortunes. Money, that is what Jacob Beam would have called him, Mr. Money.

He let go my hand and waved towards the door. A woman was coming into the room; she paused in the shadows of the doorway then stepped quickly towards us. "My wife," Perestrello said, as if confessing. "I would like you to meet my wife, Felipa. Theodore Beam."

"I'm very pleased . . ." Her costume was carried one stage further than her husband's: a sparkling blue gown that plunged from her shoulders to her belly, revealing a long triangle of smooth olive skin; pale transparent jewels that glittered on her fingers like wet eyes; narrow gold-hooped earrings. Her hair, black and shining, was drawn back from her face and fell in a long curtain that glowed in the candlelight. She clung to my arm as if the whole day had been leading to this moment. Soon Perestrello and Lise were standing to one side, drinks in hand. Meanwhile Felipa had involved me in the process of pouring and serving; my first drink quickly disappeared in favour of my second. I began to notice things about her. I imagined she looked Spanish, like her husband. But where he was strong and radiated vitality, Felipa seemed almost frail: a woman no longer young, an unhealthy pallor beneath the surface of her skin, flashes of gold where teeth had been fixed or replaced. Before-dinner drinks gave way to wine. Aside from laziness and curiosity, one of my worst vices is occasionally drinking myself into oblivion, usually when I least expect it. I remember Felipa standing closer and closer, her arm growing into mine, her voice working its way into my bones and blood.

"I keep thinking you're someone else," I said to her. "I keep thinking you're a movie star." I could imagine her face on the screen, looming up against chalky cliffs, her pitch-black eyes close together, the skin beneath them darkened by dissipation and suggestions of unspeakable vice; she might have played anyone at all. But mostly I was attracted to that long triangle of skin. In the midst of this room filled with clatter and food, my own confusion mounting as glass after glass of red wine was added to my otherwise empty stomach, that warm olive belly looked like a potential oasis.

It drew me magnetically. I found myself standing closer and closer to her, perpetuating our conversation by long pointless jokes and gossip about Salem. I even reminded myself of a Salem drunk, tottering about in the hotel, going on endlessly to whoever happened to be nearest.

And yet in the tiny part of me that was still sober – the part that can never get drunk, only increasingly detached – I thought I was being extraordinarily clever. After all, here I was in the midst of the revolution, led in as a virtual innocent, threatened on all sides by war, the undoubtedly maniacal Perestrello and the memory of the Vancouver police – here I was in the midst of the greatest danger of my life, and in order to fool those who pursued me I was pretending to be drunk, to bump into an insignificant triangle of stomach, to be far too much of a fool to participate in Perestrello's violent games.

Supper came and went. I wouldn't have noticed it if the plate of food hadn't been replaced by pastry, then the pastry by coffee. "Excellent meal," I mumbled to Felipa. "I can't remember anything like it." I touched my hand to her stomach. It was too late; I was so drunk my hand was numb.

"Mr. Beam," Felipa said, "you are suddenly so silent."

I was trying to think of something to say when Perestrello turned out the light. There was a brief silence, then the train whistle sounded: a shrill electric howl that was so close it seemed to grow right out of the walls. Perestrello opened the blinds. We were passing from the mountains into the foothills – a vast expanse of undulating snowy ground stretched out in front of us, like an infinity of breasts and hips stuck hopelessly together. The whistle howled again. As I passed from drunkenness to absolute sobriety, I had a sudden vision of us:

This long multi-engined train with its freight cars piled high with weapons and explosives, and its coaches crammed with people, the food they had rescued, the clothes and memories they could carry with them – a vision of us all being joined together into one live being, flesh and metal joined together by our frantic speed and fear, making us into a long and rabid mechanical wolf, raging across the country from west to east.

Our own dreams of discovery turned back at the Coast by famine and fear, so now the dream had become nightmare, this high-pitched sound that had already carried us from the ocean to the great plains. And now we were heading east again, returning to the heartland, as if only the centre of the continent, where the dream had been spawned, could soothe us.

The moon had risen higher, and with its rising had shrunk and receded to a smaller more intense white. I could remember standing on the shore of the ocean watching this moon, waiting for it to let go its grip, leave the tide slack enough for the small journeys we used to make by boat. And I could remember the stories of Indians who could conjure themselves from the forest to the moon – an easy trick, it was said, if the night was long and the rain held back. Vancouver seemed that far away now – the past few months compressing themselves into one brief dream of quiet.

In the silence of the train's noise there were only Perestrello's footsteps, a catlike restless pacing about the car, as if he had now made himself the master and spirit of this particular animal. He stood in front of the window and pointed outside, like an explorer who had just discovered the world.

"Look," said Perestrello, "space. Empty space. Last summer grain grew there. In twenty years it could be a desert, a coal mine, a city state, a prison camp. What do you think will be there twenty years from now?"

A jumble of images came into my mind – men and women travelling by foot and by horse, searching the plain for live animals: meat for the winter, skins to make clothes against the cold, to make shelter from the wind and the snow.

"Nobody ever thinks of the future," said Perestrello. "Yet to the man who knows how to think, everything is possible. One man who knows what he wants has more force than a thousand who don't want anything."

Perestrello was a romantic, worse than Lise with her wide green eyes falling in love with a man because he died, worse than myself who believed in nothing at all, nothing but what I could touch or had touched me: Lise's warm fingers, Felipa's belly, the policeman's fist twisting into my gut, Jacob Beam's stolid march through life, day joined to day only by the force of will and habit.

"There are times in history," said Perestrello, "when everything hangs in the balance. No one can see the future. The prospect of death is meaningless. That's the worst thing. If a man can no longer hold his own death in his mind, if a man cannot balance the meaning of his death against his life, then he cares about nothing."

But who needs excuses for not caring? We all have the same secret, the same one secret beneath our many secrets: we're all terrorists now. And though for some it means the destruction of the old, and for others it means the creation of the new, at bottom it is the same, the same for you reading these words as it is for me writing them; it's one second after another, moments strung together in long irregular chains, and we all know, if only in our dreams: it's simpler than it ever was – the force of one single life, of one single moment of living and breathing, of one long impulse to live thrown against the random net of history and chance. The man with a million dollars in the bank and the man with only enough food in his stomach to last another hour are finally equal – pure survival is their only calculation.

Perestrello stood in the centre of the room, piles of words

and ideas surrounding him like paper clothes that have gone out of style. There was a burst of static from the radio. He sat down at the desk, began playing with switches and knobs, the static growing louder and sharper until finally it broke apart into words: "Calling, Red Thomas calling, calling . . . Please come in. Please come in . . ." And as Perestrello picked up the microphone and began to speak, his low musical voice soothing against the electric noise, Felipa showed us to the door.

I let Lise help me down the darkened swaying corridors, through the crowded passenger cars, through the bar cars, dining cars, the long faceless corridors of compartments until we came to her own. Where she leaned me against the wall as she searched for a key. Drunk: I was getting worse than my father, turning into him to get back to Salem, drinking three nights in a row; and this time my stomach felt uneasy and swam in layers of wine and brandy. Lise leaned forward and kissed me, her breath and skin still fresh. "Good night," she said. "I'll see you tomorrow." She smiled as if she were about to thank me for dinner. Then she changed her mind, opened the door and helped me into her compartment. We lay down on her bed, squirmed to fit each other's arms. "A week," she whispered. It didn't matter. I was asleep already.

SIX

I was in the room of interrogation. It was comfortable and warm. There was no tension or anxiety here. But I was out of place, fidgeting nervously in the armchair they'd given me, looking at the suit now so faded and dirty, the greying cuffs of my shirt. Even my hands had betrayed me: they were blotchy and sweating, as if they already knew what would happen. In front of me stood the first detective. My throat remembered his arm pushing me back against the wall, as my belly remembered his fist punching out the air.

The detective smiled. His teeth glittered and he waved a cigarette. They had put on music so that no one would be disturbed by my screams. The room was bright at the centre and I was almost blinded by the light. The edges faded away into shadows, populated by rats and blades, remnants of my old nightmares. The detective seated himself on a table. He swung his legs, carefree. He was dressed formally for this occasion: black wool pants, black patent-leather shoes.

"As for ourselves," he said, gesturing mildly and calmly – including the furniture, his assistant with his omnipresent note pad, the woman inspector who attended us all, seated glacially in a dark corner. "As for ourselves, we have all night."

He had spread my luggage out on the table. My books and old journals littered the floor. Also my socks, underwear, old shirts and hairbrush I had been ashamed to throw out.

"Of course this proves nothing," the detective said, waving at the innocent luggage. "You might have hidden it anywhere."

"What?"

"What," he repeated, finding this so comical he almost choked on his cigarette. He looked significantly over at the inspector. My lungs ached for smoke. I remember his laugh – a long glissando cat's purr that left me feeling curiously helpless. "Isn't that funny?" he said when he had recovered himself. "Isn't that funny?" His voice jumped into a giggle. Where was Lise? I wanted to know. In another similar compartment, being put through these ridiculous ceremonies of waiting? Or perhaps she had reported me already.

The inspector stepped forward, out of the shadows. Her long ringed fingers preceded her, clasped across the black belly of her cape. Narrow brass hoops hung from her ears. Her broad smile flashed bits of gold as she moved into the circle of light. She looked like Felipa and yet she did not. In this dream she was older, more sinister, the shadow-side of Felipa's personality. In the light her face wavered like silly-putty, like a liquid hallucination.

"Don't misunderstand," she whispered confidentially. In this war there were no rules, no sides. We were most certainly on the train, and now I could feel the tremors of the car gliding along the uneven rails. She knelt in front of me and gently lowered her head to my knees. The others receded. At that point, to tell the truth, I was certain it was a dream. In this dream, as with all my dreams, I began to sense the process, the filaments of energy stretching from the beginning to the end. I could already imagine waking up. I could feel the pressure of Lise's warm and sleeping body against mine. I reached out for her, wanting the curve of her belly in my hand. Instead my hand met the inspector's shoulder, slid into that corner where the shoulder meets the neck. She moved; my hand was enclosed by her hair.

She turned her head and looked up at me. There was no fat on her neck. The flesh barely covered the tight corded muscles that jumped with her every motion.

"Are you afraid?"

They were forcing me back in the chair, tying a white plastic bib around my neck. "Afraid?" I was swimming in a panic of dreamfear. Even my hand on her neck was damp with sweat. Why didn't I try to strangle her? I thought of it. I even squeezed slightly. Alarms exploded inside of me.

"Stop it!" I shouted. The train shuddered. Its engine began to hum more loudly, throbbing through our car with the dull power of a ship's engine. My hand had turned round her throat. Now my thumb was against her tiny Adam's apple. I pushed. It pushed back. The train jolted forward. I hung onto her neck. In my shoulders, my arms, my thighs, I felt the desire to crush her, to choke her before anything else could happen.

But the muscles of my hands were frozen. With all my will I could barely move my fingers. I screamed and screamed until my throat was raw. I had my mouth wide open, took great convulsive gulps of air. The room faded. When I opened my eyes, everything was as it had been. Her throat was now soft and warm to my touch. On either side the detective stood, holding instruments.

"What do you want?" I asked. But what did it matter? The white plastic was chained to my neck. The inspector looked at me, despairingly, like a teacher at a hopeless pupil. Her face wavered in my mind. It could have been my own.

Once my father had discovered me in his room, searching through his notebooks. I hadn't seen him enter. I only turned when I felt his presence in the room. I was paralyzed. In one motion he had the belt whipped out of his pants, advanced on me, slashing through the air. Just before he hit me, his pants started to slide down, uncovering his polka-dot boxer shorts. Horrified at myself, so scared I thought I would wet my pants, I started to laugh. He checked his swing, then swung again, harder and harder, the belt catching me across the face and knocking me to the floor. I cowered on my knees and elbows, chin tucked into my chest and hands across the back of my neck, laughing hysterically, holding snug in the position they had taught us to take in case of atomic attack.

"Tell us," the inspector said gently. "Tell me."

"You want me to confess?"

"Yes."

"What do I know?" My mind seemed empty of secrets.

"Tell me," she insisted. The cast of her skin darkened, shadows grew around her black eyes. The pulse of her neck beat beneath my fingers. The room swam into focus again, calm and endless. For a moment I was almost part of it, almost ready to wait through this night with them.

"Tell me," she whispered. Her breath on me, searching me out, fanning my fear as the train hit a sudden smooth portion of track and we skimmed along the surface of this iron road.

"Please."

"Yes?"

"I hate pain," I said. "I'm only human."

Two pairs of arms reached out, grabbed my shoulders and forced me deep into the chair. They pried my mouth open. I tried to scream again but couldn't. A long finger, bitter and antiseptic, poked down my tongue. I started to bring up. Stopped. Swallowed involuntarily. As I swallowed I could feel a pill going down my throat. They let go of me.

"We're all human beings," the inspector said. "You and I and the thousands and millions and billions like us on this earth. We seek only justice, a chance to live. Air to breathe and the silence for making love. And if we can become pure, if each of us can be pure in our own heart, then I believe it's possible. No one wants pain; only justice and love." Still kneeling in front of me, she reached out to one of the detectives. He handed her a cigarette, me a package of matches. I lit the inspector's cigarette, gave the matches back. I clasped her shoulders. I have to admit that in a way I almost wanted her – the way a patient wants his nurse. I put one hand on her cheek, then drew it away. The imprint of my fingers remained, red and flushed.

She put her arms around my neck. There was a snap and the chain was undone. The burning tip of her cigarette brushed my skin, singed the hairs at the back of my head. They smelled pungent and unpleasant. She took off the white plastic, loosened my tie. Again the tip of the cigarette passed across me, casually, accidentally. The detectives had stepped back. "You know," she said, "I asked you not to misunderstand me. So many people confuse politics with pain."

The engine was humming, a giant bird skimming over the surface of smooth water, patiently seeking its dinner.

"People always misunderstand," she murmured. She leaned closer to me, her hands slid about my head, pushing back my cheeks. "Open wider, dear." She pulled herself forward and kissed me. She tasted of wine we had drunk at dinner, a dry red wine, delicate and faintly robust. Her skin too smelled expensive, each tiny layer deep and plush. Imperceptibly one of the detectives put his hand across my brow and held my head back against the chair. The inspector now sat herself upon my lap. "Another time," she whispered.

For a moment I supposed I was seeing deeply into her eyes.

"You feel better?" she asked. Her voice had found its way into my nerves and her face was fully Felipa's. "You're not afraid. Without us, there can be no freedom. We're like gardeners, cutting away what is diseased, leaving what is healthy." Her eyes and head moved back. A lamp replaced them, a single eye emanating from it, blinding me. Beyond it, still hovering, Felipa's smile flashed through the glare. Silver pliers appeared in her hand. Effortlessly they were inserted into my mouth, closed about a back upper molar. Jacob Beam once told us at dinner that he never took anaesthetic at the dentist's.

While the detectives held my head, Felipa pulled. There was a period of resistance. My tooth had expanded to fill my whole mouth, a thick dull mountain. When it began to yield, a sudden huge pain grew at its base, raced about my whole upper jaw, inflaming it, penetrating my entire skull. I opened my mouth as wide as it would go, even wider than the detectives' hands were forcing it, wider than the silver pliers which Felipa groaned over, and yelled with all my strength. As I yelled I reached out both my arms, one towards each detective, straining like a madman to bring them crashing together. Somehow I managed to pull myself to my feet. Felipa was sent crashing to the floor. The detectives regained their balance and slammed me back into the chair. But Felipa was still lying on the floor. Her cape had slid up to her waist, revealing long black-netted legs. In her hands she clutched the pliers, triumphant, their jaws fastened tightly about the tooth: small, white and flecked with tiny drops of blood.

Now that it was done, the detectives helped me to my feet. They slapped me on the back, their hands full of comradely affection. "Aah, she's a bitch," the bigger one said. He laughed his cat's laugh. He seemed about ten years older than me. His face was broad and pasty, with deep lines around his mouth. He had fair hair, sandy brown, that parted on one side. It was even possible to see him as he must have looked when he was younger, an athlete in high school, perhaps even class president. Reliable. The kind of man you would take hunting with you. He gave me a wad of cotton to put in my mouth and stop the bleeding. Then, his arm still about my shoulder, he led me to the table where they had been examining my luggage. From one drawer he pulled a microscope and more instruments. From another, a bottle and several shot glasses.

The whiskey hardly even burned as it slid down into my stomach, where it formed a warm pool, pumping heat through me.

"Imported," he said. "One of the advantages of being in the business." He smiled and clapped his hand heavily against my shoulder.

"I hated the job at first," he said. "But what else was I to do? Sell insurance? I guess it does some good." He reached into his suit pocket and pulled out his billfold. He was showing me a picture of himself, his wife and child at the beach. In the background was a huge lake, parasols and bathers interrupting the shoreline. His wife looked much younger than him, very slight and tanned. He himself held the child, an infant, cradled against his round stomach.

The inspector was bent over the table. They had sectioned my tooth and now she was examining the sections through the microscope. She stood up and stretched, then walked over to join us. She leaned against me, her warmth making me realize how cold I was.

"Look at his wife. She says he's away too often. She saves his dinners in the freezer."

She took a drink from the bottle while the detective put away his billfold. She smacked her lips and handed the bottle to me. "That's better," she said. "I'm getting hungry too."

I poked my tongue around my mouth. Where my tooth had been was a vast canyon of blood and whiskey-soaked cotton. Somewhere the pill was running in me. And through the pill I could feel the motion of the train, constant and reassuring, like a rocking cradle. It made me happy. The four of us were standing about, old comrades who had been through something together. Then, almost unobtrusively, as if they didn't wish to disturb me, the detectives pushed me back into the chair and I was sitting down again, blood in my mouth, the sounds of the train mixing with the beating of my heart.

I looked at my frayed cuffs, at the veins puffed and blue on the back of my hand, at the black shoes of the detective. The inspector knelt once more in front of me, her hand on mine. She had no face at all. Now I no longer feared anyone, only my own body: all these tiny bones that could so easily be broken, the millions of nerves so easily betrayed.

"You were wondering about Lise," she said. Her lips were warm on my skin. Her tongue found the inside of my wrist, circled round, soft and loving, a snake in love with its prey. I closed my eyes. She kissed my hand, each of my fingers, ran her tongue on the soft skin between them.

70

SEVEN

I slept so long that it was almost dark by the time I woke up. The train was traversing the flat prairie, and the late afternoon lay across the land, firing the snowfields red and yellow. Sitting cross-legged on Lise's bed, I smoked a cigarette and sipped at a cup of coffee. Bits of the dream still clung to me; and while I looked out the window at the flaming horizon, I found myself poking my tongue nervously around my mouth, surprised all my teeth were still in place.

Somehow Lise had managed to procure a tray of food. As I reached for the orange juice, I saw a napkin with a message written on it: Do you like me?

Through the breaking fog of the dream, Lise smiled craftily. I had begun to think her mouth was wide.

"Do you?"

"Yes," I said. Now it seemed the war had truly begun. The fields were erupting with the sunset, all shades of red and yellow jumping across the snow.

"Last night I wanted to give you this." Lise held out her closed hand and then, opening it, showed me a plain gold ring.

I picked it up gingerly, held it between my fingers to look inside it, laid it in my palm to feel its weight. 22K Gold was etched into it, as if this heavy metal could be measured for love: a year of happiness for every karat.

"Do you like it?"

"It's nice."

"It was my friend's. I don't know where it came from, but when they shot him he was wearing it. They gave it to me and I thought, Well, there's no use burying it in the ground. If you bury things too soon they just come back to haunt you."

She was always saying things like that: Lise, with her perfect clothes and her modulated voice, almost irritated me those first few days. Another time she solemnly told me that she believed in fate. According to the dictionary, fate is unavoidable; according to Lise, fate is what happens – as if to say that everything is always forgiven. But at this point, when she gave me the ring, there was nothing to forgive because nothing had happened. Nothing that could explain this gift of the ring; and in some part of me I was beginning to feel that she was trying to tie me to her, for nothing, for something to do.

"I don't want to force you," she said. "I only want to give you something."

"I like it," I said. Feeling stupid for balking over a gift. Freely given. We had promised each other the truth but it didn't exist anymore. I slid the ring on, moving it carefully over my knuckle to the base of my wedding finger, where it fit perfectly. But when I tried to close my hand it felt uncomfortable and strange.

"You better eat," Lise said.

I took a piece of toast and bit into it. It was so cold and hard that the sound of it breaking apart in my mouth made us both laugh.

Lise took two halves of toast and rubbed them together. They fell apart into bits of charcoal. She carried the plate into the bathroom. "Do not flush foreign matter," she read from the sign. "They want us to sit here, our toilet full of food, while the rest of the world is starving."

Then she suddenly looked sad and came and lay on the bed beside me, crying as I held her and waited, my ringed hand on her back pulling her closer, trying to console her and then trying to console myself too as the train sped into the night. And as she cried it seemed her voice changed: at first she cried only for herself, then it deepened to the rhythms of the train as if she were crying for everyone on it and everyone who had been lost in other wars.

Like my father – who had not been lost, only confused beyond recognition, so that sitting in a valley in Spain he had written hopeless letters to my mother:

The sea is warm here. It is easy to swim. Last week I was drunk all the time. Now I've had a headache since. I don't hope to survive.

Last night I fell asleep at sunset, lying on ground above a fast-moving stream. The sounds of the water made me think I was back home again, with you. I found I was asking God to forgive me. Then I began to be convinced you were having an affair with someone else.

Today we went into another buried town. I looked into the graveyard for the ancestors of da Bobidilla. For the first time we dug trenches. I keep having nightmares that we will dig up live bodies.

Later we sat on the bed, the maps spread out between us. "Look," Lise said. With her pen she drew a long, looping line that traced the path of our journey, from its beginning in Vancouver Harbour, up the Fraser Canyon and through the Kicking Horse Pass, out into the midst of the prairies. There she paused momentarily. Then she continued, showing where we would go, across the prairie to the Great Lakes, which we would skirt closely, following their northern shores until we reached the small side line that would take us into the midst of central Ontario and that forgotten and useless region which surrounds the town of Salem.

"Could they ever find us here?" she asked needlessly, pointing at Salem, its empire of dense bush, broken and rolling terrain, narrow streams and dead-end valleys. Although she had never seen the place, she was absolutely right. The only reason the citizens of Salem never got lost was that no one ever went anywhere. We'd hide in the old Anglican church a few miles outside of town. To distract the locals, we'd open an antique store. We'd cover the walls with barn boards and I'd make myself conspicuous in the front yard, wearing a straw hat and chewing contemplatively on a piece of grass, slowly sanding down an old pine washstand and spitting perfect bull's-eyes of green juice onto the lawn.

Our eyes had been drawn south of the border. The map showed rivers and mountains, a few scattered cities marked only by small black dots: as if nothing had changed since a few wooden sailing ships had established their tentative colonies along the Atlantic shore; as if the inner continent were still whole. But though the map showed nothing, we saw it all: the war clouds standing black and stagnant over the cities as they collapsed upon themselves, the nets of roads cast about the cities, clenching the landscape like the dead amazed skin about an ancient eye.

"They'll come up here," Lise said, sweeping over the map with her pen. Millions would stream northward on the old explorers' route, darken Lake Champlain like the seasonal shadows of the migrating birds. But by the time they got to the church, we'd have blended into the landscape. In the front yard they'd see only the antique furniture we had restored, the old wood glowing with its new varnish. They'd look at us curiously, slowing down in their big cars loaded with guns and instant food. Finally they'd stop and buy it all, paying us with their worthless money. When we ran out of antiques we'd have to fake it, build new ones out of wood held together by magnets and plastic hinges.

The train moved through the night, steel wheels hammering on steel tracks. Around her neck Lise wore a gold chain that carried a six-cornered star. When she leaned forward the star tangled in her yellow hair; with each new motion she had to shake it free. And each time that happened, and I saw her nervously brush her hair back over her shoulder, I felt a strange sense of recognition, as if we had been sitting here always, planning how to survive, as if our previous lives had been unreal and could now be forgotten.

Lise put her hand on mine. "Do you remember I asked if you would help me?"

"Yes."

"Do you still want to? You don't have to."

"I thought it was settled."

Lise smiled. Our hands were crushing the map. Tonight was to be a new beginning, and now that she had reminded me, I felt nervous and restless, wondering if the train was on schedule, if everything would go exactly as planned or if in the end we'd have gotten ourselves killed for nothing. I pushed up the blind and looked outside. The sun had been replaced by the moon, and where the prairie had been in flames before it now glowed dully, a blue-grey metallic glow. There were no towns, no houses, no signs of anything live outside. Only the occasional car, pushing yellow cones of light down the road that was otherwise invisible.

"Will I like your parents?"

"I hope so."

"Will they like me?"

"Like you," I said. "You won't believe how much they'll like you."

Lise spread my left hand out on the map. I have long fingers and wide palms; good hands, Jacob Beam used to say, waiting for me to do some work with them. With the ring on, my hand looked respectable and solid, a good citizen in these troubled times.

"It looks good on you," she said. "We'll get rings for all your fingers." She pulled me on top of her but lay quiet and passive still waiting for the week to pass.

My eyes were closed and I felt blanketed in the sweet, almost milky smell of Lise's hair and skin. The rhythmic clicking of the train's wheels seemed to hypnotize us and I began to drift into a long quiet vision of a single rainbow-coloured railway track undulating and vibrating as long strings of bright wheels rushed over it, flashing and bouncing like pinwheels. We were all joined together, metal and flesh, my finger to this ring, our bodies to this train; and nothing was different from anything else: brains, belly, arms, all felt the same, part of the same unlocated mass. The lids of my eyes were burning with the sight of myself lying on top of Lise, my elbows tucked under like the wings of an unsuccessful angel. And when I finally looked at Lise's face it was almost serene, as if she was thinking of nothing at all but had fallen back into some deep emotional pool of old wishes and dreams.

The train whistle tore through the web of our sleep. We were still lying in each other's arms; and as we started moving it seemed right that we had woken up this way, tangled up in each other's hair and limbs, as if from now on nothing could happen to us separately.

My skin now felt cold and vulnerable, needing to be encased in layers of cotton and wool. I was wearing jeans and a thin shirt. Lise went to her cupboard and began tossing out more clothes: two heavy sweaters, thick socks and gloves with leather reinforcing stitched across the palm. My bones hummed with the jolting of the train. Now we were becoming addicted to this motion; it moved through our unresisting bodies like a permanent massage.

In the pocket of the jeans my watch was waiting. I strapped it on carefully, fascinated as always by the tiny dots that glowed in the dark and the small window that showed the day and the month. It was a fancy watch, expensive and almost impossible to break. It had come with a gold expansion bracelet but I had replaced that with a thick leather strap, something suitable for working with outside, the kind of strap my father used to wear. The watch was always accurate and never needed to be wound. Lise reached for me and looked at the luminous figures: ten minutes to two.

We flattened the map out carefully and traced the path of

the railway line. I noticed now that where the arrows crossed the line there were usually indications of an old road. Tonight we were coming to the first of the arrows and in spite of all the talk and preparation, I felt unprepared. All the arrows were outside of towns, places to be passed through late at night.

"Forty minutes," Lise said. Her voice had taken on a practical turn. I adjusted the ring on my finger and lit a new cigarette; when the smoke caught in my lungs I felt reassured and stood up to stretch my legs.

"What if someone tries to stop us?"

"No one will."

"What about the police?"

Lise laughed. "The police! Perestrello never worries about the police. And why would they attack him? There'd only be a big fight and people would get killed unnecessarily."

"Exactly," I muttered, thinking of myself. I tightened my watch until the strap pinched my wrist. "This must be illegal, using the train this way – I mean, you can't just drive around the country delivering weapons and explosives to your friends, as if you were a private grocery truck."

Lise looked up from the map. "Legal," she said. Her voice was unbelieving, as if what I had asked was so stupid she didn't know where to begin. "Sometimes I really wonder about you," she said. "Don't you understand anything that's happening around you? There's no such thing as law anymore. The unions could overthrow the army in a week now. But why would they? No one wants to live in a country when it's in the middle of a famine. It's live and let live."

"Then why work for Perestrello? We could go back to Salem and grow potatoes. At least we wouldn't starve."

"Because," Lise said, patient as my dream, "Perestrello cares about people. He believes in them." She came and stood next to me. I've said she was intense. Her eyes sometimes burned with it, so convinced that it seemed she had disappeared and only this purposeful energy was left. I picked up the map. It fell together in my hand like an old wallet.

"He believes in the future, Theodore. I *know* he does."

In my arms, through all the layers of clothes, Lise felt small and frail as a child. Leaning against the door, eyes closed, holding her, I was hypnotized again by the noises and swaying of the train. It seemed we had been on this train forever, that it had grown into our bodies like any other twist of nature, sealing us together with its inevitable speed, erasing our pasts as we sacrificed them to each other. But while I was falling asleep again, Lise had moved her hand around my back and was unlocking the door.

We moved slowly through the darkened corridors of the sleeping cars. The tunnels between the cars were cold and their floors were packed with snow. We came to the dining car. It was empty; its tables were covered with white linen and the service laid for breakfast. On each of the tables was a small glass vase. In the morning they would be filled with water and red roses. The lights in this car were dimmed, and the linen glowed a surreal blue-white as we passed through.

At the end of the car was a door. Lise opened it with a key. Then we were in a small vestibule. The next door would lead us outside, to the platform between this car and the freight cars. This door was much heavier. I pushed at it gently. It began to yield, then slammed back with the wind. "Go ahead," Lise whispered. First I put my shoulder then my whole weight against it. Finally it gave way. The wind forced me back, blowing smoke and soot into my face, filling my eyes so I could only move ahead instinctively, the cold outside air blowing through my clothes and skin right into my bones. I could feel Lise close behind me for protection, her fists buried in my back. Bits of snow, blown up by the passing of the train, cut into us. There was one bad step, where the cars coupled together; then, as she had told me, there was a small platform below the foot of the ladder. When I had both feet on the bottom rung, I reached back for Lise.

Clinging to the ladder against the back of the freight car we were protected from the wind. The freezing cold and fear levelled off. To our right, the south, there were a few lights from a town we would be passing through. In the spring and fall, westbound freight trains stopped here to unload the huge elevators full of grain this empty country grew, grain destined for Vancouver and eventual export to China or Russia. Now, with the famine coming here, that would change. I moved up the ladder carefully, gripping each rung with my hands, uncertain that my boots would hold on the slippery metal. When I got to the top I stuck my head over. For the first time I felt the full strength of the wind. It slapped against my head and face, almost made me lose my balance.

I looked down at Lise. She was waving me ahead. The ladder was bent at the top and continued along the roof. I moved cautiously, keeping my head down, until I was flat on my stomach. In the movies this is always the romantic moment. Bathed in broad sunlight the hero lies on the roof, preferably with a revolver in each hand, and fights off the villains. But all I had was a knife Lise had given me, a sharp single-bladed knife that folded into itself. At least the snow couldn't reach me here.

But the wind dug into my back, gripped my ribs and pressed my chest into the cold metal rungs of the ladder. As I pulled myself along, they scraped my chest and belly, kept trapping my knees. The wind was so cold on my skull that it seemed my scalp had been laid open and the bones exposed. I looked at my watch. Five after two. We had less than half an hour. At each rung I rubbed my hand carefully over the roof, looking for the trap door. Finally I came to it. No light showed from the inside. I pushed at the door and it fell open. The car was completely dark. This wasn't the way it was supposed to be.

I edged back. There was a shot; I could barely hear it, the sound filtered dully through the wind. I had the knife in my hand now, open. Lise touched my ankle. The feel of her hand startled me so much my leg jumped. Then the train whistle sounded. From the top of the car it was so loud, magnified by the wind, it seemed the whole world had exploded. In the midst of it I sensed something moving below me. I grabbed the knife more tightly and moved forward. A head appeared. I tried to smash the handle of my knife against it. But it was faster than me; there was a moment of contact as it brushed by, then my wrist slammed into the metal edge of the door.

"Jesus Christ," the voice came up. "You almost killed me." From inside the car was the signal we had arranged – two flashes of light. Each one jumped outside like a small yellow flare. I folded up my knife and put it in my pocket. I stood up, to start lowering my feet into the car. The wind surprised me, caught me like a badly tied sail. It pushed me to one side and I thought I was going to fall over until I realized I was still hanging on with one hand. I tried again, this time backing down. The flashlight showed me the floor. Then Lise's shadow was above. I caught her as she came down. Even falling she was almost without weight, her bones hollow and her flesh starving.

In the yellow beam of the flashlight, we could see each other: Lise and I and Perestrello's son, Daniel. We pushed a wooden box beneath the opening in the roof and I climbed up and bolted the trap door closed. Now finally Daniel was satisfied. He switched on the inside light. We were in a huge and ancient freight car. At either end were refrigerators and stoves, crated up for cross-country shipment. In the centre, piled now in a U around the door where we would be unloading them, were boxes of rifles and ammunition.

"Jesus Christ," Daniel said again, as if he had just learned to swear that afternoon. He was thirteen years old.

"You should be careful with that gun," I said. Daniel was dressed in green fatigues that were too big for him. From his belt hung a shining brown leather holster. Its cover was snapped into place, bulging over the gun.

"We're expecting trouble," he said. His overgrown hand caressed the holster obsessively. Though he was still small and slight, he'd end up being big. It was easy to see in the bones of his hands and knuckles, which seemed to have lengthened and swollen even in the few days I had known him.

"Trouble," Lise repeated. She looked at me curiously. I adjusted myself with care as I sat down on one of the boxes. Now that we were inside I had forgotten the wind and the cold and my body, tired and content, was starting to remember Lise again, and that we were supposed to be lying in bed, sleeping on top of each other, trying to make our dream fit into the noises of the train.

As if he understood our plight, Daniel produced a thermos and began filling plastic cups with coffee. Sixteen minutes after two. I spread the map out in front of me and took off my gloves. My new gold ring caught on my knuckle. I pushed it back down again, forcing the edges into the sensitive skin between my fingers. It didn't feel right. Lise was watching me, as if already suspicious that I was planning to lose it.

The train was going full speed, bouncing and swaying, bumping so much that the coffee was spilling, bit by bit, small splashes hanging in the air above the cups. Lise had now found herself a corner and was sitting, cross-legged on a box of rifles, her back pushed against the wall.

The coffee was scalding. It made shallow burnt islands on my lips and tongue. I swallowed and it jumped down my throat. I was leaning on the map, my elbows pressed down against the wooden packing case. Sleep was all I wanted; it was coming through my nervous system in waves. We would soon be back in the huge bed they had given us, the blankets piled over our heads and shoulders, enclosing us in our cave. I could already feel the heat of Lise's breath on my neck, the long unwinding of my bones and muscles.

"Theodore," came Lise's voice through the noises of the train. And with it a pounding on the roof of the car, a rifle butt crashing against the trap door. The boy turned out the light, and the moment it was dark, as if on cue, the train whistle sounded again, a hollow piercing echo. Two-twenty. Exactly ten more minutes. The train began to slow. As the whistle died away we could hear the pounding again. Daniel pulled the emergency brake cord. Suddenly we were thrown across the car.

Through the screaming of the wheels we could hear a human voice; whoever had been trying to get in had been thrown off the roof. And now Daniel had the door pushed open and was lying on the floor, a rifle cradled in his arms. The train was still skidding and screeching. In this noise the shots were silent, but we could see Daniel's body snap back with each recoil. Once. Twice. Then he was on his feet again, jumping for the cord. I took his place at the door, trying to slide it closed.

A figure was kneeling outside on the ground, illuminated by the slowly passing light from a train window. It tried to stand up. As it collapsed a red spark jumped out. My hand was torn away from the door.

The centre of my brain felt as if it had been sledgehammered and my bones went stiff and numb. I swayed forward, almost falling out. Then Daniel grabbed at my sweater and pulled me back. Even as I regained my balance some part of me remembered what I was supposed to be doing and pushed the door closed. Daniel turned on the light. I couldn't tell where I had been hit. Finally I looked down at the palm of my hand. A huge sliver of wood, almost as big as a finger, was protruding from the fat part of the heel. Without thinking, I pulled it out. A chunk of flesh was missing. Gradually the vacancy began to fill with blood. I sucked at the wound and then checked my watch. Two-twenty-four. The train was picking up speed but we'd be late now. We began pushing the wooden boxes into place, in front of the door. At first I used only one hand, then I put on my gloves and used both.

The train had slowed, was now skimming along the rails like a bird swooping down over a lake. I climbed up through the trap door of the roof and lay on the ladder again. My hand was sore and stiff already. Tomorrow I would have to spend the day soaking it in water. Now it was filled with Daniel's pistol. The wind made my bones ache, drew tears to my eyes. Soon my face was covered in them, dried tears and new tears. The more I tried to stop, the more I cried, until my chest and stomach began to hurt and I had to lay my head down in my arms.

Two-thirty-two. At this speed the train flew smoothly. I took off my glove and held my hand out to the wind to stop the blood. Now it felt almost wooden. As we drew close to the lights of the town, they appeared as great scintillating globes, shooting off arms of red and blue and yellow. For the first time I was really afraid. Two cars were moving slowly along the highway. I hugged close to the roof as we passed them. Crossing signals flashed ahead. This time the train's whistle echoed like a strange and pitiful cry, trying to fill up the night. Five more miles now. Perestrello would be checking his map one last time, brushing specks of dust from his impeccable blue sleeves, trying to remember the face of his son.

The main highway turned north at the town. Looking ahead now I could see nothing at all in the darkness of the night, only a slight grey shimmer that the rising crescent moon threw onto the snow. Still, we were losing speed. I put my glove back on and fitted my finger next to the trigger of the pistol. The leather was cold and sticky with blood. The wind had stiffened it and it scraped against the open wound. Now we were coasting. There were two brief flashes of yellow light from a crossing up ahead. Two-forty-one. I took the safety off, the way Daniel had shown me. Over the humming of the wheels I heard them sliding the door open. They'd be hiding now, behind the crates, grenades in their hands as if the war might start at the slightest excuse. When I accepted the ring, Lise had looked at me in the most extraordinary way, her eyes pushed wide open, black irises split apart in surprise at finding that even this was part of the obscure plan that had jammed our lives together.

I could see the truck against the snow. Then figures jumping out of the cab as we stopped, the open door of the freight car opposite the back of the truck. I leaned over to look. A light pinned me to the roof, pistol in my hand. The finger against the trigger started to tremble. The light had caught me in the eyes and blinded me. I didn't know where to aim or whether to just put it down. The fear had grown into hopelessness. I looked away from the light. One of the men had circled to the side of the car, climbed up the roof and was coming towards me. I dropped the gun and turned to meet him.

"Theodore Beam," he whispered with great satisfaction, as if he had spent the whole day memorizing photographs. The light had caught us both now. I didn't know him.

"Let's get this fucking stuff moved," he said. We dropped down into the car and began passing the crates out to the truck. In the half light of flashlights and lanterns his face started to pull at my memory. There were four men – two in the train and two in the truck, arms swinging back and forth, a human conveyor belt. Daniel was at the far end, sorting and stacking. Lise was outside, pacing around with a rifle in her arms, like a crying baby that needed to be walked.

"Theodore Beam," he whispered again. "You have to get better."

He was tall, as tall as myself, and each time I turned back he had a crate ready for me, moving slowly to my hands so it would be easy to grab and pass on. "When you're doing this," he asked, "do you think about the revolution?"

"No," I admitted. "I'm too hungry."

In these few days I had lost so much weight that my jeans were starting to slide down my hips. My arms and shoulders were sore and my back was beginning to ache. We had passed out all the rifles and were now on the heavier crates, the ammunition. I tried to shift the angle of my back and staggered as I passed one of the boxes, breaking the rhythm of the line.

"Careful," he whispered. "In two months this will be easy."

Now I recognized him. I had seen him in the mirror of the train station coffee shop, sneaking up on Perestrello and myself, his broad face smiling as he stalked us. I took the weight of the gunpowder and metal into my hands and passed it on. With each twist I tried to guess how much worse the next one would be. The wound on my hand had broken open again. Now each box would be stamped with my blood. It was possible that no one would notice.

"Last one," he said. He clapped my back, his hand like stone against my flesh. He grinned. Some of his teeth were rimmed with gold, medals from old battles. Then he stepped across into the truck.

Daniel had pulled the cord. The train hissed and sighed, trembled and began to move. Lise was sitting exhausted on the floor, her head resting against her knees. Daniel pushed the door closed and turned on the light. Now the train was skimming again, the wheels humming against the track. Soon they began to clack and bang as they gained speed for our run through the night. I thought I heard Lise crying. I looked down and saw that she had wrapped a cloth around her head. One side was soaked with blood, matted and caked into layers. Her hair too was tangled up with it, like a mass of silk that had been thrown into a puddle and run over by a truck. I helped her stand up. She led me over to the wall where she had been standing. The bullet was embedded in it, spread apart and flattened into a tiny metal fist.

EIGHT

It was almost dawn before the train stopped for a few minutes, giving me time to help Lise back to her compartment. She wrapped herself in a thick white flannel nightgown, like a little girl secure in her mother's clothes, and climbed carefully into the wide bed. From there, drinking a glass of brandy and talking in a weak voice, she gave instructions until I found the particular shirt she wanted and tore it into strips for a bandage. More brandy was poured to wash away the blood, then I tied a soft cloth around her head. She didn't complain, only winced as the alcohol touched the open flesh. Then she relaxed and fell asleep almost instantly, the glass still in her hand.

A few hours later Felipa came to tell us the train would be stopping overnight in Regina.

"Regina," said Felipa, pronouncing the word as if it had never been spoken before. "Ree-gi-na. What a horrible name for a city. Has anyone ever been to such a place?" Along with her news she had brought us a bag full of buns, oranges and cheese.

"I hope it still has restaurants," I said. All this talk of famine was starting to come true. My stomach was getting small and shrivelled, like a muscle knotted into itself.

The skin about Felipa's eyes was dark with fatigue. The first time we had met I had been attracted to her, despite myself; now I was only tired and discouraged, trying to find some room in my belly for this food. While we ate, Felipa sat uncomfortably by the window. The train was moving with fantastic speed, as if it had gathered confidence in the night. Outside we could see a blur of snow, the occasional fence dividing one huge field from the other. "Poor Lise," Felipa suddenly said, noticing her wound for the first time. "We'll have to take you to a doctor."

Lise was still in bed, a tiny figure covered almost to the neck with a thick blanket. She sat up and unwrapped the bandage. What had merely been a bad cut above her left eye had now swollen into a fat purple egg with a thick black seam down the centre. She took a mirror from the table beside the bed and inspected herself. "It looks awful," she said, almost pleased with herself. "God, does it ever look awful."

Lise shifted herself against the pillows, then began dabbing at the cut with a new piece of cloth and more brandy. Immediately Felipa went over to help. "Look at this. Look at this. Get me some hot water and a towel. Did this happen last night? They were broadcasting on the radio all last night." Red Thomas she meant, that improbable young voice cutting through the static. I could imagine him staying up days at a time, glued to his station by dozens of cups of coffee and plastic sandwiches, his voice getting worn out and excited, indiscriminately relaying everything that had happened, detail by detail, hoping someone would make sense of it.

In Salem my parents used to have a short-wave radio in the living room. Sometimes they would let me sit in the dark and listen to it, listen to the voices coming in, a talking choir from around the world all speaking in languages I couldn't understand.

"On the radio he said the government is beginning to panic. Now they've announced more shortages – oil and fuel – and citizens are supposed to stay in their homes and turn down the heat. *Turn down the heat*. He says the streets are filled with demonstrators."

"It doesn't hurt," Lise said. "I just have a headache." But

every time the train bounced, she closed her eyes. In her hand she had a torn-open bun and an orange; and as Felipa cleaned the wound and talked, Lise kept on eating.

"You'll have to see a doctor," Felipa muttered. "Look at this. My goddamn idiot husband. You could have been killed." The train whistle howled, the pitch higher than ever at this fantastic speed.

A wind had come up and snow was gusting against the windows of our compartment. I could remember winters in the old one-room school at Salem, staring at the big clock as it dragged through the day, epileptically jerking from one minute to the next. On one side of the clock was a picture of the queen: cheeks rouged, eyes glass-blue, looking so bored she might have been stuffed. And on the other side, wearing a narrow black beard and resembling a cross between Jesse James and Jesus Christ, was Francisco da Bobidilla – founder and patron saint of Salem, preserved forever in one of those tinted, nineteenth-century photographs that make everyone look as if they've been declared immortal. In fact, da Bobidilla, with his high pomaded brow and his tinted skin, had done the next best thing to living forever – he had built houses that threatened never to fall down. Our own, for example, was set on a stone foundation four feet thick; even its walls were almost that thick, rising in cut limestone out of the ground like a permanent fortress against the infidels. "This country is built on its small towns," Henry McCaffrey used to intone, standing in front of the class in his black schoolteacher's suit. And then, as often as not, he would tell us about how his father had worked on the great railway, the iron road that connected sea to sea and made Canada a nation.

And what happened to his railway? It was drifted over with snow and there were no traces of movement. Only our train with its cargo of stolen explosives was alive, carrying them from an unknown ship in Vancouver Harbour to the centre of the country, like a giant missile turned round and homing in on the dream that launched it.

"They say everything will be back to normal in a week," Felipa said. "Citizens are requested to listen regularly to the radio for hints on saving food and fuel." She had finished cleaning the wound and now tied a new strip of cloth around Lise's head. "They like to keep you cold," she said, "cold and hungry. When your belly is empty and you shiver all day, it's hard to think of anything. They also announced that for this one week they'll keep the television transmitters operating around the clock, bringing everyone their favourite movies."

Feeling better, Lise washed her face and shook her hair free. It fell religiously about the shoulders of her white nightgown, still massed and clotted with blood.

Now that she had nothing to do, Felipa was restless again. Her eyes jumped around the compartment as she smoked a cigarette. Finally they stopped at my new ring.

"Congratulations," Felipa said.

"It was nothing," I said stupidly. Despite myself, I was blushing, and instead of hiding it I stared aggressively at Felipa. Lise seemed completely unbothered by this; in fact she was smiling, as if our engagement had just been announced. This only made me more hostile towards Felipa. Ministering to Lise, she had taken over, taken over her bullet wound in the same way I had imagined she and Perestrello had taken over her psychological wounds, using her hurt to manipulate her.

"Lise is lucky to have found such a brave companion," Felipa said. For a moment her face melted into the face that had bent over me in my dream. She kissed Lise on the cheek. My hostility kept increasing. There was something in the way she treated Lise, in everything she said and did towards her, that was supposed to be telling me that Lise was somehow less than human, that she had to be treated like a child, charming and lovable but not whole. Maybe they had made her believe this too, so that she would work for them without question.

The train whistle howled again. Through the snow and wind we could now see the occasional house. "I wish you every happiness," Felipa said.

Lise looked startled. I looked out the window. The ring felt uncomfortable on my finger and I had to resist taking it off.

"Men," Lise finally said, "they never want to get married."

Felipa smiled broadly, in control again. She put her hand on Lise's as if it was established now, the two women on the lookout for the untrustworthy man. "You're too young, anyway. If you get married now what will you have to look forward to?"

We were approaching the outskirts of Regina. There were scatterings of houses and the occasional service station, but everything looked closed down and the roads hadn't been ploughed. Felipa got up from the bed and came over to the window. "Ree-gi-na," she said. "I hate those towns. No one ever knows what they want. All they do is talk and talk. Nothing ever happens."

"Are we in a hurry?"

"I don't know," Felipa said sharply. "Are you?" Then she went and stood by the door. "When we get to town, take a room in the hotel and find a doctor for Lise. Then we'll see what happens." She nodded at us, to let us know we had both failed some invisible test, and walked out.

"Bitch," Lise said as soon as the door closed.

"It doesn't matter."

"Sometimes she makes me sick."

The train whistle was blowing as we came into the town.

I sat down on the bed beside Lise. Wounded, she seemed not frail but stronger – as if she had now proved she could survive the worst that fate could deal her.

"Did you ever want to get married?"

"No."

"I don't want to own you. What are you afraid of?" Her voice had suddenly jumped towards the edge again.

"Nothing."

She held my hands in hers. Her touch was starting to seem cloying to me now. I couldn't believe we'd ever sleep together, that I'd ever sleep with anyone. I still wanted her but in a way my body was starting to revolt against all this delay, to tell me we would never actually *do* it. Our hands tightened, hers with the sound of her own voice, mine with guilt at wanting her, wanting to leave her, when she was sick. "Theodore," she said. Her voice: so perfectly modulated, so perfectly expensive. She pulled me down beside her, started to kiss me slowly, her lips warm and velvet, her tongue shy but present, full of secret messages. I didn't dare move; I was afraid of hurting her, afraid if I moved I would move away. She took my arms and pulled them around her. "Come on," she said, "we'll pretend it's been a week. It seems like a week." She giggled and pressed her mouth into my neck. Her back was amazingly small; with my hands I could almost circle her waist. "Take your clothes off," she whispered. Her skin burned through the flannel nightgown.

Finally we were naked, hiding from each other in the broken light beneath her sheets. I still couldn't believe it was going to happen. We could hear footsteps working their way up and down the corridor, the sounds beating nervously against our skin. I held myself above her. Without her rich clothes, she was so tiny – she seemed too delicate for me.

"You look beautiful," she said. She reached up to me; her hands swallowed the space between us, twisted my hair until it was knotted as an old man's beard. Then everything was all right and I was inside her, her legs wrapped round my waist, her face shining happily through the forest of yellow hair.

"Is this better?"

"Yes," I said. "This is better." Though she was thin, her breasts were full and heavy and her nipples burned into the palms of my hands. We both looked at the ring she had given me; now it felt like a gift.

"Do you like this?" She curved and stretched beneath me, fitting into the movements of the train, her ribs running up her side like railway ties. There were more and more footsteps in the corridor, always threatening to stop outside our door. On the few long curves, the train slowed only slightly, then sped up again, travelling blind through the snow, through the prairies, a crazy mechanical arrow seeking the edge of the world. Suddenly, for only the briefest moment, the train jolted and almost stopped, as if we were passing through an extremely thin barrier; we were thrown even closer. "Go away," Lise shouted at the door. I forgot about her bandage. We *were* the edge of the world, poised on the edge of the world, wanting to fall off. The train was moving faster than ever. As it picked up speed Lise rocked me back and forth, her bones shuddering, making me shake with her, drawing me deeper inside to match the rhythm of the wheels, which slapped round and round, steel on steel, clicked and moaned with us until finally we were both flying.

Lise opened her eyes. Perhaps they had been open the whole time. Have I told you that when we made love her eyes were like the sea? And when it was good, just after it was good, she would always open them and look at me slyly, just making sure that I knew.

Later we lay on the half-dark bed, smoking and feeling the air as it explored our bodies. I felt exhausted and brand-new all at once; my skin was so happy to have all this stimulation it was going crazy dropping off layers of dead, unused cells and growing fresh ones to feel Lise that much more closely.

"What are you thinking?"

"It was worth waiting for," I said. As if it had been five years. "But it was a long time."

She sat up, crossing her legs, millions of my sperm spilling out of her as she leaned forward for her cigarettes.

When I sleep with someone, the person I knew disappears. Her body gets mixed up with mine, and even when it's over I keep having visual flashes of limbs intertwined, mounded terrains of flesh running together like strange rivers meeting. When we separate, the known woman has vanished and the new one has begun to recreate herself – partly out of me. So with Lise: from a distance she was all sharp edges – well-defined, expensively dressed, her past and present condensed into a few pointed stories. But making love she was transformed: supple, unexpected, the mask of persona dissolved in our movements, in the movements of the train. I didn't care if she had been bribing me. I didn't feel the need to leave her anymore. Even her face was difficult to recognize, alive with new signals: touch and recognition. We were in a new and foreign territory, liquid and benevolent, a neutral zone where anything could happen. While the train sped across the prairie we put on our clothes, smoked, drank small glasses of brandy, watched the falling snow diminish with the light. My body patched together with her heat.

Regina, when we finally arrived, was beyond anything I would have expected. Despite Lise's wound, the boxcars full of weapons, the radio in Perestrello's compartment blasting out news of war and revolution, some part of me still believed the old order would continue, that peace and comfort would reassert themselves like a small town shrugging off a scandal, and that when we got off the train the world would be cured, safe again: familiar and untouched.

But the war fever in Regina had gone far beyond the panic of the Vancouver train station. A state of emergency had been declared. Thousands of men, dressed in a motley collection of old and new uniforms, armed with an absurd assortment of weapons and all wearing red bands on their sleeves, patrolled the streets. The station, the hotel, all public buildings and places were guarded by this rag-tag army. Pasted to telephone poles, hoardings, any wall with an empty space, were notices of the new regulations – some of them so dense with fine print they were impossible to read. At first it seemed ludicrous that this city in the middle of nowhere could have been so infected. But even by the time we had settled in our hotel room I had started to adapt. Standing at the window I looked out to the square and the groups of soldiers that populated every corner like out-of-season Santa Clauses.

The storm which had started in the mountains had dumped more than a foot of snow here. Even the downtown roads were unploughed; and, in any case, all use of private vehicles was forbidden by the new laws. I began going through the telephone book, trying to find a doctor that had an address near the hotel. It took six calls before I found one willing to come to see Lise; and he made me promise I would walk to his house to get him. James Fine was his name, Dr. James Fine: an optimistic name for a doctor.

Over the telephone he had sounded cautious. When he opened his door, after undoing several locks, clouds of alcohol floated out into the cold air. He was a short wide man, with a wide muscular face and grey-white hair combed straight back. His eyes were large and oval: child's eyes in the face of a man who was almost sixty. I leaned forward to see them better, to see if he was drunk. They were clear, a catty smoked grey that matched the colour of his skin and hair. He grabbed my arm, his hand like a clamp, and pushed me through the hall into the living room. There he left me standing in the midst of an array of horrible gold-speckled furniture. The only light was provided by a huge colour television set. Seated on a couch opposite it, watching intently, was a squat woman. I heard the sound of locks being fastened, then the doctor grabbed my arm again and almost threw me down on the couch, between himself and his wife. In front of us was a coffee table with a bottle of rye and several glasses. '

"I'm Gloria Fine," the doctor's wife announced. "My husband is the doctor."

"Pleased to meet you." In Salem, on all occasions, these words were considered the ultimate response to an introduction – pleased to meet you. You could say them to anyone and they were sure to be safe.

"She's drunk," James Fine said. "Ha ha." At the end of almost every sentence he laughed nervously, like a dog barking in its sleep.

A movie was on television. Sounds of a car chase tore through the room – screeching tires and gunshots echoing in some Los Angeles movie set. Then suddenly these sounds were cut off and a picture of the Canadian flag appeared, accompanied by strains of the national anthem.

"We have to watch this," said the doctor. "Then we can go."

The music ended. "And now," a voice announced, "the Prime Minister of Canada." His face, familiar from thousands of photographs in newspapers and magazines, filled the screen. His eyes were deeply shadowed, his skin had almost a green-grey cast, and his lips trembled. Though he gazed steadily at the camera and controlled the movements of his hands as he straightened the papers on the desk in front of him, the impression he gave was almost funny. He looked like an actor, an actor portraying a man who had been corrupted by circumstance until he was beyond human recognition.

"My fellow Canadians." His voice was low and rasping. He even sounded like the actor who didn't quite suit his part. "This evening I would like to speak to you of matters which have been of deep concern to all of us during the last few weeks and months. I won't take much of your time; and I know you don't want to interrupt the programs you are watching, so please bear with me and I'll be as brief as possible."

He paused and coughed. And as he prepared to resume speaking, his jaw line tightened and became more aggressive. As if most of his training was in doing commercials. The doctor's wife poured more whiskey into one of the glasses. It was easy to see that the citizens of this town were preparing for an extended siege.

"As you know, there has been much talk about shortages of food and fuel. In some areas there have been actual deficiencies. And as I told you last week, we're doing everything in our power to alleviate these problems. At the same time, as you have undoubtedly seen in the newspapers, there have been increasing incidents of violence and rioting, especially in the cities of our southern neighbour, the United States. More recently, some of these same problems have surfaced in our own country, and within the past few days there have been unfortunate incidents in almost every one of our major cities —"

"— goddamn murder —" said Gloria Fine.

" — and we've had cause to join our efforts with those of our neighbour, the United States, in the restoration of peace, order and good government."

"Blah, blah," Gloria Fine muttered.

"I should say, as those of you who live near the border may already know, that as I address you this evening, the President of the United States is speaking to that nation.

"The main thing we have to report to you is that our joint investigation has revealed a plan to bring down the governments of both countries; that the riots we have witnessed – in Halifax and Montreal for example – were instigated and carried out by well-paid gangs; and that these efforts are being controlled by a well-organized private army financed and run by elements that include businessmen, unions, even familiar political figures, as well as certain underworld names well known to the police of both countries; and that the supply and delivery problems being experienced in many areas are a result of the same deliberate and planned effort."

"Goddamn," said Gloria Fine. "It must be them goddamn commies again. I told you." She smiled strangely at me, then poured more whiskey, the bottle clinking uncertainly against the glass. In the meantime the Prime Minister had consulted his papers, checked his lines, and was looking straight into the camera, almost sincere, the old actor down to his last and least convincing trick.

"Even at this time, as I speak these words, warrants are being served to the persons police have determined to be responsible. Some are prominent figures in public and even political life. Despite the fact that they have always been given the democratic right of dissent, and even the right to run for office, they have chosen subterfuge and violence, holding you, the public, ransom in their schemes. Such abrogation of the popular will cannot be permitted.

96

"We intend to act quickly and ruthlessly to preserve our social order. Although by declaring a martial emergency – and such an emergency clearly exists – we could simply throw the offenders in jail, the Government of Canada has decided to conduct public trials and, in an unprecedented measure, to show citizens all over the country the highlights of these trials on television, as they happen, so you may see for yourself the guilt of these despicable culprits.

"Secondly, in order to restore economic prosperity and equality, the Canadian and American governments have set up a joint commission that will be responsible for the production and dispersion of essential materials. All those employed in food and resource industries should be assured that their jobs will be secure under the new system, which – for the first time in our history – positively ensures that our standard of living will be guaranteed.

"Thirdly, I want to appeal to you, the citizens of this country, to help us in this crisis. It is, after all, in the hearts and the living rooms of this nation that our future is decided. How can you help? Most importantly, by believing in this nation and co-operating with the plans we have set out. Because we need you. No matter how many police we have, no matter how many armies we raise, there will still be those who will escape their survey. But with every eye and ear in the nation alerted, with each of us aware of what is at stake and what we have to lose, no saboteur or traitor is safe, no one who would destroy us can long go undetected."

Once more the Prime Minister shuffled and rearranged his papers. Now he was calm and relaxed; traces of a smile played across his face.

"During the next few days we will be rounding up those we consider most responsible for the situation we are in. Some will no doubt go into hiding. Immediately after this broadcast we will show the photographs of some of the most wanted persons. Tomorrow those pictures will be posted in public places. With your help, none will escape.

"We all know what is at stake. If we all co-operate and pull together, if we all believe there's hope, then we can overcome our difficulties and from this crisis arise renewed."

In the background the national anthem began. "Well, goddamn," said Gloria Fine. "Goddamn. I never would have guessed it."

"That's right," James Fine said. His heavy voice cut through the noises of the television set. He stood up and stretched widely.

"I'll get your coat," his wife said. But she didn't move.

The doctor got his own coat, a grey tweed that looked as respectable as his black doctor's bag and the black homburg he clapped on his head.

"Be careful," said Gloria Fine, still splayed out on the couch. Photographs were beginning to appear on the television set. "Don't worry about missing this stuff. It's just the usual bullshit."

We walked to the hotel without talking, and although the doctor was almost an old man he led the way at a fast pace. It was a beautiful night – clear, not too cold, the snow welcome underfoot. If it hadn't been for the omnipresent red armbands and the occasional snowmobile whining through the streets, it would have seemed that an unusual and benevolent peace had descended, halting all machines and anxiety and throwing the town back eighty years – into that ancient and almost mythical century when the cycles of food and seasons were untouched by governments and war.

NINE

Dr. James Fine swept into the hotel room like a giant tweed-covered insect. Lise was back in bed, wearing her white flannel nightgown and a shawl around her shoulders. For this occasion her lips had been tinted a dark red: they stood out against her porcelain skin, as did her eyelids which were now a sudden purple-blue. Altogether she presented a picture of a forlorn and desperate girl; and as Fine threw off his coat and paced about the room, rubbing his hands together with a dry cracking sound, it seemed nothing less than a major operation could do justice to this tableau.

Its creator, Felipa, was also in the room. With her black cape and shining black boots she seemed a caricature of herself, a refugee from a movie about trains and spies. She and Lise had been watching the television, which had not yet returned to its regular programming but was still showing pictures of the conspirators and giving brief summaries of their lives. Some, as the Prime Minister indicated, were public or semi-public figures: leaders of unions, members of the political opposition, even the occasional journalist. Others were completely obscure: like Maria Bonnelli, who looked exactly like Felipa; she was wanted on several counts of fraud and armed robbery, as well as for attempting to incite riots in eleven separate states. It was impossible to know what was true and what was simply the government's attempt to grab power and throw its opposition into jail. It couldn't all be lies; after all,

Lise had already told me that the train was safe from the police.

Fine was one of those short, muscular men who exude infinite energy. In the bathroom, washing his hands, he slapped and splashed and talked above his own noise. Then he came out stretching and flexing his shoulders as if he were preparing to go into combat. On first meeting him – in his house with his squat wife who might have been his sister, and in the hotel where he threw off so much nervous static I wanted to leave the room – I didn't like him. Like an insect, he wore his skeleton on the outside.

"What do you think of this, eh?" he barked. "Stupidest thing I ever heard. The government has a crop failure and the next thing you know they're throwing people in jail for it. Ha ha." He rubbed his hands together with that grinding sound and sat down on the bed beside Lise, opening his bag. "It's a crock of shit if you ask me." He leaned forward towards Lise. "Let's see what you've got now."

He slowly unwound the bandage. His hands moved with amazing dexterity and grace; Felipa had suggested the right thing. "What's this?" he asked. "What happened?"

Lise looked at him with total sincerity, her green eyes luminous beneath the darkened lids. I could have sworn she was going to tell him the truth. "I was on the train, you know. I was just coming back from the bar car and you know how the train sways back and forth, and I guess I just fell on the platform between cars. I don't know what I hit."

"Is that so?" He had cotton batting out now, a soft white cloud soaked in rubbing alcohol, and he dabbed with it at her head. "That hurt?"

"No."

"I'll give you some stitches then." He reached into his bag and began pulling out his equipment. All his nervousness had gone; his movements were now quick and precise. "People tell you the craziest stories," he said. "There used to be a couple down the street from me. Every Sunday morning the husband

100

would come to get me for his wife. Big bastard he was, almost pounded down the door. She'd be all cut and bruised, half killed from his beating. But she wouldn't say anything against him. 'I've fallen down the stairs again,' she'd say. Or, 'Look at me, I fell on a roller skate.' Then one morning I could hardly hear the knock on the door. I thought he must have worn himself out. But it was she who came to get me. I went to the house and he was laid out on the floor, his big gut sticking up into the air, his head caved in. She'd hit him with the skillet – it was lying there beside him. 'Look at him,' she said. 'He was having a nightmare.' "

Dr. Fine was already putting a new bandage on Lise's head.

"You're fast," I said.

"Have to be. I learned in the army. Ha ha." There was something about his nervous laugh, coughed up in such a forced way, that made you want to laugh with him to get him through it, like wanting to complete the word when someone stutters. Then his hands were jumping around again: his sleeves rolled down, bag packed, jacket and coat reassembled. "I'll be back tomorrow morning to make sure it's held together. And next time one of your friends points a gun at you, duck." He was out the door before I could even offer to pay him.

"God," Felipa said.

The television was still showing photographs of the wanted. I turned it off and went to look out the window. I saw the doctor emerge in the square, nod at a group of soldiers and march confidently down the street as if he owned it. And, of course, in a way he did. This was his city; he had probably lived here for decades, bringing life into the world, ushering it out, delaying the inevitable, providing whatever he could when his telephone rang or his office door opened. A noble life. In return he had a wife who was a drunk, a house full of ugly furniture and the world's biggest television set.

But despite everything, he had a home. Where was mine? Vancouver? Salem? The train? Or was it only this body I lived in, this crazy and useless body with its week-old bruise beaming out from my belly like a green-and-blue headlight, with its arms and shoulders gradually repossessed by my father's unpaid debts, and its sex still jumping around like a teenager's, quiet for months at a time and then attracted to any woman who might happen by, as if the fate of this whole conglomerate of flesh, teeth, bones and blood could be worked out in these encounters. Home, yes, we're all so stupid that we'd give up anything to attain it, to convince ourselves that this place, *any* place, is somehow where we belong. So the amazing electrically fingered doctor scurries home to his own ridiculous nest; and so Lise, Felipa and I, in this hotel, convince ourselves that this place, for an hour or a week, is somehow right for us.

Home. A hotel room in a small city that stands in the midst of a half-deserted country waiting for its war. Looking out the window I could still see the bands of soldiers, their numbers breathing with the hours as they walked in and out of nearby taverns, gaining fuel to last the night. I looked back from the window to Lise. She had slid further down into the bed, her head almost horizontal, already asleep from the pill Dr. Fine had given her. Felipa was sitting in the armchair reading a magazine. Or at least she appeared to be reading; but as the doctor had left and there was no reason for her to stay, I could only assume she was waiting for the obvious to transpire.

"What are you thinking about?" she asked.

"The weather." Maria Bonnelli they had called her. No doubt the police in both countries had spent weeks trying to find evidence of their imaginary conspiracy. And I thought, when they broke into my apartment, that they were looking for drugs. I wondered who they had hoped I might be. Maybe the dream I had had was truer than the reality: detectives demanding answers to non-existent questions, desires betraying themselves like rotting teeth, the whole nervous system on continuous alert, only wanting to be shut off, all thoughts of freedom given up – death or sleep the only hope of release.

I sat on the window sill in the old hotel and lit a cigarette. In Vancouver my life had proceeded calmly enough, from nowhere to nowhere. If I needed a home then, I had it in my mind: a few old memories of Jacob Beam, drunk or sober; of my mother, enduring her fate without complaint; of the town of Salem, ticking like a clock around its old stone houses, slowly falling behind.

"I'll tell you what I'm thinking," Felipa said.

"All right."

"I'm thinking that when you sit in the window with the lights on, you make a perfect target." She switched off the lamps and came to stand beside me. Lise's breathing filled the room.

In Salem everyone has a home, a home of some kind, if only an abandoned truck near the dump.

I became aware that I was twisting my ring nervously around my finger. I have to admit that I was attracted to Felipa, I don't know why. Sometimes I think my body can't distinguish one person from another, that it blindly seeks other flesh, other blood. Felipa put her hand on my chest, branding my skin through the thin cloth of my shirt; while my own hands stayed touching themselves, seeking reassurance in the ring, in the sounds of Lise's breathing. After all, it's natural for men and women to *want* to be faithful; I always imagine primitive scenes – a man and a woman clothed in furs, sitting around a fire in front of their cave. In my bones I know better: lives cross like vines, wrapping around each other without knowing why.

We stood at the window, looking out at the soldiers moving about the square in the yellow light of the street lamps. The weather was turning warmer. Snow was falling slowly, leaving long streaks on the dusty panes. Felipa's hand was still on my chest, resting there, neither coming nor going, as if to mark this interlude.

I felt as if all these random movements of soldiers, the proclamations pasted to walls and telephone poles, the confusion of my own existence, the pictures that had flashed on the television screen were all organizing into some inexorable series of events that would swallow up my life. And in the back of my head I could feel the echo of the hammer, the echo of the bullet slamming the wood into my hand and jolting my bones in its passing.

Felipa's hand slipped down to my belly, the warmth of her fingers growing into my skin. She and Lise seemed to be opposite sides of the same person: both burning with fanatical intensity; but where Lise was almost innocent, afraid and insecure, Felipa was older and more cynical. Perhaps she was doing this to settle some old score with Perestrello, or to make a distance between Lise and me so that when the time came we wouldn't desert them.

"We should go down to the train," Felipa said. "We can't stand here forever."

As I sit in the old church near the village of Salem, writing this story, trying to remember the sounds of our voices through the sounds of this wind blowing through the cracks of the old square limestone, I think of that moment with Felipa as one for which I've learned to hate myself.

Out in the street, we walked the few blocks from the hotel to the train station. The air was cool and crisp, and the snow falling against my face melted on contact – a warm benevolent snow. Felipa pressed close to me, her arm hooked through mine.

The clock in the hotel lobby had indicated it was not yet midnight. No curfew had been announced; and perhaps because of the turn in the weather, there were quite a few citizens out walking. The soldiers were also out in force: they were crowded onto all the corners, patrolled the streets relentlessly, stood in groups in the lobbies of apartments and taverns. The television broadcast had increased the feeling of tension. The one supermarket we passed had its windows boarded up, and even its glass doors had been broken and replaced with cardboard.

"You heard the announcements," I said.

"Yes."

"Aren't you afraid to be walking around like this? The police must be looking for you."

"The police can look up their own assholes," Felipa said.

We were coming to a corner with a group of soldiers standing under a street lamp. They parted to let us pass. As I stepped off the curb, Felipa's arm still hooked through mine, I felt someone jostle me. The smell of whiskey was heavy in the cold air. I was convinced that the soldiers had their rifles trained on my back, ready to pull the triggers. But, miraculously, we were on our way, across the street and one more block to the station.

It was new, glowing with neon and plastic. We moved as quickly as we could without seeming to run.

The waiting room of the station was filled with more soldiers and passengers from the train. There was nowhere to sit except on the rows of plastic seats. These were all occupied, as were the walls which were lined with machines for dispensing coffee and chocolate bars. To one side I could see a door marked RESTAURANT. I hadn't eaten for so long that my stomach cramped at the sign. I was almost at the door, half dragging Felipa after me, when I saw it was locked. My stomach knotted, unable to remember the last time it had held food.

I let go of Felipa's arm and walked out the station door to the asphalt platform. The train was still there, silent and dark, but soldiers walked back and forth along the platform. Further along I could see an old stone building; and in the yellow snowy light it seemed almost an apparition from Salem. Outside stood an old and battered telephone booth. The glass walls had been cracked and were held together by strips of yellowed tape. Spread out on a shelf was the telephone book. Most of the pages were torn out, the others scribbled on with pen and crayon. CHRISTOPHER COLUMBUS STINKS was scrawled on the wall in red lipstick.

I searched in my pocket for a dime, then dialed the operator. Afraid that Jacob Beam wouldn't accept the call, I charged it to my disconnected Vancouver number.

Finally Jacob's voice came through the long-distance lines. "Hello?"

"This is Theodore," I said. "I just thought I'd call to say hello."

"Theodore," Jacob said. "That's very nice. How are you?"

"Good. Things seem to be moving pretty fast. Have you been watching the television?"

"No," said Jacob. A cough. "It's not too cold here. We just put the storms up yesterday."

"Great."

"Not much new here," Jacob said. "Your mother's asleep."

"Still sleeping well?"

"Better than ever." I could hear him striking a match. Beside the wall phone he had long ago tacked a piece of emery paper for one-handed emergencies such as this. Somehow this sound also reminded me of Jacob Beam's walks which he took on various occasions. I knew that when we were finished talking, he'd sigh and put on his wool coat and the woollen gloves my mother gave him every Christmas and he'd walk through the streets smoking the rest of his cigar, stopping to look up every now and then to see if he still knew any of the constellations. The lights of the houses would mostly be out, except for the occasional bathroom light and the blue glare of television screens. When he reached the house of his best friend – the schoolteacher Henry McCaffrey – he'd stop for awhile, remembering various adventures. Then he'd circle back to stand by the river that ran close to our house, a small river that stayed open for the first half of the winter. Before climbing up the hill to the garden, he'd kneel down and scoop water into his mouth because, for some reason, he considered it unlucky to refuse.

"Ah well," Jacob said. "So it goes."

"What?"

"You remember the girl across the street?"

"Yes."

"She came home last week. We had her and her husband over to dinner."

"Oh."

"She remembered you," Jacob said. "Everyone remembers you."

I once had some small fame in Salem. One afternoon I tried to burn down the school. The project was unsuccessful. Only a small wooden outhouse, attached to the stone exterior, was destroyed.

But how would they remember me now? My mother once wrote that she had started playing bridge in the afternoons. I wondered if they compared notes, showed pictures.

"I remember you too," Jacob said. Sometimes it came to him that he wasn't being sufficiently personal and at these moments he was liable to make long speeches and declarations. "A man can't neglect his emotional duties," he used to say. On such occasions he'd smile beatifically at my mother who would simply hide her face.

"Is it snowing there?" I asked. I knew it was.

"Yes. Big, slow flakes. The back steps are already covered."

So that's how it could be when he went outside, warm and wet, the snow melting into his coat as he walked, soaking his eyebrows and beard.

"It's raining here," I said.

"Ah well, it always rains there."

I had forgotten to tell him I was on my way home. It didn't matter; even at the best of times he was difficult to surprise.

"You know," he said, "perhaps I could have been a better father." He had that familiar tone of voice: a major statement was on its way. "Sometimes I wake up in the middle of the night and I go and look in your room. It's just as you left it. Ten years now you haven't been home, and one night you call me up on the telephone as if everything is supposed to be all right." There was a pause. Another match scraping against the wall. A sharp exhalation.

"I admit it, we made mistakes. We should have had more children. Your mother wanted to – I didn't. It's me who's at fault. What am I anyway? The doctor listens to my heart and he gives me these looks worse than a dog."

I was leaning against the cracked wall of the booth, my eyes closed. "You should take it easy."

"Run," Jacob said. "The doctor wants me to run. Your mother bought me a sweat suit and insisted I run around the track at the high school."

I tried to imagine Jacob in a red sweat suit, the collar zipped up to his greying beard, the shirt bulging over his wide belly, trousers billowing about his bow legs.

"I'm fifty-six years old," Jacob said. "But it's not so easy to die. After all, no one's going to push me down the mountain."

"Are you sick?"

"Sick? No. But listen to your voice when you ask. What a long way you are from this. A wink."

TEN

I'd forgotten those long days when Jacob Beam refused to get up. He would stay in the bedroom, with the heavy curtains drawn, until noon. My mother would have to go across the street and put the special notice CLOSED TODAY on the door of the shop. Everyone knew what this meant. Sometimes after the dark morning, when the pain of his migraine only got worse, he'd dress up in an old plaid shirt and his weekend pants that were so baggy the crotch hung down almost to his knees. Shoving a felt hat over his eyes to protect them from the light, he'd stagger over to the tavern and drink with the farmers. In the same room, that is. Because at supper time, when my mother would send me to get him, he'd be sitting all alone, his table covered with beer-stained glasses. With scarcely a trace of a smile he'd stand up, adjust the dead cigar in his mouth and walk out with me, slowly and dignified, his belly swollen and swaying gracefully with beer, his back arched straight to receive this extra weight, this extra uncertainty, that he carried with him like a sign.

He would insist on leading the way through the streets of Salem, his pace slow and plodding, an agony of will behind each step. He'd precede me into the house and march straight to his place at the head of the table. Where he'd sit down and resume the position I had found him in; hat now sunk to his very nose, chair pushed back at an angle from the table, shirt sleeves rolled up to reveal his arms, thick with work and stained with dye. They appeared to be made of tough, hairy wood that was equal to the oak table he banged for service. My mother had learned that on these days it was best to cook something that could not be lessened by carving. So Jacob Beam, maintaining his distance of maximum dignity from the table and serving himself with a huge spoon, would methodically empty bowl after bowl of the thick stew my mother made. But even when he was so drunk that each spoonful had to go through strange spastic dances on its way to his mouth, he always managed to make a neat pile of bay leaves beside his plate.

It seemed strange to me that my mother wasn't angrier. In fact she seemed to prefer him drunk to sober; and if the dance of the spoon got out of control and ended in a shower, she'd laugh and rush out to the kitchen for a rag. At the end of the meal she'd set a pitcher of coffee on one side of his plate and a bottle of apple brandy on the other. Mixing them half and half, Jacob Beam would do his best. When he could drink no more he'd push himself back from the table a few more feet to give himself room to manoeuvre, then he'd stand up. Having at no point compromised even a shred of his dignity, he was not about to lose it now. Very slowly, his feet wiggling in his shoes as he teetered, he'd raise his arms high up and stretch until his spine popped. Then, taking my mother's arm, he would permit himself to be led upstairs, leaving me to do the dishes.

Standing in the kitchen, to the sounds of the muffled thumps and groans and laughter from upstairs, I would sullenly clean up from supper. By the time I was finished, the long silence would have begun. For the first time in hours it would be possible to hear the tick of the old pendulum clock that stood in our front hall beside the coat tree, guarding it like a sentinel from the horrors of the future. I'd go and stand in the hall at the bottom of the stairs and watch the clock advance upon itself, minute by minute. If it was cold, I'd slide down the narrow trap door into the basement and stoke up the wood furnace with a couple of the elm logs that Jacob had piled along all four stone walls. There, at the very bottom of my spirits, I'd wait out the evening.

At midnight I'd stoke the furnace once more. By then I'd be sleepy, mesmerized by the sounds of water and fire; and after I added the final logs I'd stand in front of the open firebox and watch the new wood catch and suddenly break apart in the pressure of the fire. And without fail, while I watched, the house would wake up again, and I'd hear the bedroom door slam against the wall as Jacob Beam opened it and clomped down the stairs. "Theodore," he'd shout, "where are you?" I'd come upstairs and meet him in the dining room.

On the last of these occasions he was standing at the table with his hands in his pockets, staring at the snow which blew in gusts against the window. "It's time I took my son for a walk," he said.

He went into the front hall and began putting on his parka and boots. I followed him. Even as we opened the door, the wind pushed into us, cold and bitter, scoured the heat from our faces. Jacob went ahead, bent down against the snow. I pulled the door closed and made my way down the steps. It was one of those nights so cold the snow blows more than it falls, grinding away at all exposed areas, filling up the hollows of your eyes, trying to force its way into every chink. There was a ghost of a moon that glowed coldly from behind the clouds, turning the night into a bowl of whirling snow.

Instead of going to the outskirts of town, as we usually did, Jacob went towards the centre. I thought only that he was too drunk to know we were aimed the wrong way. Every thirty or forty steps he'd stop, curl his shoulders against the wind and take out the remains of the bottle. He led us through narrow rutted alleys, even climbing over fences. Our passage threw the town's dogs into a frenzy of barking. But it was too late and too cold for anyone to care. The snow bit into my collar, worked its way down my shirt into my chest and back. When

Jacob offered me the bottle, I accepted, trying to get warm, hoping we could soon turn around.

We emerged onto a street where one house had its lights on. Without hesitation Jacob plunged forward and knocked on the door. There was no answer. He pushed it open and we went inside. Through the door of his library we could see Henry McCaffrey, the schoolteacher, seated at his desk. As we went inside we saw he was accompanied by two women, extra-ordinarily dressed.

"Jacob," Henry McCaffrey roared. I could hardly believe it. I'd never seen him drunk – or with a woman. His whole face had been transformed. Where his mouth was usually pinched and narrow, pulling his cheeks taut and leaving little furrows in them, it was now relaxed and slack. And his glasses, which were always perched precariously on his nose – so far down he had to squint even to see through them – were now pushed back right up to his bloodshot eyes. He greeted me with such enthusiasm that he almost fell over the top of his desk.

"Oh, Henry!" One of the women leapt to her feet and helped him back into position.

"Ah, yes," Henry finally allowed, having recovered himself. "Ladies, permit me to introduce Mr. Jacob Beam, the elder, and on his right, the young Mr. Theodore Beam."

The two women bowed and clapped their white-gloved hands.

"And," the teacher continued, "allow me to introduce my two sisters to you gentlemen: Miss Rosalie McCaffrey and Miss Mirabel McCaffrey."

"Henry," they cried, beside themselves with delight, and clapped their hands again.

In the library of the schoolteacher's house, a calm descended. The sound of the wind was broken against the roaring fire in the stove. With the exception of Henry, who remained behind his desk, we were all seated in comfortable chairs spotted along the book-lined walls. Goblets of brandy appeared in our hands. Jacob, who took possession of the bottle, emanated

112

a massive silence that blanketed everything else. Opposite him sat Mirabel. Beneath her plumed hat, dark hair hung down in long ringlets. Her mouth was well-lipsticked and even her teeth were stained red. These she showed frequently, as she gripped and re-gripped her cigarette holder.

While my ears thawed out I turned towards the other sister. Whereas Mirabel was dark-haired and well-coloured, Rosalie was an absolute albino. Her hair and eyebrows were stranded between blond and white. She was also dressed entirely in white, so that she seemed almost an absence. Her eyes too were colourless: at best a pale pink and blue which was hardly visible because most of the time they were closed, revealing thick white lashes.

When she finally spoke, the pinkness of her tongue and gums seemed to explode from her mouth. "Pleased to meet you."

"Don't mind her," Mirabel said. She smiled flirtatiously at Jacob. "Men find her forward," she confided. "Don't they, Henry?"

"No," Henry said.

Mirabel, wearing a red satin sheath, began to undo the zipper. "I'm hot," she said. She swirled her brandy and looked at Jacob. His bottle was empty and he was searching inside his coat. His plaid shirt was spotted with beer, apple brandy and stew. He was falling into a state of disrepair.

"Shut up," he said.

"My word," Mirabel exclaimed. "What a nice voice you have." Jacob smiled sleepily. Mirabel got to her feet. She went to a shelf then came to stand beside Jacob, a new bottle of brandy in her hand.

"May I?" she asked.

Jacob held out his glass.

With great care she filled it to the brim. Then, her long and ratty string of fur flouncing as she moved, she returned to her chair.

Jacob sipped delicately and swirled the brandy about in his

glass. It spilled over the edge, slid thickly down onto his hand. He appeared not to notice. "Henry," he sighed. "What is youth but desire?"

"What indeed," Henry agreed.

With that, Jacob stood up and carefully set his glass on Henry's desk. Then he stretched hugely, his thick arms extending fully, his spine snapping as he arched his back. As if by pre-arrangement Mirabel stood up too. Together they walked out of the room and up the stairs.

For a few minutes the rest of us sat in our chairs. Henry continued to peruse the anatomy text on his desk. Rosalie dozed, saying absolutely nothing. I had begun to wonder if she was some sort of idiot when she jerked her eyes open and leaned towards me with a capacious smile. At that moment we heard a tremendous noise from upstairs, then silence. Rosalie smiled again. "Pleased to meet you," she said. The schoolteacher looked at me hopelessly.

Rosalie came and sat on the arm of my chair. She was wearing a strange perfume that smelled of late-blooming flowers. She put her hand on my shoulder. I studied my drink. Save for the sounds of the fire, the house was quiet again.

"We need some more wood," Henry said.

I got up and went out into the hall where I put on my coat. Rosalie followed me. Then we went back through the kitchen to the woodshed. My ears had only begun to unfreeze. Almost instantly, they went numb. I felt a pressure at my side. Rosalie, wearing a white Eskimo parka, was pressed into me. I tried to ignore her, feeling along the rough pine wall for the light switch. Before I could protest, she began frantically kissing my ear and sliding her hand inside my coat. I tried to ignore this too.

"You chickenshit monster," she hissed. My eyes were growing used to the dark. I found the logs and an ax. I grabbed them and dragged them outside. She pursued me. I set the first log up on the chopping block. The snow had stopped. The sky was clear now, bitter cold, the stars shining brightly, the moon right above us. For the first time I began to feel I was in the wrong army. I had a tremendous desire to suddenly turn around and hit Rosalie. I set the ax down carefully, then I whirled about. Before I could do anything, she threw her arms around my neck and tried to sink her teeth into my cheek. I pushed her away. She clung to me like a snake. Somehow I got my coat in her mouth. Then she slid one of her legs between mine and we both went sprawling in the snow. I landed face first, my mouth filling up with snow and the taste of blood. I lay still for a moment, letting her settle into my back. Then I rolled over quickly, trying to catch her with my elbow. But she was too fast for me. And as I struggled to my feet she jumped up and down, clapping her hands like the miserable white wraith she was.

Now I had the ax in my hand. I swung it high in the air. The wood jumped apart with the first touch of steel, razor brittle with the frost. When our arms were full we staggered inside and dumped the wood beside the library stove.

Jacob and Mirabel had come back downstairs and Jacob was lying on the couch at the far end of the room, his massive head in Mirabel's lap. He appeared to be snoring. She stroked his forehead and hummed. While she did, I sampled the brandy in deep swallows, letting it burn into my stomach, and kept a guilty eye on Jacob.

Henry McCaffrey was also asleep, his head resting on the text he had been studying so devoutly.

Then Rosalie and I put wood in the fire and, knowing our duty, went upstairs.

There were only three rooms on the second storey of the house. The first was Henry's bedroom. Books and papers were spread everywhere over floor and bed alike, as if now that his wife had left him there was no further need for pretence. The second was the room that Jacob and Mirabel had used. It was small with a huge oak bed. The bed was split down the middle and lay on the floor like a broken smile.

We went into the third room. Once Isabella, the servant

employed many years ago, had lived there. It was still furnished as it had been then: a bed, dresser and a sewing chair with a seat that lifted up. We turned on the light and closed the door. The lamp shade was decorated with ships painted onto its parchment. Through the centre of the room rose the stovepipe from the living room.

Rosalie stood in front of the dresser and inspected herself in the mirror, then began brushing out her long pale hair. In the light of the lamp shade it was not entirely awful. I began to wonder what the rest of her would be like, if it would be possible to see the veins and arteries through her skin. I sat on the bed. Our eyes met in the mirror, floundered, met again. Eventually she sat down on the chair, her legs stretched straight out.

From the library we could hear movement. The door of the stove clanked open and shut: more wood being added. The bedroom grew warmer. I took off my shirt and shoes. Rosalie looked at me speculatively.

"Don't be afraid," I said.

"All right."

It wasn't her fault that her eyes were pink. I began to feel sorry for her. The room was swimming with heat.

"I know I'm ugly," she said.

"It could be worse." Actually, I was thinking of myself.

"Look at your father," Rosalie said, "right away he preferred my sister. It's always been that way."

"I know," I said. "I mean, he's married. He doesn't know any better. You know how it is."

"Yes." Her face took on an expression of absolute simplicity. She began pulling down the zipper of her white satin dress.

"Are you married?" she asked.

"Me?"

"I always fall in love with married men. I don't know why. There must be something wrong with me."

"I'm sorry," I said. "I guess I just haven't met the right person."

Even with the light on, the stovepipe was beginning to glow. Rosalie took off her dress. Her body was pale and unmarked. I looked away. Then I walked to the door and locked it.

"I just did that," I said.

"I know."

I sat down on the bed. I began to feel sorry for her. My legs were stifling hot inside my pants.

"Do you think I'm ugly?" she asked.

"What?"

"Look at me."

Beads of moisture were beginning to appear on the walls. I looked at her. She stood up and turned around slowly, modelling herself. "Well?"

"You look okay," I said. It was hard to know what to compare her to. It must have been difficult for her when she was younger. I took off my pants. Then, as if it didn't matter, I took off the rest of my clothes.

"Now we're both naked," she said.

"Well, actually," I finally admitted, "it's my first time."

"Aah," she sighed, "your first time." From the library we could hear shouts and stomping, as if the three of them were trying to invent a virginity dance.

She looked at me sadly. Even her pubic hair was transparent. She sat on the brocaded sewing chair that Henry's ex-wife had made. I sat on the bed. Sweat streamed down my back. Though the door was locked, I wanted to push the dresser against it too.

"We can wait for a while," I said, "then go down."

"All right," she agreed. She looked so mournful I had already forgiven her for attacking me outside. I lay down on the bed. At least the sheets would be soaked. She came and sat beside me. Her belly sagged unhappily. I put my hand on her thigh to console her. My palm was wet with tension.

"This must feel awful," I said. "I'm sorry."

"You can't help it. Don't apologize."

I looked at the lamp shade. The orange sails of the ships seemed to billow in the heat. There was something strange about doing this in a room with such a light. She put her hand over mine.

"Rosalie," I said.

"Shh."

She lay down beside me. I got on top of her. She reached down with her hand. I felt as if I was swimming in a hot bath. I realized my eyes were closed. I opened them. Rosalie was staring at me, her pink pupils turned red with heat. The stove-pipe had started to burn itself out. Small pinholes appeared and flames were shooting past. I twisted to look at it better and realized I was inside her. How had it happened?

"This is it," I said.

"What?"

I moved back and forth. I remembered reading something about it being like rowing a boat. I couldn't figure out what to do with my arms.

"Hey," Rosalie said.

I'd forgotten about her. It was so hot and wet I could hardly feel anything. I knew that something spectacular was supposed to happen. The room was filling up with smoke.

"Now," she said.

She was wrapped tightly around me. I was trapped like a sausage in an intestine. She began to caress me in long undulating waves. My spine had turned to liquid. I closed my eyes against the smoke.

She squeezed again and again. The muscles of my back and legs had gone rigid. We could hear them calling us from the library. Then suddenly some resistance gave way in her. I could feel her insides pouring over me. Her thighs tightened round my hips and drew me in deeper. I sighed and then finally, after all these years, my bones and muscles contracted in a feeling far sweeter than – say – Jacob Beam's apple brandy.

Perhaps I tried too hard. A man tries to be a good father to his son. Perhaps this education was too sentimental. It might have been the other way. I could have taught by example, never even speaking to him. As it was I spoke to him every day, always something, if only to ask him to do some small task or come and help me at the shop. You don't expect gratitude but at least you can hope that one day, perhaps when he's in the same position, he'll understand what has been done for him. Is that so much?

Rosalie seemed to have fallen into a deep sleep beside me. Finally I put on my clothes and went downstairs. The library was empty. In the front hall I could see Jacob's coat and boots. Exhausted, I sat down in the armchair and continued to drink the brandy I had started hours ago. The lateness, the brandy, the numb buzz that vibrated through my body, all somehow combined to put me to sleep. When I woke up, my neck was stiff and my chin practically on my chest. The library was dark; all the lights in the house had been turned off. I started to get up, then remembered, checked myself and tried to listen for the sound of breathing. There was none.

With infinite caution, letting my feet sink slowly into the rug with each step, I stalked about the pitch-black room, feeling ahead with my hand. Finally I came to the desk. I rested my palm on its surface, the cold leather momentarily surprising me. It seemed eons before I located the lamp and turned it on. I was alone in the library and there was no sign of the others.

It was only when I had my coat on and was at the door that I saw Jacob's coat and boots still in the hall. I realized what might happen if I went home alone at this hour without him. So, embarrassed and resentful, I went back to the study to wait. I sat down at Henry McCaffrey's desk. The diagram which had last held his attention was one of the human eye. Many long arrows, like porcupine quills, stuck out from its different areas. "How marvellous is the human eye," the text read, "for without it we should hardly be able to survive. Beside being endowed with the faculty of seeing, poets have often thought the eye to be the window to the soul . . ."

At the end opposite the desk was the stuffed velvet sofa. I lay down on my back and began to contemplate the ceiling. As I shifted my position, I became aware of something unusually hard beneath one cushion. I rose and inspected it. Then I saw a black casebound diary. In place of the title were the words NOT TO BE OPENED.

I listened. I could hear nothing. I closed the study door and used my shoes to brace it, so that I would be alerted to anyone entering.

Scrawled on the first page was the sole word ISABELLA. The second page was blank. On the third was a sonnet. I turned the page.

Two nights after Thanksgiving, in the year nineteen hundred and forty-nine, I was sitting at my desk working on the History when JB came to see me. We had a habit of strange conversation, so I was not surprised when as soon as my wife left the room he said to me: What is youth but desire? But before I could reply or even allow him to amplify on his little joke, he said he had a favour to ask me. It seemed that while he was on a business trip he had made the acquaintance of a young woman. As she would not be welcome in his household, he wondered if she might find a home in mine, especially as he understood we were in need of a servant. After further discussion, I agreed to at least meet her, which we arranged for the following Sunday.

She introduced herself as Isabella Hanley. She said that her mother had recently died and that her father, a doctor, had moved his practice to Arizona. Mrs. McCaffrey soon took her aside to tell her about her various illnesses and so, more easily than I had expected, it was settled.

Oh, Isabella! What thighs! What knees! Of all parts your knees are the most infinitely desirable. So soft! So smooth! After you, my wife's knees scrape like pillars of salt. What exquisite torture. Come back to me. . .

Knees? No wonder they had no children. I skipped a few

pages, then I came upon a black-and-white snapshot of my father on Henry McCaffrey's stuffed velvet sofa, Isabella sitting on his lap. In the background was a face that remarkably resembled my mother's. Beneath, the caption: JB and friend.

When I awoke it was full daylight.

"Good morning." In the doorway of Henry McCaffrey's library, dressed in their Sunday best, were Jacob Beam and my mother. They came to stand beside me. We looked out the window. The snow from last night's blizzard lay white and dazzling on the streets of Salem.

ELEVEN

My father's last drunken spree, at least the last one I witnessed, took place that night at the schoolteacher's house. The rest of the winter passed slowly, with me counting the days until I would graduate from high school. And when June finally came and it was warm enough, I left Salem. I just packed a small bag with the clothes I had planned on months before and walked out the door and down the road to Salem's lone highway, heading west, a road map of Canada hidden in my back pocket.

When I got to Vancouver it was high summer. I was seventeen years old and knew only one trade, the one I had learned from my father; so I took a job setting linotype on a weekly newspaper in suburban Vancouver. Obituaries, bingo games, church socials: they were my specialties. After a couple of months I learned how to embellish the copy and so while I was setting the words I would elaborate on them, letter by letter, word by word, blowing everything up to fill as many columns as possible. The woman who ran the paper appreciated this.

"People like to read," she said. Her name was Terry McTigue – Terry, as if she were a schoolgirl, though she must have been twice my age. In my mind I called her Scarlet Tiara. What she meant about people reading was that if there were more words there could be more advertisements to place between the words. Soon she fired the reporter and sent me out to find news items. In a plaid jacket and a starched white shirt, I made the rounds of church basements and summer sales.

"You have a way with words," Scarlet Tiara said. She was a red-haired Scotswoman with sharp features and a red nose, and she tried not to drink at lunch. It seemed that the whole adult world was running on alcohol. I began to broaden my horizons and write up car wrecks caused by drunken driving. I even did a series on Alcoholics Anonymous.

By the time fall came, Scarlet Tiara began staying away from the office days at a time, leaving everything – even a young and disapproving secretary – for me to run. I remembered the columns I used to set at my father's shop and dredged them up from memory as best I could.

The long rainy winter went by with me writing the copy, setting it on the linotype machine, translating the strangeness of this city to its slow rhythms, to the sound of type rattling into place. And of those long months the times I liked best were the nights I spent alone in the office. Then I'd do my work with great care, every letter carefully considered, made alive by its place in the centre of the world. Sometimes I'd turn off all the lights and listen to the cars swooshing by in the rain. And when it got so late there were no more cars, no more passing lights, I felt like the last man in the world.

On one of those nights in Scarlet Tiara's office, at that late hour, there was a whining of brakes, a door slamming. In she came – drunk, I suppose, but not drunk the way Jacob Beam used to be – floating in all directions. I was sitting in the dark behind her desk. She turned the lights on, seemed not at all surprised to see me, then turned them off again.

"Teddy," she said, "Teddy Good-good." She came and perched on the desk. No, not perched. Scarlet Tiara was too solid to be a bird, at least not a tame bird – though she might have been a mutant eagle or a giant red pelican. The street lamps sent in long yellow triangles that glowed in the dark, like in an old spy movie. "How good to see you, Teddy Good-good. Are you happy?" She shook her head and her hair came free. Then she lay face-down on her desk. "I'm so tired," she said. "Rub my back. Please rub my back."

In the morning, when the secretary came to work, she found the office empty, though the curtains were mysteriously open. Scarlet Tiara's desk was swept clean, but on the floor were two broken lamps, various notes, letters, unpaid bills, copy that was supposed to be checked, a few wadded-up pieces of Kleenex. It was almost closing time when I showed up. By then the lamps had been sent out for repair and the desk restored to normal.

When a year had gone by I decided to try university. Guiltily, Jacob Beam sent me money. Guiltily, I accepted. His monthly cheques paid for rooms in a string of boarding houses near the university. It began to feel as if I'd left my body in Salem. While others drank and pursued the loss of their virginity, I sat in my room and read. Of course, I was already a man of the world. But what had I experienced? I didn't seem to know. At times I thought my father had felt he was doing his duty. And at other times I simply hated him.

To console myself I read. Books, endless books. There had always been books at home – good books that lay about the house exercising an osmotic influence; and the paperbacks we actually read, hiding them from each other, noting the turned-down pages and the cracked spines.

In my third year at university I quit cashing the cheques and got a job cleaning fish. After a couple of years of doing ridiculous work and travelling around the Coast, I finally found my way of earning money – writing government reports. I had to stop thinking of words one at a time and just write them down as many and as fast as possible, the more obscure and jumbled-up the better. "Words are like true love," Jacob Beam once said, "very intense, but you have to live in the spaces in between." For government reports, nothing had to live; everything was filled with facts, details, qualifications, headings, sub-headings, addenda and further facts. I wrote reports on everything from fish to immigration. After a while it didn't matter; my brain turned into a pliable kind of cheese that sifted anything through it and forgot everything immediately. Even train stations: I wrote one report on the future of train stations. It was one of my best, near the end. By that time I was forgetting the purpose of these reports and would amuse myself by writing Dickensian introductions: "In the evening light the low wooden building looks like an apparition from the past, and in its lee can be seen young children playing in the shadows of battered garbage cans ..." My typewriter broke just before they were going to fire me.

Now, with the war, there would be a temporary suspension of reports. Too bad: this Regina train station would have made a perfect subject. I stood on the cement platform, surveying it. Here, as in Salem, the snow was beginning to fall again: soft large flakes that melted on my face and hands. I felt dizzy and faint. I began to walk back to the station house. Daniel and Felipa were coming towards me, walking quickly, almost running. But each of my steps was slow. I kept thinking I was going to pass out, right now, on my feet, and with each jolt of the pavement against my bones I could feel a black cloud pushing up inside me. In her hand Felipa was carrying a shopping bag. I had a sudden craving for tomatoes, warm tomatoes – in our garden at home I had sometimes eaten them from the vines; I was so hungry now I could taste what they had been like, hot from the sun, seeds exploding in my mouth.

"This way," Felipa said. In the snow and yellow station light she and Daniel looked less like mother and son than sister and brother. She linked her arm through mine and led me towards the old stone building that was the former station house. Of course the government report would have to deal with the fate of a building like this – in a special appendix. It would say the building was uneconomical, difficult to heat, its roof ridge unaccountably sagging, practically an eyesore. I always admitted that in the long run such buildings would have to give way to the future, to the splendours of plastic and huge sheets of glass – but for the moment, since it was a particular example of rare architecture, and since it could be used for functions that would only take away from the shiny rightness of a newer building, perhaps it could be saved. Saved.

The soldiers standing outside, with red armbands knotted to their sleeves, recognized Felipa and without question let us pass into a crowded room filled with smoke, more soldiers, men and women all talking at once. It seemed almost two hundred people were packed into the tiny space. The noise was unbearable. It rose and fell in waves. Perestrello, uniformed and bizarrely well-groomed, was standing against a wall, beneath a giant map of the continent – all the lines of power and transportation marked in – as if his whole idea of the future had been imposed on the continent in one giant red-and-blue stamp.

Regina, or, as Felipa would have it, Ree-gi-na. The report would open with a literate touch – a description of the town, of the way it sits in the midst of the flat prairie and rises up out of the earth in an amazing conglomeration of high-rise buildings, grain elevators, television antennas, creating its own little mound of civilization in the midst of land once covered with tough sweet grass: unfenced. And then the report would have to say that Regina, in addition to being the wheat capital of the West, had once been known as a centre of socialism; that Canada's own socialist party and labour movement had focussed here in the midst of the Great Depression and composed a manifesto declaring all men equal. Property Evil. The Dawn of A New Age.

In the centre of the room was a big conference table, with about twenty men and women sitting around it. Their discussion was drowned out in the general noise, but they carried on anyway; like insects with a cellular means of communication, everyone seemed to be able to talk at once and somehow still progress. They were arguing about the distribution of food to various parts of the province. I couldn't concentrate on the details, only the bewildering variety of faces, all of them intense, haggard, bright-eyed – as if the memory of the

126

police riding through the streets and breaking up strike lines lived in each one's imagination, recurring over and over again, every second of their lives, like a huge rock that forever shapes a river.

The meeting was being run by one person in particular – a middle-aged, grey-haired woman with sharp white teeth, an equally sharp tongue and big muscular hands. She was stout, and her lungs and throat must have been made of leather, because even in this room her voice boomed and rasped, a voice meant to carry to the edge of the largest crowd, a voice that could bounce off buildings and turn any street into an echo chamber. Every time someone made a comment she approved of, she'd laugh and give the table a whack with the flat of her palm. It was almost an hour before she banged the table for silence and introduced Perestrello.

He stepped forward, bowed to her as if she was the most fragile creature, and waved suggestively at his map. "This," he said in his most formal and musical voice, "is what they call the scene of the crime." There was scattered laughter and a loud approving slap against the table. "At least they tell us we have committed a crime – and that we plan many more." In this room, in the midst of this gathering of makeshift soldiers, farmers and townspeople, Perestrello was an imposing and immaculate figure. With a sweep of his expensively uniformed arm, he indicated the West Coast from Los Angeles to Alaska. "These areas we already control," he said. "And now there are buses and trains – like our own – going across the continent, bringing food and weapons to resistance groups."

I began to feel claustrophobic and wanted to get out of this crowded room, to walk through the snow to the deserted streets and look around the city: at the houses that had been built here, at the big spaces in between them, at anything except this room. But when I turned to leave I saw I was trapped by new arrivals, more soldiers who had squeezed in the door. Sweat was springing up on my skin. Felipa's elbow dug into my ribs. A soldier with the washed-out blue eyes of an old farmer and a hard dry voice had somehow made everyone else quiet.

"We've been screwed by every government this country ever had. Why would you be any different?" He was talking to Perestrello, not angrily, only stating a fact.

"Not me," said Perestrello, grinning as if that was enough to charm them. "I don't want to tell you what to do. I just want you to co-operate with me because there's someone else – " he pointed east and everyone in the room laughed, captured at last – "who would like to shoot us all, you and me together."

The body heat made the room smell like a sales barn on a winter's night, and the windows were covered in condensation. Felipa's elbow was grinding into my bones. I tried to manoeuvre away but there was no space. I wanted to be alone. It seemed like years since the police had awoken me and exiled me from my slow life, years since I had been on this crowded train sharing every second with hundreds of people I didn't even know. I wanted to be back at the hotel, sitting in the bath with the door open, looking out into an empty room.

"We need a government," shouted a short red-faced man without a uniform. "Who's going to pay us for our crops?"

"What crops?" shouted another man. He was plain and dry-voiced, wearing a uniform with no insignia. It had been a bad year for grain, with drought in the summer and heavy rains in the fall. What hadn't been killed by the dryness had been rotted by the damp.

"At least we have crop insurance," the red-faced man shouted.

"I never got any crop insurance," the uniformed farmer finally said. His voice, so tough and dry, reminded me of some of the farmers who lived around Salem, cantankerous old bastards with necks wrinkled like plucked turkey skins and hands swollen from decades of freezing winters and – as my father used to say – squeezing cows' tits twice a day. "Anyone here get money from their insurance this year?"

"I did," claimed the red-faced man belligerently.

"Anyone else?"

A long silence.

"Ass-licker," came a voice from the side of the room.

"Harry Ass-Licker got his cheque," another voice called out.

Waves of laughter swept through the crowd.

"You could have got yours too," Harry defended himself. His red face was turning redder, a deep flushed scarlet. "Any of you could have had yours." The attitude in the room had changed from laughter to hostility.

The tough old farmer now put up his hand for silence. There was something impressive about him; his face, his hands, even his uniform, were so plain it seemed he must be without vanity or pretence. "I'm with *him*," he said, nodding at Perestrello. "Anyone else that is, raise his hand." A forest of arms shot up. Only Harry, the odd man out, his face redder than ever, kept his hands by his sides.

"All right," the old farmer said to Perestrello. "We'll do what you say. For now. And in the meantime Harry better wait in the closet, before he forgets where he is."

"That's right," said the woman at the table. Slap. Her hand slapped hard against the polished wood. Harry was suddenly surrounded and the whole room jumped with a new tension. Two soldiers dragged him through the crowd and out the door. Voices rose and the hand slapped the table again and again. The room was deep in stale smells of smoke and endless discussion.

I awoke at dawn, feeling newly born – so perfect, so relaxed, that the events of the previous night fell into a new and rosy perspective. In the station house something mysteriously good had transpired; instead of being enemies – soldiers and civilians – we were now all comrades, joined in a common cause. The sight of that old and cynical farmer – a man as skeptical as my own father – finding himself on the same ground as Christopher Perestrello, moved something in me. It seemed that in the midst of this empty country something had actually happened, a change more real than a face or a television screen mouthing banalities and lies.

Maybe there are a few mornings in your life when you wake up feeling perfect: once, once more, just to remember how it was. I remember how it was. I was lying in the hotel bed, Lise beside me, listening to the sounds of our breathing and the squeak of hard boots through the snow.

There was a shout. More shouts. I paid them no attention. In this strange town people were always marching, playing soldier, looking for a war. It was all right; we were all together; we had conspired to be human.

Then the sharp explosion of rifles. It lasted forever. It found a space between my ears and bounced back and forth like an image sandwiched between two mirrors. And then it was gone. In its absence the vacuum was filled, a thousand tiny noises sucked into the aftermath, and knitting them together was the movement of air itself: the wind brushing through the window, Lise's breathing, still rising and falling undisturbed. The new silence forced me to my feet, and I went to the window.

Standing in line, rifles held loosely in their arms, were the soldiers; they were facing a lamppost in the centre of the square. The dead man was tied to the post with ropes around his chest and thighs, and his wrists were bound behind. No blood showed through his heavy coat, and his eyes had been blindfolded. Feeling his pulse, his hands moving fast and sure to certify that life was over, twelve bullets dead, was Dr. James Fine. The dead man was Harry – the farmer who had spoken up at the meeting.

In the early morning, a pale, almost delicate light fell on the square, the sun still low on the southern horizon. This man had died at the beginning of winter, the ground only slightly frozen – easy to dig out for his grave.

"What's wrong?" Lise's voice. Then, when she saw my face, she twisted sharply, up and out of bed, and came to look for herself.

130

I felt some part of me had died and I had been hurled into the future – my past demolished – like one of Jacob Beam's carefully grown tomatoes thrown against a brick wall.

Some of the soldiers were cutting down the body. Then finally they wrapped it in a white sheet and dragged it to a jeep at the edge of the square. There was one place in the snow where the blood still remained; otherwise there was no sign of what had taken place. And standing at this window, looking out at this scene, we might have been anywhere, in any of dozens of cities that have seen revolutions and coups, reprisals and executions.

I told Lise about the meeting last night and how the soldiers and townspeople had lined up with Perestrello, who had not been present for this ceremony. I remember sitting on the edge of the bed, fragments of my perfect morning still clinging to my nerves, pulling on my shoes and talking, feeling sickened and exhilarated at the same time. The blue morning light lived like a ghost in the room. The blood on the snow was only a dark stain.

TWELVE

In the hotel cafeteria, the sombre winter colours were dissolved in fluorescent glare. I had always thought that the external world would plod along forever, unchanged – a comfortable and amorphous bureaucracy, surrounding my life like a giant marshmallow, a giant excuse. Now that was fading away and I was beginning to feel responsible for every moment I lived.

"It always happens this way," Lise said. "History catches up to people."

"Bullshit."

"It's not. How people live and die is what makes things change. One day it will happen to you and me. Or did you expect to die of boredom?"

A waiter came. There was food today but it was rationed – two pieces of toast, one egg, limitless coffee, milk only for children. All prices had been doubled. In the government report something would have to be said about restaurants in times of famine: *It is bad for morale to double the price of non-existent items. It is bad for morale to wake up feeling perfect on days set aside for executions.*

I looked down at my hands. Eating one meal a day had begun to melt the flesh away from my fingers. My hands were becoming big and bony, like a priest's hands. My father and Henry McCaffrey had always made jokes about priests, about men who valued their faith more than their bodies. As if their own bodies – Jacob's stout and falling to unnecessary layers, and Henry McCaffrey's dried up by decades of teaching school – were too valuable to be ignored. "Priests' hands," they would say contemptuously – meaning hands that were thin and bony, hands that had wasted away from keeping to themselves instead of seeking out their natural friends. Scarlet Tiara's hands had been stubby, the backs covered with freckles, the palms amazingly soft. She had frightened me then – it was too much, like drinking straight cream. With Lise it was different. We sat in our island, not talking, watching others who drifted in and out of the cafeteria: everyone was quiet, avoiding the same patch of snow. Finally the waiter came back with toast, eggs, cups of steaming coffee.

If I was getting thin, Lise was on the verge of starving. Her wide green eyes glittered, almost feverish, and dark hollows were starting to form in her cheeks. Her hands were wrapped desperately around the hot cup, as if no longer able to keep themselves warm.

"Eat," I said. "You have to eat." I pushed my toast towards her and scraped my egg onto her plate.

"I'm not hungry."

I was still wearing Lise's ring, a plain gold band. I made it click-click against the table, a tattoo, wedding ring – a priest's ring. At least I knew I wanted to live. The knowledge that I was going home had settled in my stomach, a promise I needed to keep for myself. I wanted to see the town again, my parents; but most of all I wanted it to be winter. I could put on my old snowshoes and tramp through the bush, be alone and outdoors, soaked in the winter light that filtered in the trees. I could breathe in the colours and the squeaking snow of the late afternoon, test my body against the cold that had stripped the trees of their leaves, sucked the summer out of the air, laid snow between my feet and the earth as if it could never heat up to spring again.

Despite her protests, Lise ate almost everything. I took our coffee cups to be refilled at the counter. Through the window

I could see the square; passers-by and soldiers were walking about calmly, as if nothing unusual had happened. The sun had risen fully and burned white against the snow. There were no stains, no marks, no unsightly splotches: only a lamppost in the centre of the square around which the pavement had been shovelled clean.

When I got back to the table, the doctor, James Fine, was sitting beside Lise. Touching her wound through the bandage. His face was white and pallid, shaved clean as cement.

"There," he said. "There? There?"

"I can hardly feel it," Lise said.

The doctor nodded at me. With a fast and agile motion he stripped away the bandage and laid the wound bare. The stitches stood out from Lise's skin, black and bristly, like a boar's hairs.

"Don't forget to take these out," he said. "Ten days." He looked at me. "You make sure she does it."

In one night the swelling had almost disappeared. It was amazing how exact fate could be: if the farmer had kept his mouth shut, he'd still be alive; if Lise had moved a half inch, she would not.

James Fine leaned forward. "I wish I could come with you," he said. He took out a new package of cigarettes, his fingers undoing the cellophane and slitting through the revenue stamp as if it were a trick puzzle.

"Of course," said Lise. "We need a doctor."

"I hope you're not planning anything that would require a doctor. I hope there won't be anything like that." He forgot to bark, and his hard voice had become so soft and sincere we both almost laughed. He made Lise a new bandage – a smaller one this time – then lit himself a cigarette.

"But you do feel welcome," Lise insisted.

"Oh yes," Fine said, "but I can't leave my wife."

Lise laughed. "Well, then you should bring her with you." I remembered going to Fine's door, the triple locks, the smell of Gloria Fine's whiskey so strong that I thought he was drunk too.

"She doesn't like to travel," Fine said. "And unfortunately I have no vices, not even leaving my wife, ha ha." His face had turned red with embarrassment. It was now possible to imagine him as a boy, small and nervous, uncomfortable with the freakish speed of his hands.

"Have you been married a long time?"

When Lise asked him this question, it made me nervous too and I twisted the ring on my finger.

"Twelve years," Fine said. "An even dozen. We're a marriage of old age and companionship."

"That's all right," Lise said sympathetically. "It's hard to live alone."

Fine nodded, as if this small reprieve was more than he deserved.

"I was downtown," he said. "The government offices are giving out news bulletins in place of newspapers, which they say have been suspended in order to conserve energy. Indefinitely suspended, ha ha." He reached into his bag and pulled out two handbills, giving them to Lise and me.

The Ministry of Agriculture wishes to make the following announcement:

The minor and temporary food shortage which was announced last month will now persist until early in the summer.

The extension of the shortage is due to railway and shipping strikes, and illegal black-market activity.

The army is now engaged in moving supplies of powdered milk and grain to the poorer areas of the country.

Citizens are requested to remain calm and limit their consumption of food to one small meal and one large meal a day.

Emergency legislation has been passed which makes the illegal sale or purchase of food a crime punishable by hanging.

As I finished reading this, Lise slid hers across to me and we exchanged.

The Ministry of Justice wishes to make the following announcement:

Four men and two women have been caught attempting to smuggle rice onto Vancouver Island from a vessel of unknown origin.

The cabinet has decided that if they are convicted, there will be no commutation of the death sentence.

The trial is scheduled to begin this morning and will conclude within three days.

The final speeches of the defence and prosecution, as well as the delivery of the verdict and the execution, will be seen on television at a time to be announced.

"You see," Fine said, "you should never underestimate the power of the government. They won't give up easily."

What he should have said was that they wouldn't give up their television programs, their reports, their bulletins, speeches, commissions of inquiry. What he should have said was that the government was addicted to its own propaganda.

Fine carefully folded up the handbills and put them in his pocket. His voice was altogether wrong for government: beneath the careful lies and omissions it was too alive, too human.

And then Felipa came into the cafeteria, confident and renewed – pausing at the door for effect, then coming straight towards us. Her high boots clicked happily against the hardwood floor. "What a victory," she said. "What an amazing victory." She sat down, smiling broadly, her teeth metallic in this fluorescent light.

I looked at her, not making the connection, then of course remembered – the meeting in the station, the body hanging like wet laundry from the post.

"Tonight Regina, tomorrow the world," said Fine sardonically.

"It is a great moment," Felipa said. "Nothing like this has ever happened."

After the first few days of paranoia and indecision, Lise and I seemed to enter an oasis of perfection: sex. We were ridiculous. Our bodies were covered with plumes of dried love. We wanted to be touching all the time. Even from the hotel to the train station we stumbled all over each other. And once we were in her compartment we sat in her new chairs like royalty, holding hands and waving to the townspeople on the crowded platform as the train slowly pulled away.

When we reached the outskirts, the engines began to pick up speed, the whistle blew a long sad note and the whole train shuddered: alive again, awake from its day-long rest and ready to continue its flight into the east. And if in the mountains this train had been a marauding metal wolf, speeding through the canyons under the cover of night, here on the prairies it was a lion, solid and defiant, daring all in a full daylight of clear sky and glittering snow.

"Are you really going home?"

"Yes."

"I'll miss you."

"You should come with me," I said. "My parents want to meet you. My father is even trimming his beard."

"What about yours?" Lise asked.

It was days since I had shaved. I went into the bathroom of her compartment to inspect myself. A blond-and-red fuzz carpet had begun to grow unevenly on my face and neck. If I let it grow, I would look like a younger, honey-coloured version of Jacob Beam. I filled the sink with water and covered my face in shaving cream.

Jacob Beam had never used instant shaving cream or a safety razor. He had an old shaving mug filled with soap, a brush made of genuine horsehair, a straight razor and a leather strap. The strap was seldom used except to sharpen the razor for the occasional trim or to pursue me in a fit of temper.

With everything shaved except my upper lip, I went in to show Lise. "How about a moustache?" I said. "Wouldn't I look handsome in one?"

"I like moustaches. I used to have a boyfriend with a moustache."

I went back into the bathroom to shave it off. It was amazing how quickly I got used to things. Even the ring no longer chafed my finger; and if I sometimes caught myself nervously twisting it around, well, such reactions were to be expected.

"Have you had a lot of boyfriends?"

"A few," Lise said.

"Women are wild about me." I had reduced my moustache to a small Hitler-style decoration. We Jews have a weakness about Hitler. "For example," I said, "I was once in a store shoplifting a pair of nylons for my mother when I got caught by a lady detective. It was love at first sight." With two careful swipes the moustache was gone. Who wants to be Hitler? I could stuff my face with doughnuts and be Winston Churchill instead.

I was starting to feel cooped up again, as if we had been on this train forever. I lit one of Lise's cigarettes. Here I was in her compartment, smoking her cigarettes, wearing her ring.

"I don't know," she said, "I'm just not feeling well today." She looked at me hopelessly, as if all these changes were too fast for her. Once, only in passing, Lise had mentioned her parents, making clear they were dead. Her whole past was either dead or, like her child, out of reach.

"I wish I knew what you were like," I said. "I mean, what it's like to *be* you."

"You can't talk about those things."

"Yes, you can."

She looked at me, suddenly sad and exhausted. Her hands reached out for mine, her fingers burrowing into my palms. The invisible walls between us were beginning to drop down. "Sometimes I feel small," she said. "I shrink down inside myself and wait for everything to go away. Sleeping helps. Or meditating. I used to meditate but I can't do it on the train."

For the first time, I wondered if Lise and I might grow old together. She would become thinner every season. Her hips would grow sharp and her legs long and stringy. And myself? The smaller she became, the larger I would grow, gradually turning into a comfortable bear. And the time would come when I'd turn grey and fat and be released from all this random desire.

She leaned against me and our hands remained locked. Yet, behind the curtains of our own skins, of our own unexpected rushes of feeling and desire, there were other currents, pools waiting to trap us. And now we found ourselves on Lise's bed, our arms around each other, searching, our bodies still covered by trophies from previous wars – and we weren't quite ready, didn't quite want to carry through.

"It's not right," Lise said, drawing back. "Let's wait."

"It's been a bad day."

She smiled at me. Consolingly. She looked beautiful and distant, the way she had looked that very first night. "I wish we had some wine," she said, her voice going through another quick change. "I feel depressed." As she lit a cigarette, the yellow flare of the match illuminated her face: eyes puffy, mouth set as she sucked in the smoke. The train had slowed down again; it was gliding through the plains, and I was beginning to feel it would be forever before we arrived in Ontario.

"When we get home," I said, "we can drink my father's apple brandy. After you drink that, you might never want wine again."

"You still want to take me home?"

"Of course," I said. "Why not?" I put my hand on her back and could feel her skin tightening, trying to turn itself into armour.

This journey had gone on for so long now, I could hardly remember how it had begun. Even the bruise on my stomach was starting to fade; after reaching its peak in a gorgeous blue and dark yellow flower, it had now diminished into a pale splotch, the imprint of a remembered sun.

At the last moment Fine had decided to join the train; my own place had been given up to him and his wife. Now I was stuck in this room with Lise, our sudden changes in mood; and the ring she had given me which sometimes seemed to have already grown into my finger and other times – like now – was only an imposition I didn't know how to get rid of. Not that I wanted to leave her. I never wanted to be without Lise – not now, not then – and yet I couldn't help asking myself how I had gotten to be twenty-seven years old and still remained an absolute fool about women. After all, the mechanics of these things aren't hidden when you grow up in a small town and see all kinds of relationships flourish and die – from those brief ecstasies consummated in a back seat in the empty lot behind the hardware store to all the marriages where the couple stick together like two pieces of mismatched old taffy. And in the end, that's how it always was in Salem: despite what happened on the occasional hot and drunk summer afternoon, despite the agonies of indecision, adultery and questionable parenthood, in the end, for reasons far too mysterious for anyone to fathom – perhaps simply necessity – the marriages usually lasted, even if they had to be greased by daily visits to the liquor store or other arrangements of mutual convenience.

Lise was sulking, sitting rigid and staring out the window at the unbroken snow. When my mother got depressed, a monthly occurrence Jacob Beam had explained to me early on, Jacob would get dressed and leave the house, either for one of his serious visits to the hotel or for a walk over to the schoolteacher's. "Let her sit," he'd say. And why not? She left him often enough. It was only because we were in this train, afraid that at any moment we'd be blown out of our skins, that Lise and I felt trapped this way.

I turned off the lights and lay down on the bed beside her. Perhaps if we lay quietly together in each other's arms, we could somehow grow strong again.

The engine was mounted with blades to plough through the snow that had drifted onto the tracks. At the rate we were going, it would take days to cross these prairies. Still, I was reassured by the sound of the wheels moving rhythmically against the tracks, the slow swayings and creakings of the cars. At least we were moving again; and every motion, every pile of snow thrown aside, drew me that much closer to home. Ten years I had been away, but couldn't imagine living ten years more. I'd be lucky to get through this winter; I'd be lucky to get through this next one thousand miles. Lying on the bed with Lise in my arms, I promised myself to put together a survival kit, so that when this train finally stopped, we'd be able to continue our journey on foot. I dozed off with the image of Lise and I stranded in the bush, hunting rabbits, boiling tea out of bark and snow, trying to make a stew with a frozen partridge and two handfuls of dead leaves.

There was no real sleep, only a blurred succession of dreams, old memories, speculations about the future, all strung together by the slow progress of the train as it hissed and bellied its way through the snow. With my head buried in the pillow I could almost erase the picture of the red-faced farmer slumping down in the low morning light, his body held only by ropes. They had moved towards him and surrounded him with slow deliberation, a cannibal's dance.

I woke up with my hands clenched, holding my breath. And yet some part of me, some tiny part of me, was not involved at all and was looking down and laughing contemptuously. Theodore Beam, it seemed to be saying, what an idiot you are. And later that evening when Lise woke up, we found our way together again. I felt so close to her, every pore of her skin, the light jumping from the shadow of her eyes, the blond wave of her hair encircling us both. But when I kissed her and said I loved her, loved her, I was still divided, and that skeptical part of me stood back and watched – touched and drowned in this but still reserved, waiting.

THIRTEEN

The cold air scrapes our faces, bites at the inside of our lungs. The moon lights up the vast white plain, and to my eyes it's so strange, it might be the moon itself: mysterious and white, absolutely flat. Hollow noises move through the cold; spirits of animals that human eyes will never see.

After a day of crawling through the prairie at a snail's pace, we were stopped in the middle of the great plateau that stretches from the west of Regina to the edge of the Ontario bush. In this empty night, the temperature had dropped into the middle of winter. Even in their gloves, my hands were frozen from trying to wrap themselves around the edges of the wooden crates that I was passing out of the freight car to the man next in the human chain.

When we started, he asked me my name.

"Theodore."

"Theodore, eh? I'm Steve Wirkowski myself." He buried my thinly gloved hand in his nylon-padded mitt. "We heard you had quite a time in Regina."

He and fifteen others had come to meet the train in their snow machines. Now they were drawn in a circle beside the door of the freight car, trailers being loaded with crates of automatic weapons.

"I wouldn't want to be shooting anyone," Steve Wirkowski said. He was dressed in a quilted nylon outfit. Occasionally his sleeve brushed against the canvas of my parka, making a dry scratching sound, like a chicken digging at ice. "My older brother was in the war, in Korea, and he shot three men. He said it was all right because they weren't even human. But then he had nightmares all the time and his wife had to leave him. Everyone is human, you know – even that Harry St. John who got shot in Regina."

This was the first time I heard his full name.

The wind was coming across the snow from the north. Not a strong wind but cold enough to reach through the skin and make my bones ache as if they'd been touched by metal fingers.

"You travel with this bunch, eh? Lucky man."

Perestrello was walking among the trailers, rubbing his hands together for warmth and conferring like a general with the two men half a step behind him.

In the freight car Daniel clambered among the crates to select what was needed, as Lise called out instructions to him. She was sitting at the end of the car, with a clipboard and a thick sheaf of lists, keeping track of what was gone and what remained. Beside her was James Fine. This stop was our third and – Perestrello said – our last of the night.

"I wouldn't be out here," said Wirkowski, "except for my wife. She's a Métis, you know – a half-breed – and she hates the government worse than anyone. When they came on the television saying they'd be having trials and putting people in jail, she brought out pictures of her great-grandfather – him with his old buffalo-hunting gun and one arm blown off by the police when he fought in the rebellion. And she said I might as well come out and help because if I don't they can always find an excuse to hang me anyway." He laughed, obviously not believing that a threat could jump out of his television set and touch him personally.

And then we were at the last crate. Wirkowski slapped me on the shoulder with his padded hand and grinned.

I saw his face in the light of the freight car's single bulb. His beard had gone untouched for days, the stubble shot through with grey, and there were gaps in his front teeth. Getting old, but for him war was still only a story about his elder brother and his wife's half-Indian ancestor.

We stood in the snow while he finished telling me about his brother who had been in Korea. First he had nightmares, then he began waking up with hallucinations, running through the house, shouting and breaking things. Finally his wife left him. He was afraid to live alone, so he moved back to his father's house. Every morning he went into town to work at his job at the hardware store. In the evening he drank ale at the hotel until it closed, then drove back to his father's in the old Ford, the same Ford he had bought when the war was just a rumour.

"It was a fast car, eh. He bought it to be fast, and he used to race with it on the highway, dragging with the other fellows. That was before he got married, before the highway turned into the Trans-Canada Highway and got filled up by tourists and cops."

On the last night, his brother left the hotel early, saying he didn't feel well. He drove home in his old Ford, turned into the driveway, then accelerated as fast as he could: past the house, the new drive shed, the new silo, straight towards the old cattle barn, smashing into the stone foundation.

"Crazy man," Wirkowski said, and to shake off the remembered vision slapped me on the shoulder again and held out his hand.

"Good luck, eh. And try to stay alive." He grinned at me and turned to walk towards his snow machine. We were still climbing back into the train when they took off, their engines roaring and coughing in the night as they went speeding across the snow, disappearing into the dark like a long line of metal insects.

By the time I got to the dining car, Lise was already there, sitting at a table opposite James Fine. Beside him was his wife. Her stubby, smudged features were arranged in the same expression she had the first time I saw her – a strange mixture of aggression and contentment. She was asleep.

In front of him James Fine had a package of cigarettes which he was gradually disassembling in order to amuse himself. The cellophane had been ripped into neat, narrow strips and tied into bows. The silver paper had been shaped into little stars.

Although he was about the same age as my father, James Fine seemed almost a different species. Even ten years ago, Jacob Beam had already become distinctly seedy. His clothes were falling apart, his beard straggled, the frames of his reading glasses twisted and held together by a safety pin. I had never thought this represented carelessness on his part, only his idea that it was the true destiny of man to spend the first half of his life puffing himself up as big as possible and the second half gradually collapsing.

By comparison, it was James Fine's fate to exude the air of an overly neat and successful salesman of encyclopaedias. A success which had not touched his wife; for she was not only asleep, she was also – as they used to say in Salem – absolutely varnished. Her eyes were closed, and through the noises of the train we gradually began to discern her snores.

"Well, now that I'm used to things, I'm glad we decided to come," Fine said.

"Me too," said Lise. "We hoped you would." She smiled at him bravely. "My cut is almost better. Tomorrow I'm going to take the bandage off."

Fine leaned across the table and touched her head lightly with his fingers.

While I'd been outside, slinging heavy crates and freezing, Fine and Lise had been making their lists – and, no doubt, charming conversation, inquiring after each other's health. The snores of Fine's wife cut across the sound of the train's engines. Fine stood up. "I'll get some tea," he said. He looked at me solicitously, as if he had been reading my mind. "You must be cold."

"I hate doctors," I said to Lise as soon as he was out of ear-shot.

And then Fine was back, proudly holding a pot of tea in his hand, as if it had been born there. Paper cups, spoons, sugar and milk all magically emerged. "God, I'm tired," Fine said. "I'm getting too old to stay up this late."

I too was tired. My eyes were sore and raw, and a muscle in the centre of my back didn't want to settle into place no matter how I wriggled and stretched. I took off my watch and placed it on the table; fifteen minutes after four. There was a small crack down the centre where the watch had been smashed against the door that first night, and drops of water were beginning to collect under the crystal. We had been up half this night with the three stops: the first at one o'clock; the second a little over an hour later; and now this final one that returned us to where we had begun, sitting at a table – hungry.

In the hours between our shifts, Fine had quizzed me on the organization of the train; and as he did, adding information of his own, I began to realize that Perestrello's system was much more sophisticated than it first seemed. Daniel, Fine, Lise and I: we were now one cell. We knew, in addition, about Felipa and Perestrello – but no one else. There was at least one other cell – the people who had worked at the second stop – and most likely there were more. All this could have been obvious, but it was Fine who pointed it out and also observed that parts of the train were completely sealed off from each other.

With hot tea in his belly and the night's work behind him, Fine grew more alert. He had now completely destroyed the cigarette package: the cigarettes themselves stood on their ends in two lines, filter-tipped soldiers facing each other. Between them were the treasures: silver stars, cellophane bows.

"It's very clever," Fine said. "There must be one cell in each sealed section of the train. The rest of the passengers are legitimate – the perfect hostages. If they bomb or derail the train, thousands of innocent people will be killed and there'd be a public outcry. If they stop the train and search it, no one knows anything. At worse, they find a few carloads of illegal weapons, but no one is responsible."

"Perestrello would be caught," I said. "Everyone knows he was in Regina. He could report us. We could report him."

Lise laughed. "Perestrello would never report anyone. And he's not worried about what you might say – or the police."

"That's interesting," Fine said. "You have to admit that's interesting. Who else these days is unafraid of the police?" And now I remembered that when I sat in his house with him, watching the Prime Minister announce the plot that threatened this whole continent, the uncertainty seemed to fall away from Fine's face.

"And then," Fine continued, "you have to consider the real problem." He pushed over one of his cigarette soldiers, making the whole row topple in a slow chain reaction. "Where is all this going? After all, a man like Perestrello must have a plan. Right now we're relatively anonymous: a train passing through the empty spaces of a country crippled by a huge snowstorm. But what happens next? Eventually we'll arrive in the cities of the East. He must have an alliance with the unions and with these police whom he does not fear."

Lise yawned elaborately. Her faith in Perestrello was complete and she seemed to have an utter lack of curiosity about the details. She started to get up but put her hand on mine to restrain me. "I think I'll go to bed," she said. "You stay here and talk if you want. I'll see you later."

Felipa was sitting a few tables down from us, alone, watching Lise and waiting. As Lise passed her, she spoke, then they left the car together.

After they were gone, Fine lit one of the fallen soldiers, then began to arrange the others in a new box-like formation. When the train jolted, they all fell and he had to start over again. Sometimes his wife swayed towards him, and he'd prop her up against the window again where she continued to sleep, her snoring broken only by the occasional mumbled words.

Fine divided the dregs of the lukewarm tea between us, then he got all his soldiers into position. It would soon be five o'clock – that point in the night where it doesn't matter what time it is and even the fatigue seems to lift. I helped myself to one of Fine's soldiers, a sentry that had drifted away from the main formation; and in a swirl of smoke and warmth I tried to think out what he had been saying.

What would happen when we finally arrived in the cities? Did Perestrello have an alliance with the unions that made him invulnerable? Had the unions and army already joined to take over the country? Or, most ridiculous of all – but possible – maybe Perestrello was simply bluffing, riding out this journey knowing that other things were happening at the same time, hoping somehow the revolution would precede him wherever he went.

The train whistle sounded, a long languid note. And almost as an echo, we heard the whistle of another train. In the stone schoolhouse, where Henry McCaffrey stood beneath the picture of the Queen and told us about the way our country had been made, we had learned that for much of the Canadian railway system there was only a single set of tracks. But we weren't slowing down in search of a siding; in fact we were picking up speed, the wheels clicking and clattering against the rails in a noise we hadn't heard for days – as if the train was now turning itself into a long metal arrow drawing together the endless years of strikes, shortages, summer riots, outbursts of violence, into one last spectacular collision.

The two whistles now shrieked in unison, like yowling cats stranded halfway between fighting and mating. Fine had set the teapot down on the floor and braced his arm around his wife while she slept on, oblivious. All his cigarettes were rolling about the table.

Then there was a long thundering sound as the other train, on a different track after all, began to pass beside us.

The passing train was shorter than ours. With my nose

pressed to the glass I could see it had flatcars carrying cannons and tanks; in two of its cars uniformed soldiers played cards and drank. Friendly, knowing nothing about us, they waved to us as we passed.

"We'll smoke another cigarette," Fine said, "then go to sleep. In the morning we may still be alive."

When I got back to the compartment, Lise was sitting on the edge of the bed, looking out the window. The moon was still up and the edges of the sky seemed to be growing lighter as if dawn was not so far away.

I lay down on the bed. Lise had turned out the lights. With my eyes closed, I began to think of bread – toasted, covered with cheese and bacon. Fresh-baked whole-wheat bread like my godmother, Katherine Malone, used to make, still warm from the oven, steaming as it was sliced open, hot enough to melt the skins of butter that ran into its surface. Wheat-germ bread that I used to buy in a Vancouver health food store, its crust dotted with golden-brown sesame seeds, wrapped by one of the dozen indistinguishable employees – all long-haired and healthy with their perfect diet.

"God, I'm hungry," I said. "I feel like I haven't eaten for weeks."

"We ate in the hotel. Don't you ever think of anything but food?"

Lise's voice sounded irritated. She had finished one cigarette and was starting another. Then she turned on the lights again and began rummaging around for something to read. The gap between us seemed to be growing wider. I was trying to convince myself that I could discover the secret of how Lise and I could preserve ourselves. Family life. I had never written a report on family life. I had the idea it involved being very still, perfectly quiet in the centre of the nervous system.

"You seem bored," Lise said aggressively. "Don't you have anything to do?"

Every family needs a hobby. I looked out the window.

"What do you do when you're alone?" In her new jeans and

expensive sweater, Lise looked as if she was on her way to a ski resort. Even her bandage added to the picture, a discreet white band peeking out from beneath her perfect blond hair.

"I eat banana sandwiches," I said. "I take bananas with brown dotted skin and crush them into oblivion — "

"Fuck off."

I started to laugh, couldn't help it – hearing Lise swear was too absurd. And then she too was laughing and we were lying on the bed holding each other, with Lise whispering in my ear "Love you, love you, love you – " And her voice reached into me, through my bones and nerves and into my secret rooms, sharp and almost unbearable as I slid into her, wanting to come right away, to be released, to flood into her. I sucked in my breath and closed my eyes, poised on the edge, on the edge of the sharp line that drew us together, on the edge of Lise, her edges, the muscles that enclosed me, held me in and out at the same time.

"Do you love me?"

"Yes," I said.

"Do you?"

"Yes."

"How do you love me?"

"In deep like this. And here, waiting." Waiting. I was arched above her. I opened my eyes. Our bodies converged on each other like fingers from a single hand. The noise of the train, our breathing, the small sounds of our bodies, all melted together. There was no need for me to hold back now. I felt as if we were on a vast plateau, an infinite current of nerves and sensations that could carry us forever, that could hold up our world, our world that was my hand in the small of her back, her flesh around mine. And then, like the first time, we began to hear noises from the corridor, noises of boots rushing back and forth.

But now there was something different, an intensity that was greater, voices talking then shouting. Then crying out in pain. Until finally there was nothing for us to do but give up.

With my body still drawn and tense, so awkward and bumbling I might have been drunk, I threw on my clothes and shoes then went out into the corridor where a man had a woman pushed against a wall. He was slapping her face back and forth so her head whipped from side to side, knocking against the metal wall. And before I knew what I was doing, before I saw the others in the car, I was grabbing the man, pulling him away from the woman – Felipa.

As I turned the man around, sex and anger were mixed in my blood, half of me sluggish and the other half in an uncontrolled frenzy. And when a knife appeared in his hand, I suddenly had his wrist clamped, my knee buried in his groin, as if I had done this all my life. Even when I saw the others moving towards me, I kept at him, got the knife in my own hand and suddenly it was my arm that was up in the air, driving the metal towards his flesh and bones. As if I had been born to it. As if Lise's breath and the touch of her womb had prepared me for it. I was watching his eyes, watching them as the knife came down. Waiting for him to turn away. But he didn't, couldn't, only held his eyes to mine. And as the knife pierced the cloth of his coat, my arm stopped, cramped. Wouldn't do it. Now I could hear other things, other people: Daniel's voice screaming for everyone to stand still, Lise's whisper in my ear, my father over the telephone, asking me if I was sick. "A wink," he had said. That's how far away I was from being an old man. A wink away from death. From giving death. From my own consciousness as something smashed into my head and turned everything into a cyclone of remembered images, bloodied flesh, release finally of my own blood, a warm flood on my scalp and neck.

FOURTEEN

The first memories are sounds: the noises of birth, the loud winds of breathing, the creak of century-old wood receiving each slow step, the all-surrounding wall of my own crying. After that there are places in my mind that have become photographs of the past: pictures of the house when I was young, a dog across the street, neighbours' children, a wall so high it curved up and over me. But the first long memory, the memory of an extended event, is the time Jacob Beam took me to the old-age home to see my grandfather.

I was five years old. We took the train to Toronto and passed through hours of wallowing green fields, towns that exploded in smoke and cement, then more fields until we came to a town so big it never ended, only got thicker and thicker until we reached the centre where we got out into an unprecedented jumble of people and smells and smoke – so much smoke I thought the station must be on fire and kept closing my eyes and pressing my head against Jacob Beam's black wool coat as he dragged me into the street.

That night we slept in a hotel, a real hotel with deep mattresses and pillows with starched slips. And in the morning we walked along the streets until we came to the home where my grandfather lived. Nothing had prepared me for Toronto, for the existence of a city, for a place different from Salem. I was struck with panic, overwhelmed, amazed. I wanted to live here forever.

"You might as well see him alive as come to his funeral," was all Jacob Beam had said on the train.

I remember going up the walk to the home. It was a flag-stone walk, the longest I had ever seen, as the home itself was the biggest house I had ever seen – a huge red-brick building plastered all round with white porches and eaves, making it look like a red cake with vanilla icing.

Just before we got to the entrance Jacob Beam crouched down so his massive head was level with mine. He reached into his pocket, then put a small black cap on my head. "You might not like this," he whispered.

"I do." I thought he meant the cap.

"We won't stay long."

He took me by the hand and led me up the wide wooden steps to the glass front door. I can still see the reflection of myself standing there, reaching up to hold the hand of my father, gradually feeling the fear that he felt in the heat of his palm.

Then the door opened and an old man stood in front of us, an old man so small he seemed hardly bigger than myself. It was my grandfather and he was laughing, rocking back and forth in his huge shiny brown shoes and laughing. Then he reached out and grabbed my hands in his. His skin was like warm canvas. He was so old he had turned into something else, into another species; and after that whenever I saw the ancient great-grandfathers of farmers standing in the sun out-side the Salem liquor store, I was reminded of him.

"Theodore," he said. "Theodore." He spoke my name with a funny accent but I recognized it. Then he pointed at himself, "Theodore," and at me, and I understood we both had the same name, that we were each different versions of the same person. In between the repetitions of our name he laughed; and while he laughed I inspected him, drank him in, every detail unexpected – the grey trousers a foot too long that crumpled into his shoes, the baggy white shirt held to his arms by gold bracelets, the pale blue eyes that I recognized as my eyes but a thousand years old, my eyes shining out of his face.

We went upstairs to his room and while Jacob sat on the bed and watched, my grandfather showed me the different things he had: old books, piles of starched white shirts, suits, gold-framed pictures of people in funny clothes. Except for saying my name and laughing, he never talked. We went through all his drawers and cupboards, taking everything out, piling clothes and strange souvenirs on the floor. There was one thing he gave me: a thin gold pocket watch with gold arrow-hands that ticked with a soft confidential murmur. I sat in the midst of my grandfather's clothes, holding it to my ear, listening to this sound I had never heard before.

A woman came and brought us a tray: three glasses of grape juice and some cookies. My grandfather and I sat on the floor and drank our juice and ate the cookies. He drank the same way I did – carefully, using both hands, tipping the glass back slowly so it wouldn't spill. Still, he ended up with a long purple line down the side of his shirt, with a dot under it, like an exclamation mark. Jacob didn't drink his juice at all; I had to divide it between my grandfather and myself, and we drank it for him.

All the way home on the train I listened to the watch and wore the black cap. When my mother asked us about the visit, I said I wanted to go back; but Jacob didn't say anything, only went to the sideboard and got his bottle of apple brandy. I thought he was sulking and I told my mother it was all right, Jacob was only angry because he didn't know how to play. As I lay in bed and waited for sleep, I held a secret in my mind – that my grandfather and I were the same person, that I had seen myself in the mirror of the glass door, then the door had opened and he stepped out: me in disguise.

Sounds and sights. Eyes. I was lying on my back, aware of the feel of warm air on my face, the sound of static creeping through the web of my dreams, the feeling of my eyes in their sockets, the feeling of my eyes as they used to feel when I was a boy, when I'd wake up and remember I had my grandfather's eyes. Now that he was dead I was the sole carrier of the eyes; everything had to be registered and recorded by me until I found someone to pass them on to. The way he had passed them on to me. The way he had given me his watch.

In the back of my head where the muscles slope down to the neck, in the thin bones of the spine that carry up from the back, there was a dull ache. No edges. I had to lie still, not move, not risk the sharp line of pain I could sense somewhere, waiting to trip me like a wire in the dark. I opened my eyes: Lise's face bending over me, concerned, eyes round and filled with tears – as if I were dying and she were already crying for me.

"Am I all right?" I jerked around, trying to wiggle everywhere at once, twisting to see if I was all there. And as I did, I found the line – not a sharp edge of pain after all, only a wall passing through my nervous system, a place in the centre of my neck that hurt so much I was knocked back into a long winding drift.

I was lying in a bed that had been dragged into Perestrello's compartment. Perestrello himself was talking into the radio at Red Thomas, his voice alternating with the static of the radio. Then from the next room I heard other voices: Daniel's which was demanding, and the voice of a man who was begging. A scream. Then Fine: "Stop it, for Christ's sake." Daniel started to reply and the door slammed shut, cutting off the sound.

Lise's eyes were over me, a deep sea-green.

"Are you all right?"

"Yes. Help me sit up."

Lise put her arm under my back and I struggled up. Aside from the feeling that a nail had been driven through my neck, everything felt perfect. There were sparks jumping in my eyes. I kept still until they went away. Perestrello was sitting at his radio table, furiously writing. Felipa was in a chair, smoking and watching us.

"You were lucky," Lise said.

Now I remembered the fight in the corridor, the feel of the knife digging into my palm, my own sudden need to put the steel through a stranger. *Thou Shalt Not Kill.* Easy to say.

Lise's hand was in mine, then her fingers slid along my arm. "Fine gave you a shot," she said. "You're supposed to be asleep."

Her lips brushed against my cheek and neck as she helped me off the bed. I wasn't asleep but it was like being asleep, every movement slow and fluid. I wasn't dreaming but it was like dreaming, the webs of energy connecting every person and every thing, the slow warm current that carried me from moment to moment. And in the next room, where the muffled voices had given way to silence, it could have been my own nightmare being acted out, my old nightmare being lived out by someone else.

Finally I was in a chair, drinking coffee, the taste and smell cutting into my mind.

"We have to thank you," Perestrello said formally. "We're in your debt."

In your debt. I found it hard to imagine them owing me favours.

"Daniel came upon you in the corridor and killed the man who was attacking you."

"That's nice." My hands were shaking. The more I tried to control them, the worse they shook, until my coffee cup was almost empty. I pushed up the blind, trying to distract myself. There was nothing to be seen outside but the rectangle of light from our compartment sweeping over the snow.

"There was another man," Felipa said. "You didn't kill him."

She said this in an odd way, almost as if it was too bad I hadn't.

"You don't know what you're doing," she said. "You have the right instincts but your mind gets in the way."

She extended her arm to me. I stood up and she led me into the next room and switched on the light. In one corner Daniel was seated, cross-legged, his rifle over his knees. And in the centre of the floor, lying on his side bound and gagged, was a man who was familiar – the one who had attacked Perestrello in the train station restaurant, the one I had passed crates of weapons to on the very first night. He had recognized me then. I wondered if he had recognized me again – when I had taken his knife and tried to kill him. Now, though his eyes were open, he didn't appear to be seeing. Then he rolled over towards us, his feet kicking out uselessly.

"The life of a man who betrays," said Felipa, "is not worth having." She spat on him then left the room.

I stood in the same spot for a long time, watching this man thrash around weakly on the floor. I saw the blood on his chest where my knife had entered. It would have been better if I had killed him.

"You know," said Perestrello when I returned, "you're one of us now."

This seemed as much a threat as acceptance.

"We're a tribe," Felipa said. "We look out for each other."

"We survive," Perestrello corrected. As if this was different, a whole quality of life. "After all, some of us live at one end of the club, some at the other."

"You make it sound like pure force."

"Pure force," repeated Perestrello. He laughed. "It is pure force. It's exactly pure force."

And now I saw that his face wasn't cruel at all, not malicious, but only knowing, the face of someone who has reduced everything to what can be understood, what can be taught in arithmetic lessons.

"It was exactly pure force that got us here," Perestrello said. His voice the hawk, my mind the prey. "After all, this continent, this new world, was never truly ours. We needed it because we had already destroyed the old. But before we came, men lived here as true men, and every human knew the meaning of his own life. And while they lived here with their gods and their forests, we were breeding and fighting like locusts, all pushed up into one corner of the earth.

"I remember how it was for me," Perestrello continued. "My father brought me here on a boat. He said there was no place left at home for us to survive, no place for us to live. We were kicked out of Europe like so many ants chased from the hill. When the shadow of Spain finally disappeared, we stood on the deck and sucked in the air until our chests rattled. We rested our eyes in the clouds and the wind blew hope into our faces. But the old fears stayed with us. Secretly a part of us was always sniffing for burning houses, burning crops, or our own flesh burning like so much pigs' hide."

Even though I had been born here, as had my mother and her mother, there was some part of me that recognized what he was saying – that the mixed-up set of European races had eaten away at their own history, at their own imagination, so that finally they belonged nowhere at all.

"By the time we arrived, there was nothing we would not take for our own. The land was waiting for us. It was ripe and fertile. Summer mornings the sun rose early, burning spaces between the trees. The wood smashed into the ground like old cities falling. No one had ever seen so many trees. No one had ever seen earth like this, earth that yielded to the plough with such eagerness."

Perestrello shrugged and leaned further over the table and the map this world had become. "Of course, we were wrong. The future was only the past in an elaborate disguise. The continent was ruined as easily as a wife or a child. With the slaves and the killings we poisoned ourselves. We began to realize that the new world had already become the old. There was no place to receive us. We could only go round and round, repeating ourselves.

"I still have hope," Perestrello said. "Somewhere inside us there's a place that has never been touched and is still innocent, waiting to be discovered. When we've suffered, when the violence is over and the false governments have fallen, when we're simple men and women again, standing on the face of the earth, there'll be something we can reach for, something noble inside us."

Words are easy. There's nothing that can't be said somehow or other. It's the voice that's hard, the sound of someone who believes in himself, a voice that can let the world run its own random way.

FIFTEEN

I dreamt we were standing in the snow together: Perestrello, Felipa, Lise, Daniel, myself – even the man who had begged for mercy – and we were watching the sun come up, waiting for something. As the light grew I could see we were part of a larger crowd. The sun began to send up long flares of yellow; we were made brothers and sisters by the light that joined us, small patches lying on our sleeves and faces – every one of us the same. Then those of us who were going climbed onto the train. Its motors sped up and soon we were moving, accelerating until we flew through the fields, wheels banging, steel on steel.

When I opened my eyes it was dawn. Lise was huddled in the far corner of the bed, away from me. My neck and back were stiff but I could move if I was careful. I sat up on the bed and began to smoke one of Lise's cigarettes. The snow was blue and pink, a wildly optimistic colour that came through the window staining everything, turning even the smoke into a slow-moving statue of hope. As I watched Lise sleep I realized I was finally beginning to share the confidence she had in Perestrello. Because, to tell the truth, I had hardly ever met anyone who believed in the future, really believed in it; and Perestrello, despite his money and strange formal personality, had the courage to look ahead. Not like my father, Jacob Beam, who had been so frightened by the war – and his glimpse into the machinations of the world – that he had retreated with his letters and diaries into a small town that closed its eyes to the present, let alone the future.

And what would Perestrello think of Jacob Beam? With his farmer's belly that sagged with the food he had saved from winter to winter, his thin hair and unkempt beard, he'd seem like a failed grocer to this immaculate ambassador from the revolution. But at least Jacob Beam had had the courage to fight for Spain – risking his blood long after Perestrello himself had deserted. If in his small town he had tried to escape, at least he had given me a home.

And now I could feel it in my bones, feel the excitement of coming closer, crossing the last few miles of prairies and entering into the heartland of the continent. There was some part of me, something infinitely older than this absurd body and twisted-up mess of memory and desire – some part of me that could already sense the great sweep of forest, and the lakes that split apart the belly of this whole hemisphere, their northern edges pushed up like dykes by the glaciers, and their guts now filled up with millions of gallons of water. As Jacob Beam once said: God had to spit all day to make these lakes.

And if I couldn't believe in myself, at least I could believe in all this water, in the giant rock cliffs with the Indian legends scratched on them so deeply they couldn't be touched by thousands of years of wind and storms. And I could believe in the trees crowding and swelling down from the tundra into the very edges of the lakes, growing even where their roots reached around the iron-soaked rocks to live, trees sticking up out of the ground like a million rigid fingers.

Dawn had turned the breaking prairies into rolling purple hummocks, framed now by the beginning of bush, a ragged line of spruce growing up into the sky. Lise seemed entirely lost in sleep. I leaned down to kiss her; she stirred briefly then settled back into her dreams.

In government reports there's seldom direct mention of people, of feelings between people. Even reports on mental health treat feelings as a problem to be solved: something simple. Perhaps they're supposed to be too simple to mention. But with Lise my feelings were only getting more complicated. It seemed they were growing in two opposite directions – love and detachment. More and more I wanted her. But more and more I was getting ready to write the concluding section: How It Ended. Our bodies were growing uncomfortable in the same bed. When she woke up we'd be surprised to find ourselves together; and every time we made love there was a wider gap to be crossed.

I got dressed and went to the corridor to walk about the train and stretch my legs. My back and neck were still stiff and sore.

If we ever arrived in Salem it would be nearing Christmas. When I left this train I would walk until my legs gave out. With Jacob Beam's snowshoes and a pack on my back I could spend whole days on trails through the bush and the roads that connected farm to farm and lake to lake. If the snow was deep, so much the better. I could already feel how it would be, sinking in with each step, the sinew tops of the snowshoes covered with slabs of crusted snow, flipping them into the air as the curved fronts lifted up and forward.

To be going home after ten years. It was starting to seem so long since I left Vancouver that I couldn't remember how the journey had begun. Jacob Beam's voice had captured me. Maybe he had known that this time, when he gave me my annual birthday message, I was ready to be brought back to the fold. Theodore Beam, the prodigal son returned. "I could have been a better father," Jacob Beam had said. He was right. At times he was worse than useless. And I could have been a better son. Perhaps I should have told him that.

In the coach cars, the blinds were drawn. Only cracks of light showed through, revealing a jumble of sleeping passengers, coats and blankets. Some couples slept in each other's arms. Others had retreated for privacy into their makeshift tents, and bits of bare limbs protruded where the coverings had slipped away in the night. Even the children and infants were still magically asleep, as if the train's movements cast a spell on them they could not resist.

When I came to the dining car I saw Felipa sitting alone at a linen-covered table. In front of her was an ashtray overflowing with the butts of filtered cigarettes. I didn't mean to stop. I began to nod to her in passing.

"Theodore," she said, as if I had been searching for her. "What brings you here at this hour?"

"I was just walking around."

"Join me for just one drink."

I hesitated, wanting to be alone. Felipa's fingers, long and nervous, twisted restlessly as she rolled up the label from the wine bottle in front of her.

"Please," she said. "One drink won't hurt you."

I sat down on the chair opposite her. The train was moving at its full speed, hammering its insistent rhythms into the rails. It was now deep into the rolling Ontario bushland and was beginning to climb and descend small hills. With each passing minute my feeling of home, its closeness, my desire to get there, was growing stronger; and I couldn't help thinking that this was what I had wanted for years, that by being thousands of miles away I had only been shutting myself off from myself, like a sullen and sulking child.

And with each passing minute the sky grew brighter too. Now the air was beginning to glow white with the rising sun. I felt tired and grimy. Felipa looked worse. Her hand shook as she poured the dark red wine into her glass and pushed it across the stained tablecloth towards me. Her face was sallow and her skin swam with shadows. Even her eyes looked weak and bloodshot.

I sipped at the wine. Dry red wine, almost sour. "French Piss," Jacob Beam used to call the expensive red wine my mother sometimes brought home from her shopping expeditions to larger towns. So I felt refined. Like a man eating fish when he wants meat.

I wanted to be in Salem, with Lise. The first night we'd sleep in the room in which I was born; cold white linen sheets stretched across the wide bed – we'd almost be lost in so much space.

Felipa had filled the glass to the brim. Now that I was here, I would have to drink it all, and drink it slowly or she'd pour me another; but the wine, though it was sharp on my tongue and throat, burned warm in my stomach. I felt flushed and embarrassed.

"Well?" she said. "You're making me nervous, Theodore Beam. My husband says you're indispensable. Lise says you're wonderful. Even the doctor admires you. Such a good Samaritan, Theodore Beam. I wonder why you don't like me?"

When she was young, she must have been beautiful. Even now, tired and aging, in this unkind morning light, she was handsome in a remarkable way.

"I don't dislike you," I finally said. "I hardly even know you. I mean, we're not exactly . . ."

"Lovers," she finished for me.

"Well, that too."

Now I was filling my own glass. This conversation was uneasy, with no obvious destination. Felipa smiled and lit another cigarette. I looked around the dining car, hoping someone would come in.

Felipa's hands were nervously working their way across the table, the fingers slipping sideways, like crabs approaching their prey.

"I didn't mean to frighten you," she said. "Sometimes I'm honest in the wrong way."

"That's all right." I took one of her cigarettes and pushed my chair back. Now that the distance was established I looked at her again and tried to smile, as if we were old friends talking over the times we shared. I began to wish I had acted differently the previous night, had stayed in bed making love with Lise and left Felipa to her own fate. The climax still felt trapped in my body, needing to be released.

"Your husband seems well," I said.

She nodded. "He is well. All this activity agrees with him." She pressed her hands to her neck, then ran her fingers through the back of her hair. She shook her head and her hair settled down again, black and complacent, framing the long triangle of her face and resting lightly in the hollows of her shoulders.

"He's very persuasive," I said.

Felipa laughed. "He should be. He used to be a priest." And then, "He likes to torture himself."

Her face darkened as she blushed an impossible red. I noticed that my glass was empty again. Somehow my hostility had gone. I pulled my chair forward and leaned towards her – almost feeling sorry for her. She was looking out the window, withdrawn, like a strange cat half sleeping in the sun. And for some reason I thought all this was being seen by Perestrello: myself leaning towards his wife, my hand wrapped round an empty glass of wine; and his wife, vulnerable and stripped of her marriage, eagerly discarded like an old coat.

"I admire your husband," I said. As if this was to be my only public statement on the matter. Perhaps he was one of those men who are immensely complex in their public life, but privately wish for the same thing as everyone else – a wife who is plump and compliant and patiently bears his children while he sails around in his dreams.

We became aware of James Fine only when he was standing right between us, his hands grasping our arms. His face was red and for once he was dishevelled – his hair sticking up from his scalp like wiry ferns, his unshaven face coated with a thin white stubble.

"A terrible thing happened in Vancouver." He stopped to catch his breath. "The army returned and defeated the unions in a big battle. Hundreds have been killed and wounded – they've set up a detention camp outside the city – and the government has announced a counter-offensive against all other cities refusing to obey the law.

"It was on the radio. The government forces attacked the union headquarters in Vancouver. They bombed it first then moved up tanks and cannons. Of course it all happened in the middle of the night. They said it was a great victory, that the battle lasted less than an hour. Today at noon the soldiers are going to march through the city in a liberation parade."

As he spoke Fine's agitation disappeared and his eyes grew narrow and calm. The union headquarters must have been crowded, hundreds of men trapped. Fine ran his fingers through his hair, pushing it down close to his scalp.

"They're bastards," said Felipa. "There's nothing they wouldn't do."

"I'm not afraid to die," Fine said. His voice was professional and the only tension left was in his fingers: he held a new package of cigarettes and was beginning to operate on it, opening the cellophane with a nail file.

When we got to Perestrello's compartment, Red Thomas was jabbering incomprehensibly through the static, while Perestrello sat at the table playing uselessly with the controls, talking back to the noise with no indication that he could be heard.

The door to the adjoining room was closed. Without thinking I walked over and opened it.

The room was dark. It took a moment for my eyes to adjust to the shadows, to see Daniel sitting in the corner on a bed, the rifle still cradled in his arms, grinning as if he had stayed in the same position all night just to surprise me. But there were no traces of the man who had lain in the centre of the floor, the man I had failed to kill.

"Up early," Daniel said. "Couldn't sleep." He was at that age when his voice was changing from a boy's to a man's. Whenever he said more than a few words, it broke back and forth. If I hadn't known him better, it would have made his rifle seem ludicrous.

"Where's our friend?"

Daniel looked down at the floor, at the spot where the man

had been lying. He had on that embarrassed, curious expression that a particularly intelligent dog will sometimes wear when it has killed something it wasn't supposed to.

"You know how it is," Daniel said. Dann-y-ell, his mother called him, his mother's son. His father's son. In the few days since I had met him, he had killed or tried to kill three men.

I sat down on the cot opposite him. I felt like a visitor to a zoo who's been accidentally trapped in one of the cages. In his hands Daniel's rifle was neither toy nor weapon: it grew out of him.

Perestrello had given up trying to talk to Red Thomas, so from the other room came only waves of static – sometimes rising to create crests of concentrated birdlike gabble, at other times only a low murmur of bass sounds.

Fine came in to join us. He pressed his thumbs into the top of my spine, gently, letting me try to move around the pressure. And traced the place on my scalp where I had been cut – a quick shallow bleed, he explained, the kind that feels more impressive than it is.

"You're lucky — "

"Not lucky," Daniel interrupted. "He's tough." Then smiled at me, a big smile that I had never seen from him, a smile that showed his white teeth and split apart his face – so I could see him as a young man, the dark and flashy soldier he would be. "You're a revolutionary now. A fighter."

"Lucky," Fine said. "Even a revolutionary is lucky to be alive."

Then he stepped into the centre of the room, produced cigarettes and a pack of matches. With his day-old beard, his shirt tieless and undone, the flare of the match glowing in his face, he looked exhausted. While Daniel was turning into the warrior ready to remake the world by the sheer force of his youth, Fine had become the resigned old man, muttering over bad news, disapproving of everything, nothing left to do but try to patch up other people.

He juggled away the cigarettes and matches, then stepped

to the window and pushed up the blind. It was fully day now, an intense yellow day that roared through the trees, lit up the snow and made the grey-green bark sparkle. All signs of the prairie had disappeared. We were winding through dense rolling bush, broken only by the occasional swamp or outcropping of rock so violent that even these northern trees had gained no hold. On days like this the glittering snow squeaks under your weight and digs into your eyes. And in the bush outside of Salem, the bright winter days always bring out the hawks and eagles, and the sharp sounds of their hunting are like blood-threads in the cold air.

In Vancouver there were no real winters. No doubt the union men had died in the rain. I wondered what my landlady thought of these strange new disruptions, if they shattered the hourly rhythm of her long march down the hall. For Mona Oh No the attacks would only be her dreams come alive; I had deserted her.

Carrying rifles, Perestrello and Felipa now came into the room, laid them down on the floor and began to disassemble them, showing Fine and myself where they needed to be oiled, where they could stick and threaten to blow up. I had used rifles and shotguns to hunt small game, but these were completely different – bullets guaranteed to shatter whatever they touched, travelling so fast they stayed flat for almost a hundred yards.

Perestrello showed us once then we had to do it ourselves. The room was filled with the clicking of heavy metal.

When it was done, I stood at the door, holding my rifle in my arms.

"The passengers," said Perestrello. "If you walk around like that you're going to frighten the passengers."

It was true, I had forgotten there were still hundreds on this train who thought we were merely making a hungry winter's journey across the country.

"You can take this," offered Felipa. From the bookshelves she drew a black metal case. It opened to reveal a pistol and some cartridges. She showed me how to load it, then closed the case again and put it in a brown paper bag.

We were all clustered around the door, like guests reluctantly leaving a party. Instead of music, there was the radio, its unremitting waves of static punctuated now by electric whines and whistles. Fine and I stepped out into the corridor. Then the door was shut behind us and we were walking through the train again, its sounds, its swaying, drowning out all else.

SIXTEEN

I was in a trance, a light dreamless trance. In its centre I heard Fine's footsteps; they thundered down the corridor of the train like a protesting drunken giant. Then the sound faded and my sleep fell deep and unconscious. When I awoke Felipa was sitting in the chair and smiling sadly at me in the half-dark room.

"Fine?" I asked, knowing.

"Yes, he died this afternoon." Lise's ring cold on my hand. It didn't seem fair that James Fine, the one among us able to heal, was the first to die – presented to oblivion with a hole in his chest.

"I'm sorry," Felipa said. "I should have stayed here with you."

"It doesn't matter."

"I know you liked him. But there was nothing that could be done."

Nothing that could be done. She was starting to sound like a doctor herself. It was true that I had liked him. He seemed to have an amazing ability to live gracefully in the midst of the most ridiculous circumstances, denying nothing.

It was late afternoon and I was lying in a compartment near the very front of the train, a place Felipa and I had finally found. It was less than two days since Perestrello had explained the mechanics of his rifles. In that time I had watched him get wounded, watched Fine get shot trying to rescue him, and even spent an hour in this bed with Felipa – a cold hour that had ended with me closing my eyes and her leaving the room.

I got out of bed, awkwardly keeping my back to her, and dressed. The sun was beginning to set, and while I had slept away the afternoon and James Fine was dying, we had moved into a terrain of bush and hills. The track cut a swath through the thousands of small trees that crowded up to the edge of this strange moving knife. Sometimes there were eruptions of old glacial deposits and rock. Felipa stared intently at all this. I wondered what she saw when she looked at this landscape – it might have been like Mars to her – a weird and inhospitable place not suited for human life. But to me it was different. The trees all had names: birch, spruce, pine, aspen and poplar crowded together in a contest to see which could replace the primal forest that had been logged off long ago, when the railway was first put through. The birch, aspen and poplar were bare and leafless, their thin frozen trunks waiting for the next brief summer when they could shoot up a few more inches. The green needles of the pine and spruce were beginning to turn brown as winter froze deeper into the earth. It was growing closer to home, but it was desolate anyway, the frozen images of thick trees and cloudy sky broken only by the occasional crow, and the sound of our own passing.

My stomach was empty. Cooking and stealing, hoarding and starving. Signs of war. Temporarily at least, for the length of these cigarettes, a truce had been declared. We shifted positions, looked out the window, put bits of ash in the metal tray that was built in beside the window. There was only this short time we had been able to carve out between us; and this room, set aside for so long, was beginning to reassert itself and remind us that our cigarettes were almost finished, that we should soon have to let the dust and disuse obliterate our brief play. We looked at each other uncomfortably, Fine's death between us.

"I'm sorry," Felipa said again.

"How is your husband?"

"He'll survive." And now suddenly we had caught sight of the lake, its surface on fire from the setting sun – painted red and black, the colours of war. They spread from the lake in a great cloud across the landscape, laid down across the fields and sealed off the day from the night.

A small plane flew close to us, so loud and near we could hear its motors over the sounds of the train, see the pilot's head as it craned towards us.

Farms, houses, signs of civilization, were all beginning to appear. Lake Superior, which had been to our south all day, was now behind us, to our west, every second glowing brighter, the sun's great scarlet streaks shooting across its surface. To us, the survivors.

It had been a routine stop. One of many. Then suddenly from the edge of the bush there came an outburst of gunfire. As easily and quickly as that, Perestrello was down, wedged between a truck and the train. And as soon as he was down, Fine jumped after him, rolling him over in the snow, then picking him up.

The train took a slight twist and the sun fell across Felipa, splashing her red.

"So," I said. Feeling like my father. "So he'll be all right. But he must be wondering how he got involved in this."

"In this train?"

"In this war."

With each turn in the track, the sun moved back and forth between us, sometimes firing Felipa, at other times so strong in my eyes I could only close them and let the heat blanket me, as if to protect me from itself. And when the sun was on Felipa and she smiled, she looked almost like a goddess, so still and controlled in this light.

"Mr. Theodore Beam," she said, her voice with a new and

sudden edge. "This war, you say, *this war,* as if it had sprung out of nowhere, as if it had been called into existence by a few people so tired of peace and contentment that they had to start some trouble. Listen, Theodore Beam, do you know why Perestrello became a priest? Because he was brought up by priests. Because his father died in a cell for political prisoners in Mexico. And you may be sure he did not pass away from old age. And do you know how many thousands and millions have died in this century to serve one man or another, to put fancy food in the mouths of a few while half the world starves? *This war* is nothing new. The only thing new is that this continent, which has spent the last two hundred years dancing on top of the rest of the world like a fat ballerina falling down the stairs, is now catching the same disease as everyone else: hunger.

"Perestrello never joined *this war;* he was born to it, and he has lived it all his life. The mission where he was brought up hid and manufactured illegal guns. The day he became a priest they sent him out in the fields to organize the workers. Just as he had been doing the day before. And when I came to him in his parish, that was what he did; every morning after his night of dreams he'd go into the orchards – explaining to them with one hand why God had meant them to suffer this way, and with the other hand pointing to brotherhood and revolution. After all, God is more patient than men. When he left the priesthood, he was offered a job with the railway union, and that suited his purpose."

Scattered houses were growing into clumps, with gas stations in between and the threat of suburbs. On the roads, cars and trucks moved slowly through the coming dark, their yellow lights dotted across the landscape. And the lake was subsiding, now just a dull red glow in the background.

We had come quickly to the town; we were already among warehouses and lumberyards. The train was speeding up to run through this place and the whistle howled out its warning.

Felipa stood up. "I never talk about the past," she said.

"But in the last week, I've made one new rule."

"What's that?"

"Don't get killed. And take care of Lise. Enough have died already."

The train had slowed down. The town had turned on its lights. We were in the rail yards; bits and pieces of half-assembled trains stood about on sidings. And we saw that among them dozens of soldiers in uniform were walking, rifles held casually towards us.

We pushed open the door and began to run down the corridor. The train's whistle joined with the screeching of the wheels – and we didn't have to look outside to know that the track had been blocked up ahead.

Felipa stopped at her compartment. She started to say something as she opened the door; but the screeching of the wheels and whistle drowned out everything else. As the door opened, I could see Daniel anxiously pacing about the room, the nose of his gun waving in the air. "Red Thomas, Red Thomas, Red Thomas: this is Red Thomas speaking," exploded over the radio. "Can you hear me? Can you hear me?"

"Run," Felipa shouted. "Go on, run."

She slammed the door behind her. First walking, I quickly began to run, through the dining cars and coach cars, almost knocking over passengers who still crowded the aisles, unaware of what was happening. Then I made my way through the cars of compartments until I reached our own. As I opened the door the train jolted, seemed to fly briefly through the air, then crumpled in on itself. I was thrown into the room with the impact. Then I got up and locked the door behind me before seeing Lise, who was getting up off the floor.

She nodded at me strangely, then continued what she had been doing – pulling on her boots and coat. "What's happened?" she asked. She had a rifle laid out across the bed.

The train had come to a complete stop, but the whistle was still sounding, a long outraged shriek. I kept thinking I heard the first shots, but they were still only in my mind, my own fears starting to explode.

Lise seemed unperturbed. She just kept getting dressed and then, when her boots were laced and her coat buttoned, she picked up the rifle and started towards me.

"Where are you going?"

"It's time to fight," she said.

"Fight who?"

But now we could hear the first shots. Two loud shots, each followed by the shattering of glass.

"The army," Lise said. "For Christ's sake." She was coming towards the metal door, carrying her rifle, which looked absurdly big for her. "Excuse me, please," she said, talking in the same strange way, clipped, as if we were again meeting for the first time, but this round her decision was going the other way.

"Lise," I said. My voice as if I were pleading with a child.

"What?"

"You can't go wandering around the train now, with a rifle. You're liable to get killed."

"Yes, that's right. When you fight, it's possible to die. And what are you going to do, hide under the bed?"

"No." We could hear the slamming of doors, people shouting, footsteps running down corridors. There were voices outside too, and in the midst of all the noises, which still included the high whine of the train whistle, there were occasional isolated shots. And now I knew exactly what I *was* going to do, my eyes desperately scanning this room like a stranger's. My heart was pounding, shaking in my ribs. I pressed my back against the door. Finally knowing what had to be saved – and what had to be betrayed.

"I knew you'd never make it," Lise said contemptuously. "Not when it came time to risk your life."

"Only a fool throws away his life for nothing," I said. "There's nothing to gain by being killed today. There's hundreds of them out there."

"There always will be," Lise said, starting to cry but still looking determined and advancing closer on me with her rifle.

"You're just afraid. If they don't kill you, I will."

"I'm ready to die," I said. Which was a lie. I expected to die but didn't want to.

Then we heard more shots, clear and unmistakable, the whine of metal tearing metal. There was an explosion from the front of the train. A long silence.

"Let me go," Lise said.

"It's over."

"No, it isn't."

A volley of shots rang out. I shut the light in our compartment. There were more footsteps, voices, heavy boots running in the corridor.

"You fucking coward."

"I love you."

More shots. A larger explosion that shook the whole train. But this time I kept my feet, my back almost glued to the door. Lise pushed the muzzle of the rifle into my chest. I knew I should grab it and push it away but somehow I was paralyzed. Lise was sobbing, the rifle moving back and forth against me.

"Out of the way," she shouted.

"No."

"They're dying for us." Didn't she know about Fine? Among all the random shots and explosions, there were no human voices. "Move," she screamed hysterically. Her voice was filled with hate and despair; hate for me, and for herself also, for somehow being unable to get rid of me and for wanting to survive, despite herself.

"Put the rifle under the mattress," I said.

"Goddamn you."

Then she seemed to regain control and that moment I was convinced she would shoot me after all. I pressed back hard against the door. It was almost pitch black in the compartment, so dark we could only see each other's shadows. But I didn't have to look to know where she was; the sound of her breathing was enough. "I'm sorry I called you a coward," she whispered.

"I am."

"Everyone is."

We waited. The train was ominously silent.

"What have we done?" Lise whispered. "They trusted us. They never would have left us like this." She stepped back in the darkness. I remembered Fine's face. The last time I saw him he was still unconscious from the operation: his face was grey but serene and distant, as though he was confident he would live.

Then, like the thunder of Fine's steps in my nightmare, there came the plodding of heavy boots down the corridor. Our door bounced into my back first, then smashed the tender spot on my skull, sending me forward, face-first, to the floor.

Awareness came back in slow waves. First I thought I was once again in the room of interrogation, lying flat on the floor, waiting. Voices came in and out of range – one of them was Lise's. Then I drifted off again.

Finally I opened my eyes. The light jabbed into them. "What happened?"

"Didn't you hear?" Lise crossed over to the lamp and shut it off. "I thought you were just pretending."

Then, as the train moved through the dark countryside, we sat on the floor holding hands and Lise told me how she had played the outraged bride, pointing at the soldiers and asking what they were doing and what they had done to her husband. As if she had never seen a gun. Her own rifle securely under the mattress, waiting to be discovered. In the end they apologized to her, explaining in confidence that we'd been in great danger because this train was being illegally run – hijacked, in fact – by a group of union rebels who were using it to steal food from the government.

"They told me all the rebels had been captured and shot," Lise said hysterically. "Didn't you hear them? Didn't you?"

I pushed up the blind and there was enough of a moon so we could see each other's faces, our skin frozen white as it had been that first time we were together thousands of miles and almost two weeks away; and like that night, the moon was a quarter moon, a crescent that burned so liquid white it jumped out of the sky towards us.

"Fine died this afternoon," I said.

"I know. I was there."

"We've got to start thinking ahead."

"Do you want to know something?" Lise's voice could skate around the breaking point, crawl out over the edge and take me there with her, whether I wanted to go or not.

"What?"

"He looked at me then framed his lips, saying your name – Theodore." Then Lise lost control and cried it all out, shaking in my arms as it passed through her. Fine's death was now just stuck in me, an ache, an absence, something I would have to live with for a long time.

"Do you want to know something else?" This time her voice was secure and rooted.

"What?"

"I know you were with Felipa this afternoon."

"I'm sorry."

"Don't be sorry. I asked her and she told me." Lise leaned forward and kissed me. Her lips cool on mine, neither giving nor taking, eyes wide open, curious. "I never liked her," she said. "I know I shouldn't say that. She might still be hiding on the train."

And I remember asking myself if this was how marriages are built. Love growing up in the midst of a secret garden of destroyed lives and betrayals. Or maybe this was only us, needing each other now, needing to share what we had gone through.

Lise turned on the lamp and went into the cupboard for her suitcase. Then she opened it and began to transform herself. First she pinned up her hair so it was wrapped around her skull, then covered it with a dark-blue kerchief. Next she took out a pair of blue rhinestone glasses and a heavy sweater. Then with make-up she darkened her face and eyebrows, used lipstick to thicken her lips, and finally put twin spots of rouge on her cheeks.

"How am I?" she asked.

"My parents will love you."

She took out her briefcase and we tried to locate ourselves on the map. We were coming into central Ontario, still somewhere atop that great chain of lakes that is set halfway into the continent. It was a copy of the map Perestrello had left on the counter in the Vancouver train station, covered with all his plans and destinations. "We're close," I said, "only a few hundred more miles to go." I read the names of the towns we were near and had already passed through, some of them as small as Salem – Wawa, Marathon, Atikokan, Linko, Sault Ste. Marie. They were all familiar, towns that had been on the same map as my own for so many years I felt I knew the ones I hadn't seen, had lived in places I had only driven through.

Then I tore up the map and burned it in the copper ashtray. It disintegrated without resistance, leaving behind only an unpleasant acrid smell. And soon we were going through all our luggage, every drawer and cupboard in the compartment. I found everything that might identify us and destroyed it. In the end, our only incriminating possessions were the rifle under the mattress and the revolver in my pack.

The moon had gone down by the time we were finished. We sat on the floor, holding each other and smoking, huddled into the wall as if this night could never end. We were both so hungry, we were beginning to shiver. Every time I breathed I could feel my stomach tight against itself, sharp and hollow, an old stretched skin waiting to be tanned.

"This is like a wake," Lise said finally as the dawn began to rise.

We were out of the bush now and into land that was cleared – partly for farming, partly for the mines that had torn out the centre of the province. And though it was true we had spent half the night remembering the others to ourselves, fixing them once and for all in our minds, I couldn't help wondering what part of us had died with them and how many more nights would be spent like this, dozing and waking from chaotic dreams and the imagined steps of soldiers.

It was morning when the train stopped. We stepped outside, and after a few moments of hesitation started walking down the platform. Soldiers were milling about, but to no purpose. Lise was wearing her ugly uniform, her thick rhinestone glasses reflecting in the morning light. And I was dressed to match, in the suit I had brought to impress my parents and an old tweed overcoat. We walked quickly past the soldiers, in and out of the station and onto the street. Snow was falling. And we were free.

Over my shoulder I had slung the pack with a few clothes and one last reminder – Felipa's revolver. Lise had a small suitcase. Like two tourists home for Christmas we walked down the main street and into the first restaurant.

"Where are we?" Lise asked. We were sitting in a booth, planning to order the whole menu. Music was blaring warm and friendly from the radio, and the smell of coffee and toast floated thickly through the room.

"North Bay," I said.

"A nice town. I like it."

Then abruptly the music stopped and they began to read more news of the war.

The voices blurred together. It was James Fine's face that filled my mind. James Fine lying on a cot in Perestrello's compartment, the bullet wedged into his ribs. James Fine's face looking up at me, hopeful still, as I reached down, using his silver doctor's pliers to pry uselessly at the bullet.

SEVENTEEN

It was early evening by the time we arrived in Salem. We had taken a bus from North Bay – Lise in her blue-framed glasses and me in my suit and tie – then transferred to the old branch-line train that travels across central Ontario. In the ancient passenger coach, we put our feet up and tried to sleep as the train rattled through the barren countryside. We were in a belt of the province neither wilderness nor settled, which had been logged at one time and now bore the scars of small towns and generations of unsuccessful farmers. As we passed through it at our sedentary pace, I was calmed by its familiarity. But every time I closed my eyes, I saw James Fine's face, newspaper headlines declaring that new battles had started in Vancouver and Regina, a dead man tied to a lamppost.

Jacob Beam was waiting for us at the Salem station. He was sitting on the old varnished wooden bench bolted to the stone wall, reading the newspaper. When he saw us he stood up and eagerly came forward. Time had been cruel to him. He had once been stocky and imposing; now he was merely short and almost fat. His hair, which had once been red, was mostly grey, and long too, so it hung in uncertain clouds about his ears and neck. Though it was cold and windy and the snow lay in a thin crusty skin across the fields and roads, he wore no hat or gloves. His hands, when he took mine in them, were as strong as ever; and when he opened his eyes to me, they were so large and bright I thought he must have spent the whole ten years dreaming.

And how else could he have survived the changes in Salem? For while the station in the town's centre was the same as it had always been, like the inner ring of a tree, the rest of the town had run riot. As we came in, we had seen small suburbs gathering on the outskirts, and there were even two huge car lots, their neon signs burning in the late-November afternoon.

When I looked around I saw my mother had come out of the station house. She and Lise instantly found each other and were hugging like old companions. While my father had faded, my mother had bloomed. She too had put on weight – but it made her solid for once, as if after fifty years she had finally decided to exist on this earth. She came away from Lise and looked at me with an uncharacteristically total smile. I could never remember her smiling. She kissed me and her breath smelled of liquor and mints.

"Theodore," she said. Her voice was almost unfamiliar. Where had she lived in my memory? Now that we were facing each other, we were both trying to look away. Her eyes were filled with tears: round blue eyes, bland and unemotional. She brushed her hair back nervously and smiled. She had bloomed, but up close I saw she was growing older too. Her teeth were filled with metal and even her eyebrows had started to turn grey. She squeezed my arm.

Snow had begun to fall slowly, covering this evening in white. The lights of the station shone through the snow, making thick white cones. In this moment it was easy to imagine that a cutter with horses would soon arrive.

"Well," Jacob finally said, "why don't we go home?"

"We could have a drink first," I said. "And show Lise the old hotel."

In order to arrive at the Salem Hotel, the town's sole public drinking place and a resort of long and complicated history, we had only to cross the street.

"There's supper at home," my mother said dubiously. But she had already started to move in the direction of the hotel's only innovation, a small red neon sign that read: Ladies And

Escorts. As we set out in her wake I found myself feeling – after all the anticipation – disappointed at my own homecoming, as I used to feel at Christmas when my presents were particularly grotesque.

When we got to the hotel it seemed filled with familiar faces, though I didn't quite know who anyone was. Improbable names floated about the table: Lise, Elizabeth and Jacob. We would all call each other by our names. Why not? We were old friends. I was feeling uncomfortable. The more I drank, the more I wanted. Soon I found myself in the washroom of the Salem Hotel, getting rid of as much of four bottles of beer as my bladder had been able to process. In the mirror my face was yellow and askew. I couldn't remember a mirror here. Its presence seemed to go against local modesty. Maybe they had installed it for the tourist trade.

As I stood over the basin, a tall lanky man came into the washroom. His long arms and neck stuck out of his green service-station shirt, and his tattered wool pants bunched about his skinny waist. His nose was bright, every vein broken. Though summer was long past, his balding scalp was red and his skin dried out and weathered. Staggering, he gradually pulled himself up beside me. With his hands on his hips, he inspected my image in the mirror, then reaching out with a huge bony hand he turned my face to his.

"By God," he said. "By my living God."

He said this not in wonder but in his own fantastic, sly turkey-trot voice that was so drunk it crept around the edges of the room like a dog with an illegal bone. He laughed and clapped my shoulder, almost knocking himself over with the effort. "Theodore Beam," he whispered, dancing up and down with little wiggles and taps of his feet. "If it ain't Theodore Beam." In a totally unexpected manoeuvre he wrapped his arms around me and hugged until the bones of my back ached. Then he stepped away, almost slipping on the tile floor. As if he had been practising this for some time, he placed his hands behind his back and recited:

Theodore Beam
Theodore Beam
Where have you been?
And what have you seen?
And where are you now,
Theodore Beam?

Then he turned his back and poured his next verse into the urinal.

This was Pat Frank, the most renowned drunk of this poor area. This wretched parody of a man, who could barely hold himself up long enough to move from chair to chair, was actually my former violin teacher.

"You don't look much different," I said weakly.

"Jesus Christ," Pat Frank said. He turned himself around and hauled up his zipper. "The last ten years nearly killed me, Theodore. They nearly killed me."

His face had always been big-boned and cavernous, with shadows across it like an out-of-work actor, but now he looked close to death.

"I almost died," he said. "Even my brother thought I was gone. But who cares, eh? Now that it's over." He grinned at me. My mother's teeth had been filled with silver but they were scrubbed white and clean. Pat Frank's teeth were yellowed old bones.

He took out packets of tobacco and papers and set them on the marble window ledge. We rolled ourselves cigarettes then stood and looked across the room at each other, shuffling our feet and remarking on the wind that blew through the half-open window. I wanted to ask him about the war but didn't know where to start.

"A person might freeze their pecker off," Pat Frank finally said, "if they stood around in here too long and forgot what they were doing."

We pushed out into the tavern. The old low room – built from logs in the early days of Salem and surrounded by successive generations of additions and fancy coverings – was

184

filled with smoke and the haze of winter drinking.

"Will you look at the poor buggers," he said. Red alcoholic noses shone through the fog like so many fireflies. Food was short, but there was no rationing on beer.

"Hogs at the trough is what they are, hogs at the trough." He shook his head mournfully, with the same depressed hangdog look he used to have while trying to teach me to fiddle. We pulled self-righteously at our cigarettes and tried to survey our path.

In the old days, when I had to come here to fetch my father for his supper, this room had been famous for its Saturday night dances and its fights with knives and broken bottles. Now it was more sedate. The chinked log walls had long been panelled and families came here to water themselves after shopping. In the corners were television sets, once used to watch hockey games. Now, like everything else, they were converted to the war. A newscast was on. Pictures of the wanted flashed across the screen, interspersed with footage of battles and demonstrations. Yet everyone in the room seemed oblivious to it, with conversation and laughter drowning out the sound.

"There's your father," Pat Frank said.

Jacob Beam was standing up on a chair and waving a bottle of beer at the room. In his baggy coat, his straggly beard and hair, he looked more like a crazy fundamentalist than what he was – a prosperous and respected pillar of the community.

When he sat down again, Pat Frank and I began to work our way towards him. As we wove through the maze of crowded chairs and tables, more familiar faces appeared. I nodded to them, they nodded back.

Finally we arrived and sat down. Lise was trying to read the newspaper. She smiled widely at Pat Frank as he stared at her.

"You're getting to know some strange people," he said to me. His way of admiring Lise.

"You can't tell a book by its cover," Jacob Beam added. Sometimes the perfect cliché eluded him.

Have I told you he had an extraordinary voice? It seemed to contain a strange mixture of conflicting tones that finally had an effect of their own, independent of the words. Even ten years ago his voice had carried a certain conviction. Now its effect had been heightened by time and every word was so certain it was almost bizarre.

Jacob Beam. He was not only fatter and older, his hair wispy and greying, but he had also changed. His face was sliding into being a mirror of everything he had seen. His features had grown soft and rounded, the blemishes and imperfections gradually washed away as if his mind had rubbed itself pure against the stone of his own doubt and had now turned to remaking his body.

We've almost crossed this ocean. I was afraid of submarines and the weather. As it turned out, I was so seasick I almost hoped we would be sunk. But now I feel fine, if empty, and they say we will be in Halifax tomorrow. Elizabeth, I can't remember what we promised each other. Did you have the child? Things have changed with me. Now I hope we can start a better life.

"A toast," said Jacob Beam. "A toast to my son and his lady."

He raised his new bottle; Pat Frank and my mother found glasses to raise with him. It was unnerving to see my mother drunk after all these years.

"To Theodore and Lise," said my mother, and drained her glass.

Pat Frank pulled down Lise's newspaper and looked at her curiously. The wound on her forehead had shrunk from an egg to a small lump but there was still an angry scar that poked out from her yellow hair, giving her a vaguely menacing look.

"We of this town wish to extend you every courtesy," he said.

"Thank you."

In his day, Pat Frank had been the unexpected friend of

numerous lonesome ladies, widows and otherwise. "I can see you're a remarkable person, a welcome addition to this God-gobbling earth." He looked around expectantly, but Jacob was too drunk to interrupt him.

Someone put on the jukebox and music pounded through the room. Pat was looking at my mother apologetically, as he always had – and for the first time the explanation for this strange look came through to me. For a moment I could see them young together, in a sheltered corner of a field or in a barn. Passing the time while my father was away.

The low ceiling and the log walls caught the bass notes of the music and hummed with them. I closed my eyes, feeling drunk with the beer and sudden changes. I could remember square dances here, my parents whirling and gleaming with sweat, Pat playing the fiddle and calling out the steps.

People were starting to get up and filter through the small spaces between the tables to a corner of the room where they could dance; and soon the pounding of the bass was muffled by the stomping of work boots on the old elm floor. Pat was talking to my mother now, smiling and leaning close. I turned to see Jacob Beam. He was standing up, pulling on his coat, his motions slow and deliberate, waiting to be noticed.

"I'm hungry," he finally said when we were all watching him.

So we dressed and filed slowly out of the tavern. With every step my bones were jolted by the music and the noise. Pat Frank stayed behind, and when I looked back from the door he had already found someone to dance with and was wavering with her in the corner, his manure-coated gumboots stamping out the beat. In the corners of the room, the television sets were still on; Felipa's face suddenly filled up the screen – black and white – her eyes staring out at us, fixed by the camera. Did this mean she was still free? In the train her eyes had looked like this only once, opening up to me as we slid together in our one cold hour while Fine was dying, all passion and love driven out of them – nothing left but need. I could feel the cold draft from the open door. Then Lise's hand in mine, gripping tight, her nails digging into my palm.

Riding home from the tavern in Jacob Beam's car I began to feel more and more drunk. With my fist I rubbed the frost from the window and tried to remember the streets of Salem. But my stomach felt cold and damp and even though I was tired and pressed tightly into Lise, I could only think of that last night on the train, the long hours we had spent huddled on the floor of our compartment, waiting, replaying the shots over and over in our minds.

When we got into the house I hardly recognized it. While my mother and Lise rescued supper from the oven, Jacob poured our glasses of apple brandy and we sat in the living room in chairs I couldn't remember.

On the floor lay a newspaper but it carried very little real news of the war. Instead, there were propaganda stories from all over the continent about how people in various cities and towns were co-operating in the crisis of shortages. And there were two full-page advertisements for men and women to join the army. Another page was full of stories and pictures about a small town in Saskatchewan that had finally decided to "accept government aid." The headline story and editorials were all about the need for conscription of draft-age men to carry on domestic rebuilding. Of what, it didn't say. And about the train, there was nothing at all.

It seemed that Salem was a town set apart from the rest of the world. No one had mentioned the war; and although there had been newscasts and pictures of it on television at the hotel, no one had been interested in watching. Even Jacob Beam, who printed the local weekly and received bundles of newspapers and magazines at his shop, seemed to have nothing to say about it. I looked over the paper to my father. He raised his glass to me and smiled.

"Welcome home," he mumbled.

The room was so warm I wanted to yawn and stretch – I felt back in the safe comfortable world of before the war. And I felt as if I had been divided in two: half of me young and naïve, a child witnessing the world from the safe cage of Salem's easy rules and conventions; the other half turned into a soldier without an army.

My mother and Lise came into the room carrying steaming plates of food. I stood up. Compared to everyone else, I seemed gigantic and ungainly. Lise looked more like my parents' offspring than myself and was more at ease with them.

"It's good to have you home," my mother said.

With the passing years her round eyes had taken on separate lives. Blue eyes, china-blue eyes, one wider open than the other, as if going to sleep by degrees. She stood awkwardly beside me.

"Well," Jacob Beam said brusquely, "what are we waiting for?" But he didn't move.

"You look just the same," said my mother. "Doesn't he look just the same?" She seemed pleased enough to cry.

"Older," said Jacob, inspecting me. "He looks older. But I would have recognized him."

He was staring at me. What did he see? Looking at him I hardly saw a person at all, not my father who had towered over me in my imagination as I now stood over him.

My mother shook her head. "He looks the same," she said. She turned to Lise. "His kind of bones last, you know. After dinner I'll show you his baby pictures."

The rise and fall of Lise's breathing swept through the room with the long rhythm of water against sand. I folded my hands and placed them over my stomach. Lise breathed; I breathed with her. The window was partly open and the air above the thick quilts was brisk and cool. I felt soaked in the luxury of this real air, of sleeping in a room that had found its permanent place on this planet.

In this whole house, only I was awake – the way it had been almost every night the year I left home. The lives I might have lived floated through my mind in old novels. The story of a young man going home to see his parents again. His will to live is renewed, but his style suffers. He finds himself spending days and weeks in his room, writing letters to his friends, explaining why they may not yet come to visit. As he writes these letters, year after year, his friends marry and have children. They send announcements and pictures through the mail. These he pastes on the wall of his bedroom, gradually covering up the flowered paper. His letters grow longer and more profuse. He makes new excuses. He tells his friends that their children will love to ride the pony when they're old enough. Some days he's so busy writing letters that he neglects to go downstairs. Some days it seems a waste of time to get dressed. When the habit of sitting on his chair wears through his pyjamas he simply stays in bed. No one comes to rescue him and at the end of the first chapter he dies.

In the morning I woke up late. Lise was beside me, her face creased with sleep in this old brass bed my father bought at an auction. I looked out the window. In memory the apple tree had grown into a huge forest of long twisted fingers, reaching out for sun and rain, heavy with small sour apples left over from the fall. Then I saw it, dwarfed, a tangle of wood in one small corner of the garden. The ten years I had been away had been only a passing moment in its life.

The yard sloped down to the creek. It was still open and I could see the wavy black line made by the water where it cut through the ice and the snow. Across from the creek, the trees had been cut away, and a row of new brick houses, with asphalt shingle roofs and picket fences, shared the view.

I went down to the kitchen. The electric clock on the wall said eleven-forty-five; my mother would be bringing Jacob Beam his thermos of soup now, as she did every day. It was strange that she had grown stronger while he had faded; he had always seemed to overwhelm her. Through the kitchen window I could see a woman from one of the brick houses hanging out her laundry in the freezing air. The basements of these houses would have dry wood-panelled walls and insulated floors. I wondered if our house was considered a slum now. Not that it had passed these ten years without changes. There were oil space heaters in the kitchen and living room; and the wood stove in the kitchen had been replaced by an electric range.

On one of the elements was a pot of coffee. I poured two cups and took them upstairs. Lise was waking up now. I gave her the coffee then sat back in an old wicker chair and watched her drink it and push the sleep out of her eyes. The woman in back had finished hanging out her sheets. They were already swinging stiffly in the wind.

Of all the things I had dreamed of in this room, it had never crossed my mind that I might leave and come back – older but not changed enough to forget anything; changed but changed only by this woman who could make me want to love her. In those days when I lived in Salem, the possibility of love never entered my mind. Mostly I had dreamed of running away: by train, car, bus, even on a bicycle.

Some things had changed, but this floor was still cold and hard. And the glass in the window was wavy with age, giving the creek extra bends when I moved my head from side to side. Lise saw me doing this and smiled tolerantly, her wide practised smile. I could still see her as she was when we first met – a poised, perfect painting. But to see her this way my eyes had to lie: blur the edges of her sharp bones, stop the nervous movements of her fingers as they twisted each other, warm the colours of her skin and lips. It was easier to remember her as she had been when we stood at the door of her compartment that first night, and her face had re-formed from second to second with currents of alarm, desire and anger, her eyes searching me for hidden quirks and tremors.

I set down my empty coffee cup and went to lie on the bed beside Lise. Soon we found ourselves in various positions of familiarity. She hung above me, her sharp knees digging into my sides, her eyes closed, her thick yellow hair swinging into my face. At first we were quick – it had been a whole day and we were still new to each other; then it was slow. I slid deep into the bed, feeling like a fish between the clean smooth sheets. Lise's eyes were closed; I would close my eyes too. I ran my hands along her sides. Her ribs dug into my palms. In some corner of my mind I could still feel the swaying of the train, the rattling of its wheels against the tracks. The bed was squeaking, the springs bouncing so loudly against the brass bedstead that I knew I wouldn't be able to hear my mother returning. Lise grabbed my hands and pressed them into her stomach. Her muscles had started to contract. "Theodore," she whispered. But I might have been anyone.

Later we went downstairs to watch television for news of the war. My knapsack and revolver were hidden under the bed; and sitting in the living room, watching television in the full light of day, we might have been any young couple home for the holidays. Marriage, jobs, money: my parents had not even mentioned these things. If it was strange for me to be home, it must have been as strange for them to have their house possessed and reoccupied after ten years of silence.

"Look at this," Lise said. On the television appeared a man with a face assaulted by wind and weather, a voice dry and sardonic. Lise turned up the volume and we recognized the dry hard voice of the old farmer who had turned the meeting around in Regina. He was standing in a high vaulted hall and reading a prepared statement for the waiting cameras.

"To you who are still resisting, I want to say that the government has treated us with fairness, and that the time has come for us to stand behind our government in the battle against anarchy and lawlessness."

When the Prime Minister told his lies over television he looked ill-at-ease and restless, as if someone might discover him, as if it mattered. But this old farmer was lying in a completely confident manner, stopping frequently to stare right into the camera – the way a butcher must stare at the animal about to be killed – and reading in a dry monotonous parody of a boy reciting his lessons.

"In the next few weeks, as citizens prepare themselves for the New Year and sum up the lessons of the old, I personally hope that you will reassess, as I did, the feeling you have for your country, for its future, for the need for fairness and order in a world where all things are uncertain — "

Lise turned down the volume. My mother had walked into the living room and was standing behind us, as transfixed as we were at the image of this old man.

"Poor bugger," she muttered. Then louder, "I thought you'd sleep forever. You must be starving."

The face of the old man receded. The building he had been standing in turned out to be City Hall and we could see the spires rising inspirationally into the air.

"Do you want an omelette?" my mother asked. She crossed the room to the television and turned the volume back up. An announcer cut in.

"Despite the damage caused in the fighting, the citizens of Regina are hoping that life will soon be back to normal." The camera panned across a street of broken store fronts and barred doors. A group of men were working on one store, putting in new glass and repairing the sign. "The army is still enforcing martial law, and the curfew is expected to stay in effect for at least another week, to facilitate the finding of dissident elements. Meanwhile work crews of soldiers are restoring the downtown business area." The face of the announcer was now visible. He was standing in front of a hotel. It could have been the one we stayed in. He could have been standing in the very square where Harry St. John was shot. "As well, there are now identity cards for each citizen, and here at City Hall the lines are beginning to form. After one week from today, it will be compulsory to show cards when purchasing food or other items, and citizens without cards will be detained for questioning."

"Will you look at that?" my mother said. "I think those people are crazy, don't you? They had soldiers up here last week. They wanted the town council to give everyone little cards like that. With pictures on them! Have you ever heard anything so crazy? I thought your father was going to have a heart attack." She looked at Lise, hoping at least a woman could understand this male insanity. "What do you think?"

"I don't know," Lise said.

"Well, I don't either. I think I'll make some eggs and toast. At least we still have enough to eat." And she walked into the kitchen.

Now they had moved on to more news. A different city was being shown. Whole blocks were razed – there were bomb craters everywhere and groups of men and women were being herded about by soldiers. "Peace has been restored in San Francisco," the announcer said. A clip of ocean was shown. "Citizens are here being escorted from danger zones to rebuilding projects in the suburbs — " Then the picture began to fade and was replaced by our country's flag. "That was a brief news report," concluded the announcer.

EIGHTEEN

By the time we went outside, the sun was at its height, melting the surface of the snow that lay thinly on the fields. The road was bare and dry, and it was easy walking from Jacob Beam's house to the outskirts of town. From there the road curved and climbed up beside an old graveyard, fenced off now, full of stone monuments and white wooden crosses.

We came slowly to it, trying to catch the sun in our faces, letting our legs stretch out after the thousands of miles cramped up in the train. And before going in, we stopped and leaned on the new wood fence. There were clusters of different families — MacRae, Clenning, Thomas, Frank — each with its own section plotted out as surely and securely as the farms they had made. At the back corner of the cemetery, where it fell away into a ravine, there was an old crippled apple tree, a great-grandfather of the one in our back yard. For each of the springtime funerals I had gone to here, this tree had been in bloom, thick and fragrant with pink blossoms that people couldn't resist smelling and picking, poking into the lapels of their mourning suits.

From the cemetery it was only a mile to the church, a sturdy old stone building. At some point the church had been deconsecrated; then it was bought by Joe Malone, the husband of my mother's cousin, the woman who had been midwife to my mother. I remembered the church to be shiny and bare in winter, its bright tin roof always glaring in the sun. But now the roof was streaked with rust, and trees had grown up around it. It looked more sheltered than ever, as if it had spent all this time getting ready to be our home.

The hour in the cold had started to clear my lungs. My body seemed to thrive on the shock of being thrown into an eastern winter again. I could feel my back straightening and my shoulders starting to swing as I walked. But Lise was shivering. She had her hands buried in her pockets and her coat buttoned tightly at the neck.

When we came to the door of the church we saw it was padlocked.

"The house is close," I said. "We can go to the Malones' and get a key." Lise nodded, her face red and too cold to speak.

The house was set on a hill above the road. It looked faintly majestic, fronted by a magnificent falling down porch, and surrounded by trees so impressively huge that even in winter, stripped of their leaves, the thick profusion of bare branches seemed to provide shelter from the wind and snow. Like a house in a gothic romance, it was absolutely solitary. We stood for a moment on the road and admired its perspective. I could imagine the man who built the house coming down here every night to congratulate himself on this creation and be overwhelmed by his own energy. At the foot of the driveway was a mailbox; MALONE was painted freshly on it in careful black letters. Connecting the box to the house was a double set of footprints. Coming down they were strong and vigorous, strengthened by the slope. But going up they were close together, the tiny edges of snow kicked into each other as if it had been almost an impossible effort to make the small climb up.

Walking slowly, we followed the prints. At the end of the driveway was a new aluminum garage with a car in it. In the yard, where all the machinery of an active farm used to be, there were now only a few rusted implements. But when we came to the back door of the house I was amazed to see, wandering near the barn, an old black workhorse. He lifted his

196

head lazily then moved towards us. A horse that big shows ribs like steel hoops when it is starving.

I swung over the wooden gate and approached the barn. The horse, an ancient black Clydesdale, moved towards me hungrily, drawing its lips back over its broken yellow teeth and slowly shaking its head. With its dry nose half pushing and rubbing against my chest, it followed me into the barn.

I felt as if I was coming back to my own home, as if each inch of this barn had been familiar to me every moment of my life. At the back the winter's hay was piled – not very much, perhaps a hundred bales. Not enough for a big horse like this, if it was expected to live. I looked until I found a stall that was barred. Inside were two sacks of grain and old tobacco tins to feed it in. I filled a tin with grain and gave it to the horse.

Soon I was outside again. I could hear the horse snorting and puffing in the barn, and the scraping of metal against concrete as it pushed the tin around the floor, trying for one more mouthful of the grain. The barn and the workshed beside it were unnaturally clean; there must have been an auction sale here. From the back of the barn, rooted in a small depression, rose two huge corn silos.

Lise had disappeared into the house. A light was on in the kitchen, and the smell of woodsmoke was soaked into the air, soft and reassuring, as if to say this war and this hunger were only dreams and when summer came again the land would exert its revenge on this barren winter and rise up in a great fertility of grasses and cows.

The horse nudged me from behind, almost knocking me over. Its nose pushed at my pockets, hoping for more food. Then it came around to stand in front of me, staring with one huge brown eye at a time. Jacob Beam had always said that horses are as smart as you believe they are. This horse seemed to be thinking the same thing about me. It shoved its nose into my collar, licked at my neck. I began to walk around the yard. It followed me, shaking its head. When we came to a fence, I climbed up then suddenly swung on top of the horse, grabbing its mane. It had appeared thin and starving, but it was fat between my legs, almost too big to grip. I put my hand under its jowls. It turned its head, surprised I would do such a thing, and slowly focussed its eye on me, waiting for me to look back, to dare to sink my gaze into its pool of utter curiosity.

At a slow, swaybacked walk, each step so carefully put that even a child would have felt as safe as in a cradle, it went in a straight line to its barn, continued on inside, and stopped at the closed paddock with the grain bags.

When I went into the house, Lise and Katherine Malone were sitting across from each other at the table, drinking tea. Even as I knocked the snow off my boots, I knew that Katherine Malone lived here alone. Posted on the kitchen wall was the notice of the auction for the farm – less than one year old. FARM SALE the heading read – set no doubt by Jacob Beam himself, the line-by-line description of the farm equipment hand-set in 18-point Garamond Bold Linotype. And beside the sale notice was a picture of Joe and Katherine Malone and their six sons.

"Theodore Beam," said Katherine Malone. Her face, now cross-hatched with a thousand lines, each cell divided into a country of its own, broke apart into a wide smile. "Will you never learn to sit down, Theodore Beam?"

I pulled out a chair beside Lise. She was looking through one of the old photograph albums: Katherine Malone with her parents; Katherine Malone slim and young standing in front of the flowering lilacs that used to line their garden, shyly holding hands with her first boy friend; Katherine Malone in her white wedding dress, already heavier; Katherine Malone in her mid-forties, now standing alone in front of the lilacs, holding a striped cat in her arms. There was even a picture of her with my mother. I was in my mother's arms, my face away from the camera.

"Joe died two summers ago," Katherine Malone said. "He was sick one day and I took him to the hospital. The next day he was gone." She said this calmly, as if telling of a storm that had passed. The room was hot, almost suffocating. I took off my coat. I could see now that holes had been cut in the floor, and ducts for an oil furnace were installed. But she had the wood stove on too and was wearing a cardigan buttoned up to her neck.

I had remembered her as being fleshy. Now she had lost weight. Her face was still round but her neck was corded and her arms and wrists thin. Lise, with her smooth skin and glowing blonde hair, belonged to a different species.

"You must be hungry," Katherine Malone said. Before I could protest, she had heaved herself out of her chair and crossed to the counter where she found a pie and two plates. These she set on the table before lowering herself down again.

Because they had pulled me out of my mother and into this world, her hands had always fascinated me. Now they were almost eighty years old – the skin was mottled and the fingers beginning to claw. But some part of her had survived, as she had survived the death of her husband and the defection of her children.

"She says you might be wanting to rent the church," Katherine said. "There was a family that lived there last summer. They cleared out the pews and put in furniture and a bathroom so it was just like a house." Her voice was as it had been, strong and confident, gaining resonance as she spoke. Her eyes, looking amazingly like the eyes of the old gelding in the yard, had been preserved large and brown.

"When you get old, you feel the same," Katherine Malone said. "Everyone looks at you and they see someone that's close to dead, but you look at them and you feel the same as you ever did, maybe even better because it's taken you all these years to learn how to fit into your body."

She poured herself a cup of tea and added milk and sugar. "Theodore Beam," she said, "where have you been all these years? You've been gone so long I started to mix you up with someone else."

I shrugged and looked at Lise, as if there was nothing her presence couldn't explain. Lise had turned the page of the album. There was a full-size picture of Katherine and Joe Malone, both dressed in black, standing in front of the cemetery. It was a recent photograph.

"Look there," Katherine Malone said to Lise, pointing at the picture. "I'm standing with my husband at the grave of the man I should have married. I made them take a picture, though they said it was unlucky. He sat right here, often enough. He would come to see me on a day like this, in the winter, and then we'd sit here and drink tea until he got warm."

"And then?" Lise asked.

Katherine grinned. Now that she had false teeth her smile was white and knowing. "We used to go upstairs," she said. "Then we'd close the door and not come down until the stove got cold."

"That's beautiful," said Lise.

"His wife is still alive. Sometimes she comes here and sits in the same chair he did, sits and talks about him, not even knowing. Sometimes I've thought I might tell her, but it's my story, not hers, and I guess it wouldn't mean anything to her."

"It would be a surprise," Lise said.

Katherine grinned again. "Maybe she could surprise me too," she said. "I wouldn't wonder. His father was even worse than he was. Sometimes it seemed a miracle he could keep his pants on long enough to do the chores."

The last picture in the album was a large tinted likeness of Katherine Malone when she was young, wearing a white belted dress that came almost to her feet and a flowered white hat. She was standing in front of the house, pretending to look at a blossoming hedge, and smiling. In her hands, then soft and perfectly formed, she was holding a bunch of spring daffodils.

"Look at you," Lise exclaimed, her eyes going back and forth from the picture to Katherine Malone.

"That was my twenty-first birthday," said Katherine Malone.

In those days she had been immortal; her bones slender and long, her eyes tinted so they shone like bright beacons of rural confidence. The house in the background had been almost a mansion in that era of prosperity. Although now it shambled and sagged, the wood coming through the paint, in those days it was gleaming white with hedges and flower bushes that grew thick around the stone foundation walls.

"My father was a proud man," said Katherine Malone. "He used to like his house."

Unlike the houses of Salem, this house had fancy wood-work: a large porch with carved gables and eaves on the out-side, scrolled arches inside, announcing the change from room to room. She had been born here. Her parents had died here. She would die here too. Her whole life had been focussed in this house her father built. It would survive her and, unless it was burnt down for a joke on Hallowe'en, it would probably survive until the unploughed fields grew back into forest and surrounded it again.

Katherine Malone closed the album and poured us a final cup of tea. Then she heaved herself out of her chair again and took a key from a hook on the wall.

"This will get you into the church," she said. "There's wood outside and if you run out of that, there's some dead elm in a swamp near the road. My husband was cutting there; you'll be able to see."

Katherine Malone. As we left, she stood up to see us to the door. She put her hand on my shoulder. I bent down to kiss her; her cheek was dusty and dry, the skin tough with age. When I close my eyes I can still taste the faint trace of lavender laced with the smoke of maple and birch. "You'll come back soon," she said. Then we stepped out into the yard, our boots squeaking in the hard-packed snow near the door.

The horse was standing in the sun near the barn, licking its chops contentedly. When it saw us, it shook its head and snorted noisily, then trotted over to the fence. As Lise patted it, the horse nuzzled her arms and pockets greedily, in search of more food. "Good boy," Lise said. She scratched it under the bunched-up muscles of its jaws. Then we started down the drive.

By the time we got to the church, we were cold again. I lit a fire in the wood stove, while Lise stamped her feet and clapped her hands. The family who had lived here in the summer had specialized in comics and stuffed chairs. The chairs filled the whole ground floor. They were pushed against the walls, gathered in a group in the centre, piled upside down in one corner. Everywhere we looked there were war comics, the covers ablaze with heroes spouting words and long tongues of flames bursting from their omnipotent guns. The actual church had not changed much. The pews had been removed and the chairs substituted. Where the altar used to be, a kitchen had been installed. And in one corner, modestly concealed in a cupboard, there was a toilet and a sink.

"This is awful," Lise said.

"The windows are nice." I tried to imagine the room without the chairs and comics. The ceiling was a problem too: it was made of only one layer of boards and we could see cracks of light showing through. Though the stove was roaring, it wasn't making us any warmer.

"Needs a bit of work," I said hopefully. Lise was shivering. I hugged her. If she was shivering in November, it was hard to know how she would endure the coming months. Dreaming in the train, I had somehow imagined this place differently, warm and glowing with dark-panelled walls and oak tables. Actually the walls were white plasterboard, covered with children's scrawlings, and the one table had a plastic top featuring a design of red flowers.

"We'll need some paint," she said. "Or a package of matches."

I picked up an old newspaper from the floor:

The President said today that the United States of America

202

is entering a period of unprecedented peace and prosperity. "The world has never gone so long without war," the President said. "I hope that my children and the children of my children, will never know the meaning of that awful word." He also said that further troop withdrawals from strategic zones would be premature at this time.

In the corner of the room was a ladder leading up to a trap door. I climbed up and pushed it open. The attic had windows at both ends and was so bright it hurt my eyes. I went in and called Lise to follow. There were no chairs or comics here, only a mattress in one corner and a plain wooden table beneath one window. The roof rafters were exposed but insulation was stapled between them. The stove had made it warm here, almost hot. We looked out the front window. Through the trees and across two fields, we could see Katherine Malone's house, standing at the top of its small hill, tirelessly surveying its domain.

"This is better," Lise said. She lay down on the mattress. I sat beside her. The back window gave a view of the fields sloping down to a thick valley of cedar trees. The creek running behind my father's house widened into the river that passed between these trees. In the summer you could swim there and fish for bass and pickerel that came up in the spring. In the winter it was a good place for hunting. The banks were always thick with rabbit tracks, and in the old days even the deer sometimes came down to get a drink in the fast rocky places where the river stayed open.

"I think Felipa is still alive," Lise said. She was staring up at the ceiling, unwilling to look at me. "I just *know* she is. Both nights since we left the train I've dreamed about her, the same dream." She stopped and searched her pockets for cigarettes.

"You should stop smoking," I said. In the light of this room her skin was transparent and imperfect. "What was your dream about?"

"About? My dreams are never about anything." Her voice was getting irritable. She lit her cigarette and searched the ceiling again. We were avoiding so much that soon we wouldn't be able to speak at all without planning questions that had harmless answers. "I was in a building somewhere, in a city. A building with a maze of corridors and rooms. And I was floating through it, ghost-like, as if I were the one who was dead. I was looking for Felipa. I knew she was there but I couldn't find her." She looked at me, concerned, vulnerable. "Do you think we did the right thing?"

"I don't know," I said. "I couldn't help it."

"But what would you do," she insisted, "if you could do it over again?" Her eyes, usually so aggressive, were still staring passively at the ceiling. On the train her fragility had seemed somehow elusive – part of a style she affected, not a real lack in her body. But now that we were here, I felt a greater need to protect her.

"I don't know," I said.

"Yes, you do." She swung up and grabbed my arm.

"All right," I said. "I'd do exactly the same thing. Wouldn't you?" And for this last moment there was something that we shared – or that shared us – something we became, this living being that was neither of us and both of us, that lived and died as often as it wanted, according to its own unknown laws, out of our control.

But now that she had started, she had to have her answer. "Would you kill someone?" Lise asked. "Would you kill some-one for me?"

"I don't know." I saw myself one more time in the corridor of the train, my arm cramped up at the last moment; and then in Perestrello's compartment, looking at the man I had spared lying bound on the floor. From now on I would finish what I had started.

NINETEEN

When we got home the house was filled with the smells of baking. My mother appeared in the front hall, smiling, standing beside the old grandfather clock that had once so easily frightened me. We had hung up our coats and were about to walk into the kitchen when I saw Felipa. She was sitting on the couch in the living room, reading, a pot of tea and an ashtray in front of her. She turned to us and smiled.

"I forgot to tell you," my mother said, "a friend of yours came to visit."

Now I remembered the strange car parked outside the house.

As I entered the living room, Felipa stood up. She looked directly at me and, in front of my mother and Lise, I felt as if my clothes had suddenly been taken off. Then the moment passed; Felipa's attention turned to Lise and they embraced.

Later Lise and Felipa went upstairs to talk. I was left in the living room with my mother, drinking tea. I had remembered Salem as being quiet and free from traffic, but this afternoon it seemed there was the continuous passage of vehicles and trucks. Some were filled with farmers and townspeople, others with soldiers and police.

"You seem restless," my mother finally said. I could hear the sounds of Lise and Felipa talking, the occasional clicking of heels across the wooden floor. "You could go upstairs with your friends." She began piling the tea service on a tray. She was relaxed. The unexpected arrival of Felipa, the soldiers' presence in the town, didn't seem to bother her at all.

"I still feel cramped," I said. "All that time on the train."

"You could go over to the shop."

We had both changed so much it was hard to remember how we used to pass the time. Yet I liked being with her. I got up to leave. She stepped forward and squeezed my arm. There was always someone to reassure me – my landlady, my mother, even Felipa – someone to tell me everything was going to be all right. But whereas my landlady and Felipa had seen the whole world pass by, nothing had happened to my mother. I was still the baby who had been born when my father was away.

"Tell Jacob to come home early," she said. "We have to go out to dinner tonight."

Downtown there were soldiers everywhere. It was like Regina except that these soldiers were regular government issue: their hair was short, their pace was brisk and purposeful. Some had stripes and bars on the sleeves of their uniforms, but most were dressed in grey uniforms so badly cut and so drab they might have been designed by the chief propagator of the government report, the voice of bureaucracy, a blind tailor.

My father was standing over the linotype, his hands swooping down on the keys in that strange swimming motion he had cultivated for this machine. Anywhere else it would have long been obsolete, but in Salem there was still time to set type in its slow clanking rhythm. With each key he pressed his head bent forward with the force of his thick arms, as if he were bowing in obedience to this work which had filled his every day for these decades.

After da Bobidilla had started to build this town, a corps of British army engineers left over from some war had swept through it, leaving expertly constructed limestone buildings in their wake. This shop was one of them, with its windows recessed deep into the thick walls. Being inside this shop, with Jacob Beam's huge old metal type machines and presses, was like being inside a fortress, a sturdy time machine that nothing could touch. In the corner was an old wooden worktable, stained with dye and covered with scars and carvings. We went to the table, where Jacob Beam transacted all his business, and sat down. On the ledge of the window beside us was a hot plate with the perpetual glass pot of coffee, its vapour being sucked in a continuous stream onto the cold glass.

"Well," Jacob Beam said, "it's good to have you home again. We want you to know – your mother and I – that you're welcome to stay as long as you like."

He leaned back in his chair and looked away from me. His beard, fading from red to grey, his long straggly hair, his eyes set far into his fleshy face, his deep and complicated voice – all these gave him an air of such authority that there was no one who would have doubted his word. When I had first seen him at the station, it had seemed that age had weathered him, that he had been diminished. But here in his shop, he seemed as strong as ever, his thick arms as immortal as old slabs of oak, his voice filled with certainty, as if the world were still only a ship that he ran, eight hours a day, five days a week, from his control room right here.

"As you know," he said, "we've always hoped you'd come and live close to us so we could enjoy your company, perhaps even get to know you again."

He was looking right at me, leaning forward, his arms resting solidly on the old stained table. It was easy to imagine Jacob Beam and my mother ensconced in their living room, my mother with some knitting to occupy her and Jacob Beam with an unread magazine on his lap, virtuously discussing their continuing responsibilities to me, as if now I was finally being returned to them, their rightful property to play with for the next few years. No doubt Jacob Beam had become so involved in the discussion that he had forgotten my mother's dislike of smoke and pulled out one of his noxious cigars. "After all," he would have said, "he *is* my son. We must owe him something after all these years. We never should have let him leave home so early. I've always blamed myself for that."

There was nothing Jacob Beam liked better than to blame himself.

I took more coffee. "We're going to rent the old church from Katherine Malone," I said.

Jacob Beam was peeling the cellophane from one of his special cigars. He bit off the tip with his strong teeth, then spat it out and vigorously scratched his beard. On a piece of sandpaper he had installed there, he scraped a match under the table and carefully lit the end of the cigar, making sure it was going evenly before he replied. He always liked to do this, to time his response for the maximum effect.

"A church," he finally said, now that his lungs and mouth were filled with smoke. "What an excellent place for a Jew to begin his married life."

"We're not married," I said. "And we've already searched the attic for Bibles."

"Very funny," Jacob Beam said. "Your mother has always appreciated your fine sense of humour."

He looked unhappy. He disliked running into unforeseen difficulty after lighting his cigar.

"I could have been a better father," he said. "I wasn't perfect." He sighed. "You don't know how it is. The world changes so fast. Time passes. Soon you find yourself in a corner, trying to live out your life."

Now he was comfortable, talking, in control of the situation – as he used to be when things began to veer off course and he had to smother them with words and gestures. I lit a cigarette. He with his cigar, me with my cigarette. Father and son. Some part of me knew I was getting unreasonably angry, that he was trying to be generous.

"There are things a father wants to tell his son," he said. "I've often sat here making up long speeches I'd have liked to say to you. I've even written you letters."

"I guess it was my fault too." Maybe I should have said something before I left, or written letters of apology and lies. Now I was starting to imagine him in the aftermath of my departure, searching his soul and wondering where I would turn first: drugs or crime.

"The world isn't doomed," Jacob Beam said. "Even the worst disasters can't destroy what is good in us. And no matter what happens there will be some people, ordinary people like you and I, trying to survive, trying to love." He put his hand over mine. "Theodore, you have to believe in something, especially in times like these."

His hand shook violently on mine. I wanted to turn away from him but couldn't. I wanted to do the right thing, not to have to look back and wish I could live this over. I couldn't deny him now. This would be our last chance.

"Jacob," I said. Even my voice sounded like his. The room was filled with echoes, past and present

"We were only human," he said. His eyes wide open: my eyes, my grandfather's eyes, the family blood jumping down the corridor of generations. The skin on my father's palm was turning rough as canvas; one day mine would too. Our hands pulled away. This would be our only chance.

"You were all right," I said. "That was how we were." Words. The truth was in my voice, which had broken open, jumped out painlessly from my belly as if it had always been there.

Outside the wind was blowing, freezing the ground to prepare it for more snow. We smiled at each other across the table. It would be a long winter. We would have to live on these reserves.

Then we put on our coats and stepped outside, my father and I. "We're going to Henry McCaffrey's for dinner tonight," I said to him. "We were supposed to pick up some wine."

All of downtown Salem was connected in three long blocks that stretched from my father's printing shop at one end to the train station and hotel at the other. In between were a variety of hardware stores, small supermarkets, gift shops and gas stations. All of these survived mostly by the grace of summer tourists. The one exception was the government-controlled liquor store. A palace of linoleum and cement, it did more business in one day than the rest of the town in a week. We had already pushed open the doors and were stepping inside when I saw that in addition to the usual crowd there were several soldiers standing at the counter.

They came towards us immediately, surrounding us with a kind of careless efficiency, asking to see identification.

"What?" Jacob Beam said. "Who are you?"

The soldiers laughed. They looked out of place in Salem – no farmers' sons or country boys. Their drab grey uniforms hung uncomfortably on bodies that had never worked, cast grey lights on their tired faces and shadowed eyes – refugees from the guts of the city. By the time Jacob had refused them, I had already withdrawn my wallet. One of the men stepped forward and took it out of my hand.

"What the hell are you doing?" Jacob Beam demanded. He grabbed the wallet back and put it in his own pocket.

The other men in the store now moved from the counter and mingled in with the soldiers, pushing them towards us so that the circle around us closed in tighter. The soldiers looked at each other uncertainly.

My father's arms hung at his sides, his bare hands closed into fists. He would have seemed almost laughable, a short fat man with hardly enough hair to cloud about his ears, threatening these soldiers who now looked like the detectives who had broken in on me in Vancouver – pointlessly tough, trying to convince themselves of something they had forgotten; but Jacob Beam's eyes bulged aggressively and he looked so sure of himself that it was the soldiers who finally yielded, beginning to push back among the men, all of them silent and uncommitted.

"We're supposed to be checking," one of the soldiers said, the mildest-looking of the lot. "You know how it is."

"No," Jacob said, "I don't."

With this I could feel the mood in the store begin to turn

against the soldiers. It was the same swing that had happened in the Regina train station, the same tension that had to be released by the shooting in the morning and the slack body in the square.

"Well," said the soldier, "I guess you're known here."

"That's right," said the clerk from behind the counter. "He lives here in town."

"And what about you?" the soldier said, pointing at me.

"I'm visiting."

He looked at me, at Jacob, at the men who now seemed to have united against this intrusion into the town's own blood.

"Well," said the soldier, "we were just passing by. See you later." Then he left the store, the other soldiers following close behind. Even as they were closing the door, there was laughter from the crowd.

"Idiots," was Jacob's only comment before turning to the short list of wines carried by the Salem liquor store.

And when we stepped outside again, the darkening afternoon now studded with the lights of signs and windows, he insisted we stop at the hotel for a beer. As we went in, we saw the soldiers who had just left the liquor store sitting in a corner with their comrades – there must have been nearly forty of them – drinking beer and laughing. Without hesitating Jacob went straight to his favourite table, the one near the centre of the room, the same table where he used to sit and drink alone in the afternoons. But it was only when he was well into his second bottle that his hands stopped shaking.

"I used to wonder," he finally said, "what it would be like if there was a war here."

He was speaking in a voice so low I hardly associated it with him. He looked at me speculatively, not the way a father looks at his son but the way a man looks at a stranger.

"I fought in three wars, you know." This in that same low voice, slouched down over the table, looking at me, open to judgement.

"Did you like it?" I had always wanted to ask him that.

"Yes," said Jacob. "Sometimes I did. Does that surprise you?" He tipped back his beer, then took one of my cigarettes from the table. He lit it awkwardly, the cigarette small in his stubby fingers, as if they were unused to such fragile vices. "Sometimes I liked being a visitor in other people's countries, not having to care about every blade of grass, every tree and every building as if it held my future. Do you know what I mean?"

"I think so."

"It's going to be harder for you here," Jacob said. "Civil war is the worst, where you're fighting against yourself." Voices and laughter drifted over from the soldiers' table, clear and harsh above the noises of the jukebox and television. "One moment you hate them," Jacob said, "and you can't help thinking they're pigs. But some of them are your brothers or your cousins, and you know they hate you too, the same way. In these things, nothing is ever forgotten, every drop of blood is avenged and relived until no one is left alive to remember."

A soldier came into view and settled drunkenly on one of the chairs at our table. He seemed younger than the others, his face pocked and flushed with drink and the heat of the tavern. He looked at us, back and forth, inspecting us as we inspected him. His collar was open and around his neck was a silver chain – the kind that attached to religious medals. "I wanna — want — to — buy you a drink," he said. "Be-be-cause you're so brave."

He addressed Jacob, who remained slouched over his bottle as if to tell me he had done his duty for the day.

"We were just leaving," I said.

The soldier turned to me. He had deep brown eyes, eyes like Perestrello's, so liquid that even the bloodshot whites hardly detracted from them.

"I want to buy you a drink," he said, "because you're so brave."

I stood up and put my hand on his shoulder. "I'm sorry. We're leaving."

He pushed my hand away and jumped to his feet. "Why don't you fuck yourself." He reached out to grab my coat. I pushed him away. He staggered against the chair and suddenly there was a gun in his hand. Everything else in the tavern was proceeding normally, the jukebox and the television drowning each other out in a cacophony of war news and rock music.

"You goddamned idiot," he said. He stepped away from the table, out of Jacob's reach, and swung the gun around in small tight circles, drawing imaginary holes in my chest. "You stupid fucking idiot. I'll see you later." Then he turned his back on us and walked away.

TWENTY

In the living room of my father's house we found ourselves alone: Lise, Felipa and I, standing in a corner with crystal sherry glasses in our hands.

"It's been so bad," whispered Felipa. She shook her head and stepped back. The skin around her eyes had broken into new wrinkles and the lines on her face had gone slack. "Daniel and myself survived," she said. "My husband and Gloria Fine were killed."

"Perestrello made them hide in a false cupboard in the back of their compartment," said Lise. "They stayed there all the way to Toronto before they escaped."

"I left Daniel with friends in Toronto," Felipa said. "He's already involved in new activities." A trace of a smile flickered, far away and waiting. "I borrowed a car and drove here."

I could hear my parents' footsteps in their room above, Jacob Beam's sighs and protests as he forced himself into a starched white shirt and a clean suit.

"There's a place for us," said Lise. "They want us to join them there." Her eyes were bright green and shining. The depression of the afternoon had lifted and she seemed again the Lise I had first met, active and excited. Now Felipa stepped forward, ready to be touched. Lise too seemed almost pressed against me. This was how it had been in the beginning, nervous and electric, the old order broken open and the new unknown and alive, waiting to be discovered. We drank and refilled our glasses. The energy gathered in us, drew us together; now we ourselves would have to become the train.

"We leave in the morning," said Felipa. "There are things to do."

For a moment I was convinced that I should go back to the city with them, living from house to house, moving at night, searching out people to kill and things to blow up. Then I heard the voices of my parents as they started down the stairs.

"We'd better change for dinner. I promised we'd go."

"I need to sleep," said Felipa. "You two go ahead." She stepped back.

Jacob and my mother stood in the hall, smiling indulgently at us.

It was a long time since I had seen the dining room of Henry McCaffrey's house. I remembered it only from years before, a dark and cavernous place that received our family one Sunday every month. The room was always cold and the food an interminable series of salmon casseroles and strange mixtures of potatoes and milk. When his wife finally left him we were all relieved, and from then on invited him and Isabella to *our* house for these Sunday meals.

After Isabella also left, Henry McCaffrey withdrew into himself. And my last encounter with him had been the night with Rosalie and Mirabel.

"He's remarried, you know," my mother whispered to me as we ascended his cleanly shovelled steps: my mother and I in the front rank, Jacob Beam and Lise behind us – Jacob helping Lise up the stairs with great gentlemanly show.

There was a brass knocker on the door that I didn't remember. It rattled loudly when I used it; and it was only when I wondered if the whole street would hear the sound that I noticed a doorbell, the plastic button discreetly lit with an electric glow.

The door swung open almost immediately. A dark-haired

woman in a black dress and pearls around her throat stood before us. She was plump, and even her long dress didn't conceal her stout legs.

"Elizabeth," she said, "how nice to see you."

"Good evening, Isabella," my mother answered. "This is my son, Theodore. Perhaps you remember him."

Isabella extended her hand and smiled. I had remembered her as young and exotic. Now she had filled out beyond recognition. There was a faint dark moustache on her upper lip, her glowing black hair was wrapped around her head like a turban, and she had the beginnings of a double chin.

"Theodore," she said, her voice musical and deep-toned. She kept her eyes on me as if determined that the long years would somehow be crossed. Then, very solemnly, she shook hands with Jacob and Lise and planted a kiss on Jacob's cheek.

The house had been changed by her presence. The woodwork glowed with polish and the walls were newly papered. At the end of the hall there was a grandfather clock, tall and imposing, its brass works shining as if they were someone's insides on display.

We went into the library. In its new incarnation this room that had always smelled of cigars and liquor was respectable and rich. The old sofa, where I had passed out and later found Henry McCaffrey's diary of Isabella, had been recovered in a bright and innocent flowered cloth. Antiques and small sculptures were everywhere. Even Henry McCaffrey had been refurbished. He now resembled the president of a small but extremely successful bank. What was left of his hair had turned completely white. His old bent wire spectacles had been replaced by plastic horn-rimmed frames. And his mouth, which had been small and pointed like a bird's, was now hidden beneath the spectacular sweep of his most impressive acquisition – a white handlebar moustache with waxed tips.

Lise immediately became engaged with the others. I felt far away. I went to stand by the flowered couch and looked out the window.

So Felipa and Daniel had shut themselves in the cupboard of the train like old clothes. Had they stayed there and listened while Perestrello was shot? Since I had last been in Salem, lamps had been installed on the streets. They glowed dull yellow in the night, casting small pools on the snow. They were dim now, from lack of power; and under the new regulations, they were to be shut off before midnight.

All along this small street the houses were lit up for evening, the colours varying from white to golden, some shot through with the steel blue of television sets. From their chimneys came thick white clouds of smoke, rising easily through the light snow drifting across the town. Old houses these, most of them built fifty, sixty or even a hundred years ago, many still lived in by the children of the men who built them.

I stood at the window, trying to let the day sort itself out in my mind: Katherine Malone and her old album spread open on the kitchen table – her life lived with such focus and clarity that it could be registered. And Jacob Beam at his solitary worktable, the muscles of his arms going stiff with age, his hand like wood on mine. *We were only human* – as if this were a fate too total to be appealed.

Isabella's hand touched my shoulder. And when I looked at her now I could recognize her beneath the extra weight and the pinned-up hair that once flew black and thick around her shoulders.

"Theodore, it's good to see you again."

We raised our glasses and drank to each other's health. The last time I had seen her I was about ten years old and she twenty-one. So in various ways the gap had narrowed. I wondered if she had found the diary when the sofa was recovered. Not everyone was famous for their smooth knees.

"Your husband looks excellent," I said. "Life seems to agree with him."

Isabella laughed the way she used to, loud and unrestrained. "Henry is just beginning," she said. "He had me traced with detectives. Then he appeared on my doorstep one day, wearing a raincoat and hat. I couldn't resist him."

This then was her truth: Isabella unable to live without the man in whose house she had been disgraced, passing the years in various cities, finally ending up in an apartment in Toronto. Henry McCaffrey tracking her down, appearing at her door one rainy afternoon. On that day she is alone in her apartment on the second floor of a big old Toronto house, arranging a few clumps of dried flowers and thinking about her current lover – a young man aspiring to fame and fortune, attempting transcendental meditation in his spare time.

The landlady wasn't home, so finally when the bell rang a second time Isabella went downstairs herself and opened the door. Momentarily the sound of the spring rain stunned her; then she recognized Henry McCaffrey. She offered him a drink and he accepted. Everything about him was in contrast to the life she had been living. He sat in her living room, glass in hand, utterly happy that he had found her at last. He had grown older, and there were grey hairs on the back of his neck and spots on his hands.

When his drink was gone he put down the glass, then deliberately crossed the room to her. Isabella stood up, afraid, almost disgusted by the thought that he might want to claim her again. She had friends, social obligations, things she was interested in. "I need you," he said. She was a woman now – not a pregnant girl desperate for somewhere to go, not a servant waiting out the time.

He looked around the room for traces of the child but could not find any. Everything changed, the past endlessly disguised.

She slid closer to him, leaned her head against his chest. He didn't care about money or fame; if he tried to cross his legs it would only hurt his knees. The truth is: she took him because he was there.

And now we stood beside the window, Isabella and I, our empty glasses in our hands. Winter nights in Salem were long.

The cold was moving in through the window, my back feeling stiff and chilled. In the middle of the library Henry McCaffrey still kept his old wood stove – a cast-iron box stove with designs in the sides and the words *Old Honesty* sculpted into the door. A brand-new shining stovepipe rose up through the ceiling to the room where I had lost my virginity.

"Have you spoken to my friend?" I said to Isabella.

Soon we were all standing with new drinks and talking about the war.

"You can't have too much government," my mother said placidly.

Jacob, who had risked his life so readily in the afternoon, just nodded in agreement.

"They have regulations about everything now," Isabella said. "We're lucky we don't live in the city."

The lights flickered but stayed on. There had been talk of power shortages. Oil was being diverted to supply the factories and the trucks and boats that were trying to distribute food. Henry McCaffrey lit a kerosene lamp.

The lights flickered again then went out. In the silence we could hear a motor coughing and stopping. Henry looked at Jacob Beam then at the wood stove.

"You've got one of those electric oil furnaces now," Jacob Beam said dryly.

Henry nodded. He took the lamp then bent down and opened the door of the stove. It was stuffed with old newspapers and garbage. He set a match to it and slammed the iron door closed. The electricity on the other side of the street had also been cut off. Gradually spurts of colour could be seen as candles and kerosene lanterns were lit.

"We need some wood," Henry said. He looked at me as if he remembered that in unusual situations I was the one to ask. "It's in the old place," he said, "in the shed behind the kitchen." He turned to Lise. "You know, this is a most remarkable old house. It was built by a Spaniard, Francisco da Bobidilla, over a hundred years ago."

"Isn't that extraordinary," said Lise.

"There used to be a story that he came from a family of thieves," Henry McCaffrey said. "In fact, the original da Bobidilla, the ancestral Francisco, was the governor of Haiti. He came there when Christopher Columbus had already discovered it, put poor Columbus in chains and brought him back to Spain a prisoner, locked up in the ship's jail like a mutinous sailor. Of course he was later released."

"History is full of interesting facts," said Isabella.

"You might say that," my mother said irrelevantly.

I went out into the woodshed. By the time I found a place to set my candle, and got it lit, there were footsteps in the kitchen and Lise pushed the door open. She looked at me covertly then came into the shed.

"I needed a rest," she said guiltily. "Give me a cigarette."

I handed her the package and lit a match for her. When I held it to the tip of her cigarette, she reached out and touched my hand as if to steady it. Her fingers were damp and cold. I took her hands between mine and rubbed them. The wind had increased; it hissed against the boards of the woodshed and sporadically found gaps in the walls and patchy insulation, sending blasts of freezing air against us.

"I'm sorry," Lise said, "I just don't know what to say to them."

"That's all right. They need getting used to." I took up the ax. It was a heavy double-bladed ax with a hickory handle – and although Henry McCaffrey didn't seem to burn much wood, both edges were honed razor sharp.

"What about tomorrow?" She looked at me, open and curious.

"I can't leave. I can't just leave my parents here. I feel like I'd be betraying them."

"And yourself? What do you have to do for yourself?"

"Stay here," I said. "This is where I live." I slid my hand along the wood of the ax, shifting its weight until the fat part of the handle was in my palm. Security: a man and his ax.

"I don't want to stay," Lise said.

"I know."

"It doesn't feel right." She grinned at me. "This could be good-bye."

"This could be it."

"Another question," said Lise. Now that things were out in the open she seemed more fully herself. "Do you think there's any chance for us?"

"Do you mean, will we survive the war?"

"No," Lise said, "that doesn't matter."

"Yes, it does."

"I mean, do you think we could be happy together? You don't have to answer," she said. "I was just curious."

In the half dark, with only the irregular flame of the candle, I could remember how it had been on the train, how it had felt to be isolated in the guts of that long metal animal.

"Sometimes I wonder where you go," Lise said. "I talk to you and you just stare into space. Is that how you are about everything? About Felipa? About this goddamned war?" Her voice was rising. "You'd like to do something but you just can't seem to concentrate."

She stubbed out her cigarette, sending sparks all over the floor. "I know you're not a coward. I just don't know how — how you can exist here." Now her voice had gone and I could tell she was starting to cry. "You just seem to want us to move into that goddamned church and, Christ, I can't."

"I know. But I have to."

There was a long silence.

"It's cold," Lise finally said.

"You should go in."

"I'll help you carry some wood."

I seemed to remember that there had been a moon when we set out that evening. The darkness accented the noise of the wind. I took the candle and passed it carefully along the wall, looking for the door. As the flame was blown out by the wind, I found it. I pushed it open and stepped outside. Moon or not, it wouldn't matter tonight. There was a blast of wind and snow in my face. There were no lights to be seen, no moon, no clouds – only this storm pressing against my face and eyes. I pushed back into the shed and closed the door behind me. As I did, I bumped into Lise, her skull against my chin.

"Are you all right?" I lit another match.

She was sprawled back on the woodpile. Then the door from the kitchen opened and Isabella came in, carrying a new candle. She looked at us, back and forth.

"Excuse me," Lise said.

Isabella smiled. "It's hard work in the dark," she said. She helped Lise up and I began to split the maple and birch. Most of the wood was frozen and fell apart to the weight of the ax. Between the sounds of splintering wood we could hear the storm. In my time away from Salem, I had forgotten this high-pitched singing of the wind.

With the rising and falling of the ax, I began to feel better. Isabella took in the first armful. Lise huddled in the corner, her arms wrapped close around her. The pile of wood grew under the candle. The ax felt right in my hands: a good heavy weight that did its own work. Another gust of wind knocked the candle to the floor. By the time I had it up and going again, Jacob Beam was standing in the doorway. I piled some wood in his arms, but when I started to fill my own I almost tripped over the ax. I turned to begin again. My nerves seemed to have snapped, like an animal frightened by the storm.

Back in the library they were insulating their blood with dinner wine. My father was so drunk he no longer even pretended to be polite. He and Henry McCaffrey were standing in the middle of the room, carrying on some obscure argument about the original da Bobidilla.

As I sat down on the arm of Lise's chair, I saw Jacob stagger. If Henry McCaffrey had not grabbed him, his hand would have landed on the hot iron stove. That seemed to sober him. He stopped, looked at the stove and rubbed his hand slowly, surprised that it was still whole.

"Excuse me," he said. He gave us his most dazzling smile – and seeing that my mother and Isabella had entered, pushing a wooden cart laden with food and ablaze with candles, he raised his glass to propose a toast.

"What is youth but desire?" demanded Jacob in his most Talmudic fashion. His moment of sobriety seemed to have ended. "Brief and passing," he replied in a loud voice. "Like the first days of love, it blazes in a glorious energy then, alas, falls flat on its face."

We all stood about the steaming tureens and ladled bean soup into our wide-brimmed bowls. For this meal Isabella had spared nothing. Roast beef and pork were followed by salads, jellied and green. There were pots of mashed potatoes and tur- nips and platters of every summer vegetable grown within a hundred miles, each pickled in vinegar and wild dill.

I loosened my belt and poured more wine from the decan- ter. The linen shirt my mother had found from my high school days strained at the buttons. I felt stuffed, almost numb. I had forgotten these gigantic meals that follow every day in Salem, winter and summer alike.

The room grew warmer and the storm more intense. The crackling of the fire drowned out the wind, except for the occasional gust that shook the house. But even by the light of the kerosene lamps we could see the snow packing into the window frames, gradually building up in long curves against the glass. Once during supper a plough passed by, its blue light swirling round and round in the snow.

When we finished our main courses and were slumped in the huge armchairs, big wedges of peach pie on our plates and cups of steaming coffee in our hands, Henry McCaffrey wound up an old gramophone and began to play the scratchy jazz music of his youth. In the light of the kerosene lamps and candles, with the music of the American bands and the batter- ing of the wind, it might have been a winter night forty years ago. Isabella, only an infant then, now seemed in the midst of everything. She had let down her hair; it was longer than ever and swung thick and black, shining in the lights. She walked about the room, dispensing goblets of brandy: eyes, teeth and hair all glowing with the heat of the evening.

Jacob Beam and my mother stood up and began to dance – Jacob with his back so straight his paunch hung out like a bank account, and my mother growing stout – their bellies bouncing together and periodically knocking them off balance.

When the first cylinder was done, Henry McCaffrey wound up another; then he and Isabella rose to the occasion. This was a waltz. While Jacob Beam and my mother shambled on, Henry and Isabella flowed through the room. Isabella's hair swung like a cape about her; and my old schoolteacher's white moustache gave his face a perpetual smile as he whirled her about the library, expertly avoiding chairs and tables.

At the end of this tune, Jacob Beam took off his jacket. Even Henry loosened his tie, then he put on a fox trot. The doors to the dining room and kitchen were flung open and we all skipped drunkenly through the house, dancing to the sounds of one of Rudy Vallee's greatest triumphs. We played it again and again, Jacob Beam singing his favourite verse:

Last year's thrill
I can feel her caresses still
Oh! I still have to pay the bill
For my last year's thrill.

"What a strange town," Lise said "Is everyone like this?"

"No one's like this." And it was true. Henry McCaffrey was unique, as were Isabella, my mother and Jacob Beam. "Living in a town like this," I said, "they all turn crazy in their own way. Can't you see why I want to live here?"

"Let's go upstairs," said Lise.

We went up to the landing. It was pitch-dark. I pushed my hand out to the remembered door and it yielded to the touch. We groped our way inside. The bed was where it used to be, and the stovepipe too – I almost singed my hand just brushing past it. I lit a match and found a candle.

Nothing had changed. There was still the bedside lamp with the three sailing ships, the dresser with the mirror, the narrow bed made up with the stiff white sheets. And it was still hot, the hottest room in the house, a small bedroom with the pipe from the huge stove rising straight through it.

"I like this room," Lise said. "It reminds me of something."

"Me too."

She lay down on the bed and lit a cigarette. I took the candle and stood in front of the mirror. I didn't see myself as I was ten years ago, only as I was becoming. Red-brown hair growing darker with winter; regular features getting sharper every year as the baby fat melted away, determined this late in my life to give me a man's face; eyes sunk in the shadows, only the pupils showing pinpoints of the candles.

I brought the candle over and sat down beside Lise. She reached up for me and pulled me down. The pillow was starched; I dug into it, suddenly tired. Lise's tongue circled the inside of my ear.

"I like it here," she whispered. Her breath tingled against my wet skin. Soon my hands were under her dress, searching for her belly and waist. Even she had expanded from this dinner. The records were playing again; sounds of dancing echoed through the house. I pushed the door closed and blew out the candle.

Lise giggled. She kept putting her fingers to my lips, listening for the sounds of the others.

"What will your mother think?" she whispered. "I'm dragging you away from your own party."

Our lovemaking in the morning had left us lazy and without hurry. The heat, the fullness of our bellies, the happy sounds of the music and Jacob's occasional singing, all made it easy for us to fit together perfectly.

Outside the storm howled but it couldn't touch us. As the record wound down, Jacob Beam sang along. And for the final chorus, as if they had sung this song many times before, my mother, Isabella and Henry McCaffrey joined in:

Keep the Home-fires burning
While your hearts are yearning,
Though your lads are far away
They dream of Home.

There's a silver lining
Through the dark cloud shining,
Turn the dark cloud inside out,
Till the boys come Home.

There were cheers then further sounds of glass against glass as more brandy was poured. A warm red buzz enfolded me as if after all these years and trials I was home at last, to be renewed, to begin my life again; at least for this one night while Lise was still with me. Now there were Vivaldi concertos for violin and orchestra; they drifted up, sweet and ethereal, from Henry McCaffrey's gramophone. I closed my eyes and remembered the time Pat Frank had reeled one off on his fiddle, sawing through it with amazing vigour and speed.

There was a hot feeling in my elbow as if the nerves in my arm had been pinched. "Lise," I whispered.

"Yes?"

"Are you asleep?"

I felt it again, this time a hot bite on my toe. I looked up at the ceiling then saw a spark from where the stovepipe passed through to the roof. Right away I knew the fire must be in the attic, between ceiling and roof. I had my clothes on while Lise was still rubbing her eyes. I pointed to the ceiling then ran downstairs to grab my coat and boots.

As I pulled on my boots I could see the others reclining in the library, glasses held happily to their mouths, voices humming.

Outside the storm had piled snow in drifts around the house and though it no longer seemed to be snowing, the wind was whipping through the air, catching at my open coat, fanning the flames on the roof into high-crested plumes. No one would be awake and the lone fire truck of Salem would be snowed in. But like all the houses in Salem this one would have metal fire ladders stationed permanently on the roof. If we could get up there, it might still be possible to save the house.

I ran back inside. Lise was already in the downstairs hall, pulling on her coat. I tried to slow down as I went into the library. Jacob Beam was lying on the couch snoring, his head in my mother's lap and his hands buried in his beard. I went to the gramophone and turned it off. Henry McCaffrey seemed to know immediately, and went to the hall to start distributing boots.

The lamps and candles in this room were soft and golden as an old painting, as hopelessly romantic and still as the painting I had once thought Lise was in.

"What's wrong?" Jacob asked, suddenly staring awake.

"The house is on fire."

Jacob leapt awkwardly to his feet, then we were all suddenly in the hall. With an armful of coats and scarves, I pushed my mother and Isabella outside. Two flashlight beams were running at us from across the street where Henry had gone for help.

I went round the back and climbed up to the woodshed roof then the main roof. It was too late; there was nothing I could do. I can remember standing on the ridge of the roof, looking at the fire spreading out from the chimney. Then a lick of flame caught me in the face and I backed away and went down again.

The sky was clearing. Now the moon lit up everything that the fire didn't – the thin bowl of wispy clouds that raced along the windy sky, the rows of sleeping houses. Soon we could hear motors starting up, and the plough pulled up near the house.

Men with brooms and shovels climbed up on the roofs of adjacent houses to beat down the spreading sparks. Henry McCaffrey's house – the oldest in Salem – was starting to roar and crackle like a bird on a spit.

I went back in the front door. The downstairs was filling with smoke, the second floor all aflame. My father and Henry were in the library, struggling, and I rushed in to help my father pull Henry McCaffrey away from his desk.

The first explosion came from upstairs. We let go of Henry McCaffrey and picked up one of the armchairs to break open the front window. The glass splintered in pieces. We had to keep hacking at it until a big hole was formed; then, with Jacob holding his legs and me holding his arms, we swung Henry McCaffrey out into the snow. As we were pushing another chair to the window so we could climb out, the second explosion came, knocking us both to the floor.

Jacob was down; he wouldn't get up. I tried to drag him. He was heavy, his body already dead weight. The air burned in my lungs; I tripped over a piece of debris, too exhausted to move.

Then I felt something pushing at me. I looked up: above me stood a soldier – the same one who had threatened me in the tavern. In the midst of this fire his shoulders were shaking. He was using his rifle to turn me around.

I got up again and tried to pull my father towards the window. The soldier smashed into me, knocking me away from Jacob Beam and laughing as I fell to the floor. Then there was a loud crack as the centre beams gave way and the floor tilted crazily. We were sent spinning across the room. I was flailing at the soldier while he tried to raise his rifle at me. Then the heavy lamp from Henry McCaffrey's desk was in my hands and I swung it into the soldier's head, my chest snapping free with the sound of his skull popping.

I rolled Jacob Beam to the window, hoisted him up to balance on the ledge. Then I buried my head in his back and pushed until he rolled out. Finally there was help: bodies, arms and legs to drag him further away from the house, and me too, as I fell out of the window and into the cold snow.

TWENTY-ONE

They say that things begin and end. At least that is true in books, and this story is near the end of its telling.

Now I've opened the doors and windows to spring. The sky is clear, a sensuous April blue full of the promise of warmth and summer. The few remaining clouds float around in extravagant white puffs. Jacob Beam and my mother will be sitting in their kitchen, looking out the window at the yard and creek, planning their garden.

They dragged us away from the window of Henry McCaffrey's burning house and wrapped us in blankets. We stood at the edge of the road, among the spectators and soldiers. And while the others watched Henry McCaffrey's house grow into the sky like a giant red winter flower, I thought about the man I had killed and what I would do when it was discovered.

It was Felipa who finally delivered us home. She appeared at the fire wrapped in one of my mother's fur coats; and while everyone else seemed content to watch the house burn, she summoned the soldiers to drive us and the McCaffreys to our house in one of their jeeps. Huddled between her and Lise, the fire still lighting up the sky, the image of the dead man took root in my mind; and every time I closed my eyes I saw him falling into the flames.

I had thought the loss of his home would break Henry

McCaffrey. But even that night he raved about how he and Isabella would rent the bridal suite of the Salem Hotel, to live there in style, coming down for breakfast every morning at ten o'clock.

Jacob Beam had not emerged so well. In his chair that night he was deathly pale, so tired his eyes trembled and he seemed to have trouble catching his breath. We had to carry him to bed, dragging him up the stairs.

Finally there were only the three of us in the darkened living room. We opened the curtains. The night was black; there were no remaining signs of the fire. I told Lise and Felipa about what had happened in the house, the soldier I had killed.

"I had to," I said.

"No," Felipa said. "You wanted to."

In the middle of the night then, we put on our coats and went back to Henry McCaffrey's house. Nothing showed except the double-thickness limestone foundation so carefully cut and fitted by Francisco da Bobidilla. No one would find the body until the snow melted in the spring. And then there would be nothing left but a few bones, metal buttons and the religious chain he'd worn around his neck.

"You don't have to worry," said Felipa.

But I did. I lived the whole winter long with the fear of being caught. And every time I saw a soldier or heard a truck, I thought they were coming for me. In the spring, when the snow finally started to melt, I went back to the foundation, and poked around until I found the chain. It was wrapped tightly around a piece of bone the size of my finger. I have it now, the chain with its St. Christopher's medal. I spent a day polishing it clean, tapping the medal flat and cleaning the links of the chain. In the old days, I would have hated myself for saving it; now I know myself better and sometimes wear it around my neck.

The morning after the fire, I woke up alone in bed. When I

230

went downstairs I saw Felipa's car was gone. My parents and the McCaffreys were eating breakfast in the kitchen. "Your friends left," my mother said.

As soon as I had coffee I went to the hotel, thinking they might have stopped there for a paper or to ask the soldiers for news of the war.

With this one storm, winter had truly arrived: the lawns and driveways were packed with snow, cars were blanketed, sidewalks blocked off. Most businesses were closed, their owners snowed in; and though the supermarket was open, the shelves had little food.

I couldn't find Lise and Felipa – not in the stores or the hotel lobby. The restaurant of the hotel was empty and in the tavern I noticed Pat Frank, alone at a table drinking beer and listening to the jukebox. I sat down opposite him; a bleak light glistened on the wet surface.

"Big fire last night," he said.

I nodded.

"They say you saved your father from burning."

He looked away from me and began to scatter tobacco and papers about the table. Saved Jacob Beam? I hadn't thought of that at the time, only that he was lying on the floor refusing to move, that I needed him to be alive and a crazy soldier was trying to push me away from him.

"We were almost burned out once," Pat said. "The kitchen pipes caught but my brother got them down in time."

His fingers were so big he had to roll his cigarettes with the very tips, using his long dirty nails to crease the paper under. When the waiter brought my beer, Pat pushed over change from the middle of the table. He always liked silver money, used to make me pay him for my lessons in silver dollars, one each week, weighing down my pocket all day.

"Your friends went back to the city. They drove out a couple of hours ago."

In Salem there are no secrets.

"They say it's going to be a hard winter," he said.

The door pushed open, letting in the harsh morning light, and the first group of soldiers drifted into the tavern.

Later that day I loaded Jacob Beam's car with food and clothing and drove out to the old church. That was where I had to be, with Lise or without.

In the mornings I cut wood for Katherine Malone and myself, using her husband's old chain saw; and in the afternoons I learned how to hunt again by the river, setting snares for the rabbits and sometimes lying in wait for deer, with the old rifle Katherine Malone had given me. My legs learned how to wear snowshoes again. I watched the winter grow and shrink until finally spring was beginning and the earth pushed out through the snow to meet the warming sun.

I drank tea with Katherine Malone while she went through the old albums, retelling stories about the people in the pictures. And I fed that old black Clydesdale, rationing out its hay and grain, hoping for an early spring and thick pasture. But one morning I came up to see it and I found it on its side, its lips pulled up past its yellow teeth, lying on its ribs beside the stall where the grain was kept.

Jacob Beam faded. It was as if he was only waiting for his body to run down. One afternoon I went to visit him in his shop, and found him sitting at his worktable drinking coffee and staring out the window.

"I'm tired," he said. "Sometimes I don't care if I live anymore."

He was not yet sixty, but it was possible to imagine him at eighty with a parchment scalp and an all-white beard.

"I'm an old man now," he said. "I only want to close my eyes and reach down into myself and find something. Something that connects one day to the next, or even this day to some old memory from ten or forty years ago."

He was smiling at me benevolently, as if trying to tell me I was a child he wanted to set free. But his eyes, despite themselves, told the truth. They were fastened to mine. Even now there was some part of him unchanged, some part that could not let go. He was still bound to stamp me with himself, with his own self-righteous certainty; and he would try to hold me to this just as surely as he had done everything else in his life.

The afternoon passed. We went back to the house for dinner. Henry and Isabella were there, waiting with my mother in the kitchen, laughing and joking about the food while they traded news of the war. The Prime Minister and the American President appeared together on television almost every week now, and the city newspapers were filled mostly with propaganda and blank spaces.

In the midst of a spring storm Lise returned. She pushed through the trap door one afternoon when I was sitting in this attic, writing these words. Her hands dug into me, bones and nails rooting themselves in my skin. And later when she stood looking out the window as she did that very first day, I knew I was seeing something of myself.

"Soon the snow will stop," she said. And she moved away from me again, as if her words could only tell me that in her mind lived her own private thoughts, with their own private lives; and though they might cross with me now and again, their direction would always remain unknown to me.

We are locked together, you and I. Our lives are guided by the same gods, the same laws of chance and nature. We know each other so well, we can no longer sleep together without love or kill each other without guns and bombs. My news is yours, and yours is mine. Have I asked you to admit this? We have to confess to love.

Once we dreamed of being citizens in a perfect state. The cells of our body ran wild with faith, pushing us through childhood to this place we have reached. I remember the dreams; but sometimes it can't be helped – I hear not music but armies moving in the night.

The earth will try to feed us, no matter how foolish we are. Soon Jacob Beam will sit out in the garden in the afternoons, feeling his eyes go blind, the sun crossing his face.

Old words flood through me. This hand records them – my hand, my father's hand.

The sky is clear and the sun is out. I can see Lise walking across the field, a rifle in her arms. For this day there is food again.

We will go on living here.

Matt Cohen

The Disinherited

This is the first of Matt Cohen's highly acclaimed series set in the fictional town of Salem, Ontario. Witty and ironic, immense in the scope of its conception, brilliant in its execution, *The Disinherited* can be seen in many lights.

"A finely-told story of the decay of a generations-long way of life and of the fierce family infighting over who is to inherit or escape."

Margaret Atwood

"A beautiful book about people discovering each other too little and too late."

Peter C. Newman

"The sense of warring past and present is splendidly created, the characters swell to giants as they recede into memory, and the whole novel... has a largeness of texture that leaves a massive shadow on the mind."

Maclean's

"One reads and lives Matt Cohen's *The Disinherited*... he has expressed his vision of man and the land in this corner of the continent in terms you won't ever shake off again."

The Ottawa Journal

Matt Cohen

The Sweet Second Summer
of Kitty Malone

This is the story of two lives inextricably intertwined. After twenty years of loving each other, hating each other and ignoring each other's existence, Kitty Malone and Pat Frank have reached the point of no return.

"The people in this book are all striving to come of age the second time around and the story of their struggles is both intriguing and marvellously told."

Timothy Findley

"A violent and tender story of love... human and triumphant in spirit... splendid writing."

George Woodcock

"Funny, potent, bittersweet... a work of joy and mastery."

Dennis Lee

Matt Cohen

Flowers of Darkness

Looking for an escape from their life in Ottawa, Annabelle and Allen Jamieson move to an old stone house in the sleepy town of Salem. There, Annabelle begins to adjust to the muted rhythms of a town dominated at one end by the brooding Presbyterian church and at the other by a smoky tavern.

Annabelle, an artist, starts work or a mosaic depicting the people of Salem. As autumn gives way to winter, and then to spring, they step one by one out of the mosaic and into her life.

Flowers of Darkness tears away the serene façade of a small town to reveal undercurrents of passion and hatred. Alive with the spirit of a man and two women and their haunting and unforgettable story, it is a stunning achievement by one of Canada's finest novelists.

"*Flowers of Darkness* is a strong deeply felt, adult work of fiction... Cohen writes lyrical, wide-open, yet master-fully sure and skilful prose."

Maclean's